Finding Martin Bloom

# FINDING MARTIN BLOOM

## CASEY DORMAN

**AVIGNON PRESS**
**NEWPORT BEACH**

Dorman, Casey.
Finding Martin Bloom

Literary-women-mystery-international
Cover Art: A narrow, colorful, dark alley in between two buildings with open windows and shutters.
© Rpharaon | Dreamstime.com. Reproduced with permission.

ISBN: 978-0692670248
Library of Congress Control Number : 2016904373

Avignon Press
Newport Beach, California, USA

For my wife Lai, whose beauty, strength and goodness have provided me the greatest inspiration, joy, and love of my life, and for my wonderful children Andrea and Eric, each of whom has unique gifts and talents, which have amazed me and made me proud. To my two sweet nieces, Ngan and Nhan, who gave me the opportunity to see young minds become excited by literature. And to all the English teachers who have brought the discovery of great literature to their students.

# Acknowledgments

This book has taken me seven years to write. During those years I visited Vietnam three times, trips which allowed me to sit in Saigon, mostly in the "backpacker district" near Pham Ngu Lao street, where much of this novel takes place, and write many of the book's scenes. Of course these visits were possible because my wife is originally from Saigon and has a large and wonderful family living there. On those visits, Lai, my wife fully supported my hours and even days spent on my own, roaming the city's streets and finding inspiration for my story. Back home in the U.S. I had the opportunity to assist my Vietnamese niece, for whom English was a second language, with her AP English classes in high school. I was thrilled to be able to read again such classics as *Portrait of the Artist as a Young Man* and *The Catcher in the Rye*. I also had a glimpse into the magic that occurs when young minds discover good literature. This experience provoked me to want to write a book that similarly inspired young as well as older readers in the way such classics often did. I am sure that I have not achieved such a lofty goal, but I have tried. I have to thank, not only my wife and English teachers everywhere, but the *Orange County Writers* group, who in their online and face-to-face critique groups read parts of the book and gave me valuable feedback. My daughter, Andrea, read the manuscript and gave me priceless suggestions, as did a good friend, Sara Murrieta. My sister, Noel and her former husband, Randy, both experienced editors, scholars, and writers themselves, read the manuscript and gave me feedback and encouragement. Distinguished poet, Anca Vlasopolos read, critiqued and edited the manuscript. With all of these readers and editors I have accepted some of their suggestions and ignored others, sometimes no doubt to the detriment of the story, so the final product and any errors or poor writing it contains are entirely my own responsibility.

# Chapter 1

Mom dropped dead the day I graduated from high school. After an outdoor ceremony in weather hot enough to broil us like bratwursts on a barbecue, my mother had driven us home, a blissful smile on her face, while I sat next to her, basking in the warmth of for once having made the person whom I'd been tormenting for the last eighteen years, happy. We pulled into the garage and, as she stepped from the car, she clutched her chest and turned to me, her face an expression of pain, surprise and regret. It was a look I'll remember for a lifetime. The next thing I knew, she was sprawled across the hood of her Honda and I was screaming in panic. When she wouldn't respond to my frenzied attempts to revive her, I was seized by an overwhelming feeling of guilt, thinking that the shock of seeing her daughter actually finish something had killed my mother.

For the first time in my life I was alone. The person on whom I had counted to nag me, to ground me, to lecture me, and mostly to love me, was gone, and I was plagued by the thought that it was my fault. Finally I realized that if my mother had died as a result of my success, then her death had only proven that I'd been right about the futility of doing my homework, getting good grades, kissing up to teachers and otherwise giving in to the expectations of the Kafkaesque system that had awarded me my diploma. So, despite feeling overwhelmed with loneliness, I found myself standing at her newly excavated grave, doing my best to ignore the sanctimonious intonings of the somber minister, while the words, "I told you so," formed silently upon my quivering lips.

My mother had been a regular attendee of our neighborhood church, although I had rarely set foot in the place, but a few days after the funeral the minister and his wife came to my house to "see how I was doing."

Not well.

For the three days between her death and the funeral, I'd numbed myself to the reality of losing my mother, but once I'd witnessed the first shovelful of freshly-dug earth being flung into the yawning mouth of her grave, the reality of losing her had hit me with the force of, to quote Miley Cyrus, a wrecking ball. I'd responded with the only coping skills I possessed and gone home, climbed into bed, pulled the covers over my head, and not emerged except to smoke, to pee and to grab two bags of potato chips and all the cookies and candy bars in the house, which I cached alongside me in my undercover retreat. Every time I awoke from one of my fitful dozes, I had the momentary feeling that my mom would walk into the room and call out her familiar "rise and shine, sweetie," or at least bawl me out for smoking. But she never did, and with each dying expectation of her presence, the emptiness I was feeling consumed more and more of my being.

After three days living this mole-like existence, I was interrupted by the insistent ring of the doorbell. I had to burrow a path through chips, cookie crumbs, and candy bar wrappers in order to roll out of bed and peer through the window to see whom it was. Finding that it was my mother's minister and his wife, I knew I should have gone back to bed, but I was haunted by the insistent voice of my mom inside my head telling me to "be nice to the church people," so I threw on some clothes and answered the door.

"We just wanted to check on you, Dillon," the minister said, looking around the living room with an air of suspicion, no doubt engendered by the full ashtrays, the clothes hanging from the backs of chairs and the pervasive odor of smoke in the house. The minister was an overweight middle-aged man, dressed in what appeared to be the same black suit he'd worn at the funeral. "You haven't been a regular member of our congregation, but your mother was, and we want to extend a welcoming hand to you in your time of need." He was doing his best not to stare at the tattooed snakes writhing up my forearms and to project a benevolent Christian attitude. His wife was a washed-out blonde dressed in a housedress that looked like something Beaver Cleaver's mother had worn and must have been salvaged from a church yard sale. She had a fixed smile glued to her face, while she stared at my pierced lips, nose, and eyebrows with the terrified look of someone confronting a space alien or a mass murderer.

"Oh, I'm doing fine," I lied, my thoughts totally focused on the pack of cigarettes in my pocket, as I struggled to resist reaching for them. What had I been thinking letting these two pious do-gooders into my house? I appreciated their good intentions, but really, I wasn't up to this.

"Faith can be a great solace in times like this," the minister continued, his face taking on a beatific glow—or perhaps the lingering nicotine in the air was raising his blood pressure. His wife nodded solemnly, although she looked as if she might bolt for the door at any minute. "Do you have a Bible?" he asked, leaning toward me, raising his eyebrows. I had the feeling that if I said no, he was ready to whip one out from behind his back, like a magician pulling a rabbit out of a hat.

"Of course," I answered. "It's been a great comfort to me," I had no idea whether there was even a Bible in the house.

"Would you like to read together?" he asked. He didn't pull a Bible from behind his back, but he started to open his briefcase, in the recesses of which I was pretty sure there was one lurking.

"I'm not really up to it right now," I said hurriedly, trying to stop him before he had his Bible out, poised for a reading. "I've been pretty weak since the funeral and I'm spending a lot of time in bed trying to get my strength back." *And retreating from you and the rest of the world.*

"We're having a potluck tomorrow at the church. Perhaps you'd like to come and join us. You probably haven't had a real meal since your mother passed." He looked over at his wife as if for approval. "Ethel, my wife, is cooking a ham. Her baked hams are the class of Eugene, aren't they, honey?" He reached over and patted Ethel on her thigh. She grunted something indecipherable and nodded her head like an obedient child.

Yeah, I guess ... maybe," I mumbled, hoping to convey my demurral by incoherence.

"We're going to have a special prayer session for your mother," he went on. "Everyone misses her, and I'm sure you'll feel better with a caring group around you."

This guy knew me about as well as I know the Pope. I missed my mother more than I'd ever missed anything in my life, but sharing that feeling with a group of born-again strangers? Was he out of his mind? "Do you allow smoking in your prayer groups?" I asked.

His wife's eyes widened as if I'd just asked if they had group sex during their services.

"Certainly not," the minister said. His tone of benignity had been replaced by one of righteous indignation.

"Too bad," I answered. "I can't go more than 15 minutes without a cigarette, and it's been even worse since my mother died. In fact, I've got to have one right now. Do you mind?" I dug into my pocket and pulled out a crumpled pack of Marlboros.

His wife had finally given up trying to smile, and she elbowed her husband, a look of panic on her face. Her gaze kept darting toward the front door.

"We have to be going, I'm afraid," the minister said, resurrecting his placid smile, even though it looked as if it were painful for him to do so. He and his wife both rose from the couch.

I put off my next smoke long enough to usher the two of them from the house. Then I grabbed my pack of cigarettes and stumbled into the bedroom and crawled back into bed. How could my mother have left me alone to fend off the world, I asked myself as I took my first long-awaited drag on my cigarette. I wasn't ready to cope with anything. But I knew that the emptiness in my chest caused by my mother's absence wasn't going to go away, and I couldn't just wait things out by staying in bed for the next year. What would mom have wanted me to do?

The answer was as clear as the Snickers wrapper staring at me from across my pillowcase: she'd have wanted me to go to college.

Having spent my entire high school career reading Manga comics, vampire novels, and watching foreign films on Bravo and the Sundance Channel, I'd barely made the honor roll, but I'd gotten near-perfect scores on the SAT, which had provoked the local University of Oregon and several other universities to come panting at my doorstep like hungry wolves looking for a defenseless sheep to devour. I'd given Oregon a tentative yes, only to please my mother, and even though they'd admitted me, I'd never completed the registration process. It turned out that the whole registration process could be done in bed using my computer. I managed to enroll myself for fall.

As the summer continued, I gradually spent more time out of bed, learning how to cook my own meals and even to clean the house. By the time the first day of school rolled around, I managed to drag myself out of bed before 8:00 in the morning, and off I trekked to the state university, a backpack full of books slung high over my shoulder, a pair of skin-tight jeans slung low over my hips, my blacker-than-charcoal dyed hair spiked like a pre-9/11 silhouette of the New York skyline, and bright silver rings dangling like gypsy bangles from my nose, my lower lip, and one of my eyebrows. A matching pair of tattooed snakes slithered up both of my arms. On the inside I was terrified, knowing that there was no way I was going to measure up to the world that faced me in college and that I had no mother at home to reassure me that I was more capable than I felt. On the outside I was hoping that my *Girl with the Dragon Tattoo* pose would tell the rest of the world to fuck off.

## Chapter 2

My so-called educational experience in high school, which had kept me off the streets for four years while polluting my brain with platitudes and nonsense, had taught me that education consisted of memorizing dates in history or learning how to do stupiculous equations that couldn't possibly be applied to anything in real life. My English teachers had constantly told me that a) I couldn't write a sentence that was grammatically correct, and b) I had the imagination and vocabulary to be a writer. I'd gotten my vocabulary from my mother, who'd insisted, right up to the day she'd died, that I learn a new word every day. *Myocardial infarction* (to quote the doctor in the emergency room) was the last phrase for which I can thank her.

But despite my high school English teachers' mixed reviews on my aptitude for their subject, it turned out that my college literature classes were where I felt most at home. Had Barbara Kingsolver watched me grow up? Until I'd read *The Bean Trees* in my first freshman English class, I'd thought no one else knew what it was like to be raised in a single parent home with a strong mother. And despite using books to avoid people, I'd had no idea that reading could be an antidote to loneliness. But what had hit me most were James Joyce's *A Portrait of the Artist as a Young Man* and Thomas Hardy's *Jude the Obscure*, which half of the pinheads in my freshman lit class thought was written by either John Lennon or Paul McCartney. I knew exactly how the characters in those books felt when they struggled to define themselves, despite their meager backgrounds and their limited means, even when their struggles required that they forsake their families. After reading Joyce and Hardy, I made my first ever career commitment, scaring the bejesus out of myself by doing so: I decided to become a writer.

Doctor Hendrickson had been my instructor for two of my freshman English classes, both of which combined composition and literature. His courses were my favorites, and I even signed up for his summer course on the British novel. Right before the end of the summer he called me into his office to discuss my paper on Kazuo Ishiguro's *Never Let Me Go*. Most of the other students had skipped reading the book and just watched the movie on Netflix, but I'd loved the novel and had gotten totally amped while composing my essay, allowing myself to experiment with putting sentences together in ways that pleased my ear, not just conveyed a message. Professor Hendrickson had given me an *A*.

"You have talent, Dillon, real talent. I don't know if you're serious about writing, but for sure you have an affinity for gleaning the great ideas from literature. And you've got an ear for the rhythm of language."

And I've got an ear for devious come-on lines, even from my professors, but I didn't say that. Actually, I was flattered. For the first time someone other than my own ego was validating my aspiration to become a writer. But I was also suspicious. Doctor Hendrickson was only in his thirties. His praise could just be a ploy to get into my knickers, to quote a phrase from one of his favorite English novels. I remembered my mother's warnings about men and particularly about men such as my deceased father, who claimed to be writers. Doctor Hendrickson was a poet, or so he said, and also a novelist, although as far as I could tell, no one but his own students had ever read his one published novel. He looked the part of a novelist: dressed in a tweed jacket and Levis, his long hair over his collar and wearing wire-rimmed, John Lennon glasses as though he subscribed to the theory that all serious thinkers and creative types had to be slightly out of sync with their times. He made me feel self-conscious in my jeans with holes and my T-shirt that said, "Make 7" on the front and "Up Yours" on the back.

"Is that why you called me in, to flatter me about my talent as a writer?" I asked.

He brushed his hair back from his forehead, a gesture which seemed pretentious, since it implied a lot more unruly hair than he actually had. "You have a lot going for you. You're young, pretty, smart. I'm just saying you have an ear for literature, too. I'm interested in getting to know those students who seem to have promise, and you're one of them."

"Getting to know, like how?" This guy could be nothing but a sleazeball, I heard my ghostly, but still overprotective, mother's voice warning me, reminding me of her assessment of my late father.

"Intellectually. Sometimes I take students under my wing—help them choose what to read, what classes to take, steer their careers in the right direction. You'll be a sophomore next year and you'll have to declare a major. Have you thought of a career in literature?"

"You mean like writing for a living? Or teaching?" I felt a sense of panic. What if he was going to tell me that becoming a writer was beyond my reach, that I should aim for teaching? Did I really want to teach a bunch of brain-dead, party-hardy college students, or worse yet, high school students?

He nodded. "Either write or teach, or both, as I have done. It can be a rewarding career."

He sounded sincere, and, miraculously, he hadn't dashed my hopes to become a writer. But hadn't he slipped in a comment about me being pretty? What was that about? "My father wanted to be a writer and, according to my mother, all it did for him was to make him self-centered and alone." I didn't know why I'd told him that. I'd just blurted it out. Was I trying to sabotage my own writing career before it even gotten started?

He looked interested. "Was your father successful? Maybe your talent is inherited?"

"My father died before he ever got a word in print."

"I'm sorry about that," Professor Hendrickson said. His face showed his concern. "It's interesting that one of the books on my fall reading list is by a man with your last name. And by an even bigger coincidence, he graduated from this very university. But then this man, Martin, Bloom, is still alive, although he hasn't written anything in some time."

I felt my head starting to swim. "My father's name was Martin."

"That *is* strange," he said, looking puzzled. "And your mother told you that your father died?"

"She didn't just tell me, he *did* die." I was aware of my voice sounding desperate. What was I afraid of?

"Perhaps she just told you that."

"My mother wouldn't lie to me. We were close."

"Were?

"She's dead."

His eyes lit up and he leaned toward me with greater interest, reminding me of a glittery-eyed and sharp-fanged teenage vampire lusting after the defenseless Bella in *Twilight,* while the sound of my mother's warnings echoed in my head. "So you're all alone?" he asked.

It was none of his lecherous business if I was alone or not. "Can I see the book by Martin Bloom?" I asked. "Do you have a copy?"

He leaned back, looking at me as if he were puzzled. Then he turned around and pulled a hardbound book off his bookshelf behind his desk. He slid it across the desk toward me. "This hardbound edition has a picture of Bloom on the back. It's from when he was younger—when he wrote *A Memorial to Time,* his first and best-known work. He's a recluse and won't let himself be photographed anymore."

I'd never seen any pictures of my father, but I was afraid to turn the book over and look. I read the title on the front. It was called, *A Dead Man's Tale.*

"What's the book about?" I asked.

"It's about this man who can't die. He prepares for death, summarizes his life for himself, gets all his concerns in order, and then just keeps on living, first until he's 80, then 90, then 100. He stops aging. Then he has to decide if he wants to use his extra lifetime to try to fix all those things he did wrong the first time."

The plot was the exact opposite of my father's life; he'd died young, not at an old age. But he'd left my mother and me behind. "So does he?" I asked, noticing the obvious hostility in my own voice. Way to go at concealing my feelings.

9

"He tries, but then he finds that he only causes more damage. Those whom he'd failed or hurt had all gone on and made their lives whole without him and there was nothing left for him to fix."

I decided to quote the favorite comment of my mother's Republican friends when she had told them that I was still deciding what to do with my life. "Sounds like an excuse to do nothing."

"That's the dilemma for the reader: to decide if he's right or just being selfish. But there's a larger message, which is that life goes on despite what any one person does."

"That's supposed to make doing bad things OK?" I sounded as if I was attacking Professor Hendrickson, but I couldn't help it.

He shrugged. "It's just the way it is. Aren't you going to look at his picture? Would you recognize your father?"

"I told you my father is dead."

He just stared at me, as if he were waiting.

I wanted to tell him to back his butt off, but I still wasn't sure why I was afraid. I turned the book over, trying to act as nonchalant as I could. I stared at the picture for a few moments without really seeing it. Then I focused on it. "Can I borrow this?" I asked.

"Sure.. Is it your father?"

"My father is dead." I said, staring at a male version of the same face that looked back at me each morning from my bathroom mirror. I scooped up the book and stood, then turned and left. It wasn't a great way to leave the room, but I didn't want him to see the tears in my eyes.

## Chapter 3

Martin Bloom opened one sleep-encrusted eye and looked out at the tiny cabin of his boat. The cramped quarters of the aging forty-two-foot Chris Craft were littered with the familiar hodgepodge of wadded clothing, stacks of dirty dishes, and used Styrofoam coffee cups, some empty, some with rainbow slicks of coffee languishing in their bottoms. A persistent hammer seemed to be beating against the base of his skull. He vaguely remembered staggering down the steps from the deck above, the night before. It had been late, and his faithful friend and taxi driver, Duc, had brought him home from the seedy *Cho Lon* bar where he had been wobbling on the edge of consciousness, probably soon to pass out and be robbed of the little cash he carried, had not Duc shown up. That was Ho Chi Minh City, or *Saigon* as many of the locals still called it: a city which offered little threat of physical assault, but in which robbery was as commonplace as tripping over one of the foot-high curbs that lined the crowded streets of the city's downtown business district.

He didn't remember much of what he had been doing at the bar, except drinking gin, his principal pastime for the last three years and a serious avocation for the several decades before that. Had he been seeking companionship? Sometimes he visited the bars to pick up women, but more often than not he employed such locations for solitary drinking. Every once in a while he would strike up a conversation with a stranger—there were lots of English-speaking middle-aged men drinking alone in Saigon bars—but often he was so self-absorbed that resurrecting his interest in anything other than himself was too strenuous for him to make the effort. That hadn't always been the case. In the past, a life he recalled with an uncomfortable sense of guilt, he had been a voluble drinker. The same flair for storytelling that had allowed him to become a world-famous author had colored his conversations with friends, acquaintances, and even total strangers. But that was in his past. The stream of stories, either spoken or written, had evaporated; his voice had become arid, parched ... dry as a bone He no longer had anything to say.

He swung his legs over the scarred wooden edge of the small bunk, which was barely long enough to hold his nearly six-foot frame, and, unsteadily, stood up and stretched. He peered through the dust-covered glass of the round porthole at the boats bobbing up and down on the water only a few feet away from him and at the blue sky above them, its brilliant tone muted by a dirty brown haze. A mild breeze stirred the lines from the other boats, gently caressed their furled sails, and turned their blocks and pulleys into wind chimes. Another day in paradise ... or in hell; he knew he would succumb to both thoughts at some point during the coming day. Inside his head there seemed to be a tom-tom beating a torturous rhythm. In response he reached over to the cupboard above the cabin's tiny sink and removed a half-full bottle of Beefeater gin, unscrewed the top, and took a prolonged draught straight from the bottle. He felt better.

He changed from last night's blue cotton trousers and collared white shirt, both of which bore the imprint of his night of sleep, then put on a pair of faded green swimming trunks and a washed-out orange tank top, slipped on his flip-flops, and climbed the stairs. The morning sun was bright, although it had its work cut out for it, fighting its way through the graybrown smog that perpetually enveloped the teeming city of ten million. By noon, the sun would be only a glow behind the layers of smog and the blue sky only a memory. Carrying the bottle of Beefeater in one hand, much like a child dragging along his favorite stuffed animal, he emerged on the boat's deck. It was late August, and, despite the early hour, the temperature was already in the mid-80s. Pools of sweat were already starting to form in the fat around his waist. He could smell the fish from the three or four commercial boats that shared the marina. Inserting himself heavily into one of the worn, brown canvas deck chairs, he looked around at the other boats tied up at one or another of the three docks, hoping to see one of his neighbors, feeling a faint longing for someone to greet in the morning. No one else was up yet. Most of them, probably as hung over as he was, were sleeping off their last evening's debauchery in their cabins. That was who peopled this dingy little marina on the Saigon River—expatriates who were drowning their lives and their memories in booze and women, taking advantage of the cheap prices and laissez-faire attitudes that prevailed in this Southeast Asian city.

He too, was burying memories. His past existed behind a fog so dense that everything behind it appeared like the churning surface of a distant sea, one memory washing into another with such confusion that he welcomed the blessing of gin, which allowed him to ignore whatever events might bob to the surface, as if by ignorance he gained an undeserved innocence. But his efforts at forgetfulness were not successful enough to subjugate his past entirely, leaving him overcome by waves of paralyzing anxiety, anxiety that could only be subdued with more alcohol. And without his memories, with his forgetfulness fortified by his drinking, he could not write. It was the price he paid. Despite his efforts to contradict this state of affairs with his quixotic forays with pen and paper, he knew he hadn't the will to change.

His headache had subsided to a mild but persistent pain, as if someone were pushing against the back of his head with a closed fist. He needed coffee. He went below and splashed some water on his face, considered but rejected the idea of shaving. Then he climbed back on deck and headed toward the marina wharf. He carried his notebook in his hand and a ballpoint pen behind his ear. Might as well take another stab at writing something.

Linh, the young woman who sold the coffee at the tiny marina café, which sat on the edge of the wharf overlooking the docks that jutted into the river, greeted him politely. He was older than she by at least fifteen years, but she always responded to him with motherly concern. Unlike the other men who lived on their boats in the marina, he had never tried to talk her into coming aboard his boat, nor made lewd comments about her admittedly voluptuous figure. She was married, and he was aware of the power that his small wealth—considerable by Vietnamese standards—might give him over her. Her husband was a poor fisherman, often at sea for days at a time. They lived on a tiny boat on one of the dirty sloughs that branched off the river near the center of town. Martin's relative wealth was not something that he felt lent him any superiority over Linh and her husband. They worked much harder for their meager income than he had ever worked for his. And he had no interest in exercising the privileges that wealth, even as limited as his, gave one in this poor country. Anyway, so far as he could see, Linh remained faithful to her husband, playfully dismissive of the overtures of the men she served in the café, mindful that she could not alienate them and keep their business, but resolute about her boundaries.

She placed a cup of coffee in front of him. The cup was covered by a tin container dripping hot water through course grounds of coffee into the cup below. "Another late night in Cho Lon bar, Ong Martin?" she asked, wagging an admonitory finger at him and barely suppressing a laugh. She had a narrow, striking face, with exotic, almond-shaped eyes and high cheekbones. With her ample curves and beautiful features she might have been a model if she had not chosen the path of marriage and children.

"How'd you know?" he asked, accepting the coffee and collapsing into a plastic seat at one of the rickety plastic tables that spilled out onto the dock in front of the cafe. The café was really more of a noodle restaurant, which was frequented mostly by the fisherman and dockworkers who worked along the waterfront, as well as by the boat owners whose vessels were tied up alongside his in the marina. Despite its plastic tables and chairs, Martin preferred it to the more plush tourist restaurants that lined the streets just across the river, or one of the more sedate cafes that could be found a half-mile farther away on his side of the river, amidst the expatriate neighborhoods. And he liked Linh's company.

"Your evenings show in your face in the morning."

"You're very perceptive," Martin answered, taking a sip of the Vietnamese coffee, thick and sweet with condensed milk, the way the locals drank it. But perhaps she didn't need to be perceptive, he thought to himself. His lifestyle was taking a visible toll on his body.

"It's OK, Ong Martin. You get back to writing soon. You're not like others who live here. They just having fun. You are serious. You are writer."

Was he? Linh's faith in him, her knowledge of his wishes and aspirations, gleaned from the quiet talks they'd occasionally had together, embarrassed him. "I'm just as much a low-life as the rest of them here," he answered.

"You no low-life Ong Martin. You just lonely. Maybe someday you find someone who make you feel better. Then you start to write again."

He shook his head. She didn't know the truth. He knew how low his deeds had taken him in the past. "I wish I had as much faith in myself as you do in me, Linh. But you've inspired me. I'll take my coffee back to the boat, and maybe I'll be able to write something. Maybe I'll write about you."

She lowered her eyes, embarrassed by his words. "My life not something to write about. You make up story. Rich people, pretty women, handsome men. That's what people like to read about. Reading take them away from their poor lives."

He wondered if she was right. But then he knew she wasn't. He had never written about the rich and privileged. That was the stuff of another era or of romantic trash novels. He wished he could write about the nobility he saw in the young waitress. But he didn't know her story well enough. The only story he really knew well was his own. All of his novels were about himself. Was it this self-absorption that had finally led to his paralysis? Was he just tired of himself?" Or was he simply afraid? Afraid to dwell on himself any longer for fear of what he would find.

He stood up and put a twenty thousand-*dong* bill, the equivalent of a dollar, on the table, then headed back to his boat. Maybe he'd write. He wasn't sure. He was going to have a drink, though, there was no question about that.

## Chapter 4

My whole life I had believed my father was dead. But then who was this man who looked out at me with a mirror image of my own face from the back of a book he had written sixteen years ago, while I was still a toddler? Had my mother lied to me? Had the mystery of my father's death been that it had never happened?

Or was I letting my imagination, and my longing for a father who had never been in my life, cloud my thinking?

It would have helped if I had hated Martin Bloom's writing. But instead of hating Martin Bloom's writing, I was captivated. His vocabulary was sophisticated enough to force me to look up some of the words he used: *fustian, crepuscular*. And the way he put together sentences was like a choreographer organizing the steps of an impressionistic dance routine. He was able to do exactly what I had always imagined myself being able to do with words. Maybe my ambition to become a writer wasn't just a fantasy. Maybe I *had* inherited someone's talent.

I was getting ahead of myself. On the one hand I had my mother's word that my father had died. On the other, I had this novel, written by a man with my father's name and my face. Was I so desperate for validation as a writer, or for a father, that I was willing to turn my back on reality and believe whatever made me feel better about myself?

I suppose so.

So, to quote Oedipus, I may have killed one parent, but perhaps I wasn't an orphan. Somewhere there was an egocentric, selfish, logophilic, and celebrated writer whose talented genes I may have been carrying around, like the silver 1965 dime my mother had been toting in the bottom of her purse for who knows how long. One day when she had emptied her purse looking for a Costco coupon, a friend had spotted it and informed her it was worth over eight thousand dollars. I couldn't just go back to school next year and carry on as usual with this new knowledge boring into my brain like a persistent earwig. My brain cells were too busy rearranging themselves to accommodate these revelations about the parent who'd always been a dark lacuna in my personal history.

I could no longer ask my mother if she had lied to me about my father. She'd always said that he'd died, but when she'd spoken about him it was with more bitterness than nostalgia. Had he not died? And if not, who was this man and why had I never known him?

I turned to Google. Sure enough, there was a Wikipedia page devoted to Martin Bloom. It listed his birthdate, although without a date for my father's birth, that wasn't helpful. But his age—ten years older than my mother—fit what I had been told. Disappointingly, it didn't list a spouse or children, temporarily deflating my hopes and causing me to curse myself for allowing them to rise as far as they had. But then I read the disclaimer, which said that much of the personal information on the site was incomplete, owing to the author's well-known reclusiveness, and I grasped that slim and admittedly vague piece of information as if it were a life preserver keeping me from sinking into a murky sea.

In addition to *A Memorial to Time*, his first and most famous novel, and *A Dead Man's Tale*, which Professor Hendrickson had given me, several others of Bloom's books were mentioned, along with snippets of critical praise each had received. He had twice been shortlisted for a National Book Award, and *A Memorial to Time* had been a finalist for a Pulitzer Prize. The website confirmed that Bloom had graduated from the University of Oregon. It also listed several of his previous employers: all prestigious universities, Brown, Virginia, Harvard. His current employer, if he had one, was unknown.

Since all of Martin Bloom's books had been published by the same publisher, I decided to called the publisher's offices. When I finally reached the editor whose name, Marilyn Reams, was listed in the acknowledgment section of *A Dead Man's Tale*, I was rewarded by being told that, a) Bloom's whereabouts were unknown either to her or to anyone else within her company and b) had she known, unless I'd been ready to produce a court order, she would hardly divulge such information to someone inquiring over the telephone. *Thanks a lot, you pontifical bitch.* Because the woman's tone toward me was like that of the school vice principal who had found me smoking in the girl's restroom and had proceeded to recite the entire school behavior code to me on the spot, I had tried to avoid saying that I was Martin Bloom's daughter, which of course might not even have been true. Besides, even if she had bought the story, it would have made me sound as if I were a pitiful lost child. But I finally became desperate enough that I made my filial claim, hoping that she wouldn't ask for some sort of proof, of which I had not a shred. Instead, she only replied that, 'if you really are his daughter then all I can say is that I pity you." Her pity must have been genuine because a second before I was ready to call her a heartless, corporate whorebitch, she had a change of heart and gave me the name and telephone number of his agent, "who ought to know where Martin is, but I wouldn't guarantee it."

I called the agent, a man named Sidney Duckworth, whose area code indicated that his office was in New York City. Duckworth didn't answer his telephone so I left a message, this time identifying myself as Martin Bloom's daughter, knowing that I was stretching the truth, but the message on his answering machine made it clear that the agent didn't return calls unless he knew the party calling.

While I was waiting for Duckworth to call back I began packing a bag. I didn't know where I was going, but I knew that I wasn't going to stay here in Eugene. I wasn't even sure why I was doing it. I think I had the vague and no doubt misguided idea that I'd suddenly discovered that someone else like myself existed in the world. That person *might* be my father; and if he was out there somewhere, then I was determined to find him. I had my mother's car, which had sat unused for the last nine months in the garage; I had cash in the bank from my mother's life insurance; to quote Moses, all I needed was a destination.

Sidney Duckworth was a nano-brained, patronizing asshole. That was my (hastily considered, I admit) opinion after he returned my call and proceeded to deliver me a lecture about how many young women had claimed to be Martin Bloom's daughter, lover, or wife—all of them hoping to gain a monetary reward for occupying such status. He told me that Martin Bloom had never been married, so far as he was aware, had no children, at least not legitimate ones, and had very little money, something he did know for sure. As Martin's agent, he deposited Bloom's meager checks in the author's bank account and assumed that Bloom withdrew them and spent them as soon as they cleared, since he had never known him to save a dollar in the entire time the writer had been his client. He had no idea where Bloom actually resided and was sure that, wherever it was, he wasn't interested in hearing from some ersatz daughter. The last known address he had had for the author was in Boston, where he had enjoyed a brief stint providing a graduate seminar in writing at Harvard. That was more than three years earlier and a year after his last novel had published, which had also represented the last written word he had submitted to either his agent or to any publisher.

Duckworth's words felt like nails driven into my father's coffin, further making me wonder what perversity in my personality had made me believe that Martin Bloom, the author, could be Martin Bloom, my father. "How do you know he's still alive?" I asked, becoming fearful that, even if Martin Bloom had been my father, I might have given up my orphan status too quickly.

"Oh I get an occasional telephone call..." Duckworth answered haughtily, "...in which he pleads for money. Martin assures me that he is alive and working on his best project yet. But he doesn't tell me where he is or when he intends to send me anything."

"So why are you telling me all of this, Mr. Duckworth, instead of telling me to fuck off, which is obviously what you would like me to do?"

"Because, young lady, On the off chance that you are related in some way to Martin, which your use of profanity suggests you might be, or that, related or not, you manage to find him, I want you to tell him that my patience is wearing thin and that he'd better send in something soon because his royalty checks for his previous works are getting smaller and smaller."

I guess I wasn't going to live off Martin Bloom's income, even if he was my father. And was I really going to take Mr.

Duckworth's statement that I swore, as Martin Bloom did, seriously? But I also had the picture and its uncanny resemblance to me. I told Duckworth that I would give Bloom the message. Then I thanked him for the little information he had given me and for the large amount of baditude he had thrown in with it. Despite his pronouncements about Martin Bloom having no children, I decided that the only thing I could do was head for Boston.

What?

I knew that I was making an impulsive decision. My mother would have been horrified, but it I was desperate to find out who I really was and I had become convinced that finding out if Martin Bloom was my father was the key to that puzzle.

## Chapter 5

Although I had no ties of what I would call a personal nature in Eugene, I did have my mother's condo. I felt uncomfortable just walking out without telling someone that I would be absent from it for an indefinite period of time. Mom had been immensely proud of our home, and my still raw sensitivity to her absence motivated me to not want to do anything to put her prized possession in jeopardy—even if she no longer had any way of knowing that I had.

The condo was the townhouse variety, with a gray clapboard exterior and attached on both sides to identical units, each having its own private entrance. It was supposed to resemble a neighborhood of San Francisco row houses, which is why it bore the name *Union Square*, although there was no city around it and no square within it. Probably most of its inhabitants had never even been to San Francisco, so they bought the idea like the country bumpkins they were. Within the complex there must have been two hundred units, connected by a labyrinthine network of streets. I was on speaking terms with the neighbors on both sides and a couple of other owners a few doors away, mostly because they had known my mother. I assumed that they thought that I was the miscreant brat who had driven her into an early heart attack. Every time I ran into any of them, they looked at me as if they thought that I was a druggie who might break into their houses when they weren't home and steal whatever I could in order to feed whatever disgusting habits I was into. I resisted giving them the finger.

The family who occupied the unit on the left of my house had always seemed pretty normal, although that was a relative term, considering the blue-collar, redneck neighborhood in which I lived. The father drove a pickup truck, which in Eugene was almost obligatory, and the mother had been over to visit my mom on numerous occasions. They had a son a few years older than I was, who looked like a some kind of technowierdo and I think went to the U of O and studied computers or some such nerdacious subject, although I never had seen him on campus. He had asked me if I wanted a ride to school once, but I thought he was creepy so I'd told him to go have sex with himself instead of bothering me. He didn't seem to get it so maybe he wouldn't remember.

I'd never actually approached any of my neighbors, except in the company of my mother, but if I was going to search for my father I was going to have to develop more chutzpah than I'd cultivated in my personality up to that point in my life. I'd been pretty much a loner and a recluse who had tried to project a "screw you" attitude toward a world I had always found alien and strange, with the hope that everyone would just leave me alone. My first opportunity to try out a new, more tolerant approach to people would come when I asked the Fullers, my neighbors, to keep an eye on my condo for me.

I practiced smiling a few times in the mirror, which produced an effect that reminded me of standing in front of one of those undulating mirrors at the county fair, making my mouth look as if it stretched all the way to my ears, and looking as if I were wearing a set of plastic Halloween dentures. Every time I tried to rehearse what I was going to say to the Fullers my brain seemed to flatline. I finally decided to just screw it and knock on their door and see what issued from my mouth.

Mrs. Fuller answered the door and when she saw that it was me, she looked worried. I felt like a five-year-old knocking on my neighbor's door to say that my mother wasn't home and I didn't know what to do, but I kept smiling, hoping that she would be reassured.

"Dillon, my dear, what's wrong?"

My college education had taught me to beware of numerous things: lascivious professors, bookstore buy-back policies, the Ides of March. But the scariest things of all were, to quote Holden Caulfield, well-meaning adults who "only want to help you." I was terrified.

"I'm OK, Mrs. Fuller. I just wanted to talk to you about something."

She stepped back to allow me to come into the house and then led me into the living room, which was a carbon copy of the one in our house, except their furniture was fake early American instead of being plush and modern, like ours—the payoff from my mother's lucky silver dime. Her husband was sitting on the couch watching a baseball game on a gigantic, flat screen that made one wall look like it could be a portal to another dimension.

"Turn that thing down, Phil," Mrs. Fuller, frowning, told her husband. "Dillon from next door needs to talk to us."

"I could just talk to you, Mrs. Fuller," I said, looking apologetically at her husband and hoping that he wasn't too irritated with me. Given my background, I was clueless as to how husbands or fathers reacted to teenage girls. But, in fact, his face mirrored the same concerned expression as his wife's.

"Nonsense, you can talk to both of us. Phil and I share everything. We've been worried about you over there all alone and we're very interested in how you're doing, aren't we, Phil?"

Her husband had not just turned down the T.V., he had turned it completely off, the portal to the fifth dimension now transformed into one humongous blank eye. "Phil" was looking directly at me. "Anything we can do to help you, young lady, would be our pleasure," he said, a look of solicitude plastered on his face. Mrs. Fuller came over and sat beside him on the couch.

I had become the center of their attention and I started to panic. I took a seat on a green and yellow plaid cushion on a straight-backed wooden chair. All of their neighborly concern was threatening to smother me. I experienced a flashback to a story I had read as a child. It was about a little girl, "Coraline," who found a secret door to a hidden home right next to hers, in which lived a mother and father who were just like her real mother and father except that they had buttons for eyes. They made her a prisoner in their house and wouldn't let her return to her own parents. But I had no parents—or at least I only had a dead mother and a ghost-like father whose existence was still in question—so why was the Fullers' well-meaning solicitude making me so nervous?

"I'm going away for a while, and I just wanted you to keep a watch over my condo. Maybe collect any mail that shows up, make sure nobody breaks into the place while I'm gone."

Both of the Fullers had these big sappy smiles on their faces, clouded by the worry that continued to linger behind their

23

friendliness. "You're not sick are you, Dillon? Are you going to the hospital?"

How in the heck had Mrs. Fuller come up with that one?

"I'm fine," I answered, trying to look as perky as I could. "I'm taking a trip and I don't know how long I'll be gone. It could be a few months." Since I had no idea where I was going except to Massachusetts, and whether that destination would prove to be the beginning or the end of my search, I had to be vague about my plans.

Now Mrs. Fuller's concern turned to worry. "But I thought you were going to the university."

How could I explain that my dropping out of school was a positive move? "I'm taking a little vacation. Visiting relatives, you know, renewing some old ties now that my mother is gone." I didn't want to get into the details of my quest for my delinquent and only possibly still living, father. "Since I'm all alone, I need to reestablish connections with my family." Even though I was stretching the truth, the words, which reminded me that I, in fact, had no family, stuck in my throat, and I could feel myself ready to cry. I tried my best to put on a Lady Gaga poker face.

"I think that's commendable," Mr. Fuller said, but he still looked concerned. "But won't you miss the start of the school year?"

"You know how important it was to your mother that you go to college," Mrs. Fuller chimed in, a note of disapproval entering her voice.

They were taking the role of surrogate parents seriously—they were trying to make me feel guilty.

"Some of my relatives might not live long enough for me to see them If I don't go now," I continued to lie. I was starting to get the hang of it. "My mother would be very disappointed if I neglected seeing my relatives for what could be the last time." Two could play the 'mother's dying wish' game. "I can always resume school, but once they're gone..." I broke off my sentence and tried to look wistful, staring vaguely into the air, as I'd seen my favorite actress, Michelle Stafford, do on *The Young and the Restless*.

At that moment, Randolph, their geeky son, who had probably been upstairs fondling his computer, came down the stairs. He nodded in my general direction. Randolph had been burned once trying to be friendly to me and he was obviously not going to put himself in that position again.

"Randolph, Dillon is going away to visit some sick relatives. She wants us to watch her apartment while she's gone," Mrs. Fuller said. She'd obviously bought my story about the relatives.

Randolph stood at the bottom of the stairs looking into the living room. "Are you withdrawing from school?" he asked me. Was it a projection on my part or was there a note of censure in his voice?

"Temporarily."

"You'd better do it officially or they won't let you back in." He spoke as if he were the school principal reciting the school rules to me. Dipshit nerd.

I nodded and gave him what I hoped he could tell was a patently insincere smile, although, given his socialimbecility, he probably thought I was being nice.

I was right. "How long are you going to be gone?" he asked, obviously encouraged by my fake conviviality.

"I don't know. Maybe a few weeks."

"I wouldn't do that," he said, shaking his head as if he couldn't understand how I could make such a grievous error. "Over half of the students who take time off in their first two years of college never return." He looked toward his parents for approbation, and his father nodded gravely, as if his son had just said something profound.

I felt like kicking the jerk in the nuts, but instead I said, "Sometimes family has to come before thinking about your own future. I've had to learn that, Randolph, because I lost my mother. You'll understand some day." To quote George W. Bush, let him try say something smart-ass in response to that.

Randolph's face turned red, and he mumbled something I couldn't really hear and then headed toward the kitchen.

"You poor girl. You've had to cope with so much at such a young age," said Mrs. Fuller, watching her son's back as he headed toward the refrigerator. No doubt she was wishing she'd had a daughter like me instead of a son like him. "Well, I admire you for what you're doing," she continued. "And don't worry. You just leave us a key so we can check up on the house now and then to be sure there are no water leaks or anything and we'll keep your mail for you—if you give us the key to your mailbox. Everything will be taken care of while you're away."

I thanked the Fullers and gave them the extra keys—my mother's set—that I had thought to bring with me in hopes that they would say yes to watching my house. Mrs. Fuller gave me a big hug and Mr. Fuller patted me on the back, as if I'd done a good job. When I left their house I felt as if I'd barely eluded the two button-eyed parents who would have liked to make me their daughter.

## Chapter 6

I'd never been farther from Eugene than an occasional trip to Portland with my mother so that she could do what she called, "real shopping," usually the week before Christmas. I had a map from AAA and a suitcase full of clothes—everything from tank tops to sweaters, not having a clue as to what the weather would be like driving across country—and plenty of cash and a debit card. My mother's car was sitting in the garage, unused since the day she had died. I'd used my bicycle to get to school and back and taken the bus if it was raining. I knew how to drive and I had a driver's license. It's just that the almost new, white Honda Civic my mom had driven had been her baby. She'd never actually let me drive it, although I'd driven her old Ford Taurus plenty of times. Then there was the fact that my mom had had her fatal heart attack just as she was getting out of the Honda after coming home from my graduation. I'd developed a phobia about getting into the car.

The moment I opened the driver's side door of the Civic I was faced with two things which I had been dreading: first was the smell of my mother's perfume. She had used this kind of sickening sweet fragrance, often applied quite liberally, especially when she went out. It had always reminded me of the smell inside the candy shop at the mall where they gave out free samples. One day after school in eighth grade I'd eaten so many samples that I'd thrown up into their display case. After my mother died, I had sprayed every kind of deodorizing spray around the house, from room fresheners to underarm antiperspirant, attempting to get rid of her lingering perfume smell, but here it was again, permeating her car.

Even worse was my second fear. My avoidance of anything connected to the car since my mother had died had caused me to neglect cleaning out her belongings. Luckily, she was proud enough of the Civic to have not let it become the garbage receptacle the old Taurus had been. She hadn't even let me decorate the outside of the car with signs and stickers—*If You Can Read This, You Didn't Go To*

27

*My High School; Jocks Should be Worn, Not Dated; Raise the National IQ: Wear a Condom*—as I had the Taurus. The only bumper sticker on the Civic was one my mother had chosen: *Three wise men? Are you serious?* She'd said it was from the Bible. I'd told her that I preferred Mary's line, *"I thought you said I wouldn't get pregnant."*

Inside the car there was a center console full of makeup and coins, and a driver's side door pocket stuffed with wadded up Kleenex, most of it dabbed with lipstick. My mother was more consumed with her appearance than I had realized and I felt an overwhelming sense of loss when I sat behind the wheel and thought about her. I ran my hands over the steering wheel, imagining that I could feel her touch in the warm plastic. Finally, I opened the glove compartment, and there was my mother's government ID badge from her job, complete with her picture staring up at me. When I took the badge out of the glove box, I bit my lip to hold back my tears. This was exactly why I hadn't driven the car up to this point.

I gave myself a mental kick in the butt and willed myself back into action. The engine in the car barely turned over, sounding like the motor of an overloaded washing machine, but after several tries it finally caught. Thank God, I told myself. I wouldn't have wanted to have to go next door and ask the Fullers for help, knowing that such a request would have just given them permission for another lecture. I let the car run awhile to charge the battery and added my toiletries to my suitcase, then put it in the trunk of the car. I'd saved things like my toothbrush and toothpaste and my antiperspirant, until the very last. In the words of Marco Polo, I didn't want to start a long trip with unbrushed teeth or sweaty armpits. My purse, which I planned to keep next to me on the passenger seat at all times, contained my checkbook, my bank debit card, about a thousand dollars in cash, and my passport.

My mother and I had each gotten passports the year before because she'd at least toyed with the idea of our going on a cruise to Mexico together to celebrate my graduation. The passport was another crushing reminder of what I was missing without my mom, but I took it anyway. You never knew; maybe Martin Bloom would turn out to be in Mexico or Canada and I'd need to use my passport to get there. I pulled out of the garage and left the car idling at the curb while I went back into the house for one last check around. I had this overwhelming urge to say goodbye to my mother. I wanted to reassure her that I would call as soon as I ended my first day on the road. I wandered from room to room, feeling like a lost dog who had returned home to find her family had moved away without her. There was no one to say goodbye to and no one whom I would be calling at the end of the day.

It was early September, and I'd decided to take a southern route to Massachusetts just in case there were any early snows in the Rockies. I possessed what NPR and my history professor had called the typical, poorly educated American teenager's ideas about U.S. geography and had even less of a clue about weather across the country. I'd never driven over any mountains, not even with my mom, and I had no idea what I might encounter if I headed directly east, which would have taken me over the Rocky Mountains—mudslides? mountain lions? snow? I had some tire chains in the trunk of the car, but I didn't have a clue how to put them on. I figured the safest thing was to head south before heading east. My first day's drive would get me to Sacramento. At least that was my plan.

I did have to cross one mountain—Mt. Shasta, which finally loomed directly in front of me, looking like the picture on the side of an old-time soda can, as I pushed the grumbling Honda Civic up the winding mountain highway, holding my breath while I waited for the car to overheat or the brakes to fail or some other catastrophe to either kill me or at least cut my trip short before it really got started. Nevertheless, I kept, to quote Ricky Bobby, the "pedal to the metal" to get through the high country as quickly as I could. Passing the marker indicating my entrance into California felt like a real achievement. I had never been to California and getting out of Oregon seemed like a massive first step and one that signaled to me that I really had embarked upon an adventure.

Driving through Northern California was more boring than sitting through Mr. Arnold's U.S. History class in high school. I almost had to prop my eyelids open with my fingers in order to stay awake. The only thing that kept me alert was the scare I'd gotten listening to the little Civic's engine having to work so hard climbing Mt. Shasta. I began imagining that every sound from the engine was a telltale signal that everyone but me, who knew nothing about cars, would have recognized as a disaster about to happen. Finally I stopped at a service station that advertised "mechanic on duty." The mechanic was a grease-covered middle-aged man with glasses and a head that was bald on top but with blond hair on the back and sides, which was long enough to touch his shoulders. He even had a helper—an acne-faced, equally grimy teenager who appeared mute and looked out at the world from dull, red-rimmed eyes while he chewed on a toothpick hanging from the corner of his mouth. There didn't seem to be any cars in their garage, and I couldn't figure out where their many layers of dirt had come from, except that maybe they just never washed. From the way they both smelled I guessed I was right.

I asked the mechanic if he could check my car to be sure that there was nothing wrong with it. He opened the hood, listened to the engine, kicked the tires, then glanced at his imbecilic helper and said, "I can't tell anything just listening, but if you heard something, the smart thing to do would be to let me do a diagnostic with my electronic gear."

I couldn't see anything that looked electronic in his garage except a TV with what looked like a football game dancing across its screen. "How long will that take and how much will it cost?" I asked.

"About an hour and a hundred-fifty bucks. Unless I find something wrong, of course, then who knows? Could be pretty steep. Could take more than a day to fix." He winked at the retard. "You might have to stay here overnight." He glanced over at a collection of rundown buildings behind the gas station.

For the first time, I noticed that the row of buildings behind the station was actually a motel. There was a faded sign across the top of one of the buildings and a couple of beat up pickup trucks parked alongside two of the cabins. Was this going to be where I spent my first night away from home?

I opened up Google Maps on my phone. The next town was only another fifteen miles down the road. I didn't need to debate the choice. I'd rather break down on the highway than spend a night around Moe and Curley and whatever of their inbred relatives ran the motel.

I said no thanks and got back into my car.

I pulled onto the highway, feeling smarter for not getting suckered into a bogus car repair scam by the two crackers at the gas station, but still feeling insecure about my car's engine. By now I was almost out of the mountains and the Civic seemed to be doing just fine, so I convinced myself that the whole episode had been a symptom of my fear rather than a sign of car trouble.

I had no idea when I would begin to see palm trees, but once I left the mountains, there were hardly any trees at all, just monotonously flat farmlands and, off in the distance, clusters of buildings, which I took to be bucolic little towns where all the hayseeds who populated this bleak countryside resided. The town that I'd located on the Google Map was the first of those towns, located a couple of miles off the highway, and since my car seemed to have cured itself, I took a chance and passed on the exit that would have taken me to there. None of the truck stops on the highway had garages so I just filled up on gas, stocked up on hamburgers and French fries, and used the restrooms, which, by the way, were, without exception, so yucky that I tried to avoid drinking liquids unless I was desperate. My head was filled with visions of all the creepy diseases they'd shown us pictures of in junior high school health class, and I vowed to check myself for diseases or bugs or both, as soon as I stopped for the night.

By evening the road signs told me that I was approaching Sacramento.

There was a Motel 6 next to the truck stop where I stopped for gas and I decided that, already being on the outskirts of Sacramento, and feeling as if I had ventured to another planet, I might as well call a halt to the first day of my journey. I pulled through a Burger King for my last burger and fries of the day, and then checked into the hotel. It was my first time staying by myself away from home.

The hotel clerk, an older, gray-haired man in a short-sleeved shirt and wearing suspenders to hold up his pants, looked with suspicion at all the hardware protruding from my face and the tattooed snakes crawling up my arms and asked me, with a stern look, where my parents were.

"I don't have any," I answered.

He frowned. "That's not a good answer."

You mean I was going to need parents to check into a motel? That didn't make any sense. I was nineteen years old. "My parents are dead," I said. I figured, that I was being more or less accurate, since until a few days before I hadn't even had the hope that my father was still alive.

He was still frowning. "I'd feel better if a young lady like you had parents with you."

I shrugged. "So would I," I answered, " ... but unless you can bring people back from the dead, I'm afraid it's just me."

He seemed satisfied, although he now looked at me as if I might be an escapee from an insane asylum. I paid for the room in cash, though he still demanded to see my debit card. After he finally gave me the room key, he warned me about having any parties in my room.

"I don't know a soul in this God-forsaken wasteland, and I'm too tired to do anything but go to sleep," I told him. He still looked at me suspiciously but nodded and pointed me in the direction of my room.

I locked both locks on the motel room's door and turned on the TV set for some company and so that it might sound—to any strangers, rapists or sadoperverts of the type who lurked around truck stops waiting to find young single women to strangle—as though more than one person occupied the room. I ate my burger and fries and coke, and then faced having to do the most difficult thing; I had to take a shower. I debated skipping it, but I was hot and sweaty and I was still thinking about the collection of toilet seats I'd been forced to sit on during the day. Letting my hygiene go to hell or catching a disease that left me oozing foul liquids from open sores on my ass was no way to start out my new life.

The shower had one of those soft plastic curtains, suspiciously like the one I remembered from the old *Psycho* movie my mother had ordered on Netflix and made me watch with her because it scared her too much to watch alone— so we watched the whole thing holding each other's hands. Having no mother and no one's hand to hold, I decided to leave the shower curtain open so no butcher knife wielding screwnutcase, including the cretinous fruitcake who worked in the office, could creep in and surprise me. I spent a long time scrubbing every private place on my body, but the experience, which I otherwise hurried through, was uneventful. However, the bathroom floor was soaked with water because I hadn't used the shower curtain. I nearly slipped, which would probably have broken my neck, bringing my search to an early conclusion and being a fate nearly as bad as having a fruit-of-the-loom maniac stab me in the shower.

The next morning I saw that there was a palm tree right in front of the motel. I hadn't noticed it the night before, because I'd been too tired to have looked around at my surroundings, and it barely qualified for its name anyway. The palm fronds at the top of the tree drooped as if they were exhausted, and they were covered with big orange rust-like patches, making it look as if the palm tree had picked up all of the diseases that I'd thought I'd contracted by using the gas station restrooms the day before. I imagined it as a sort of *Dorian Gray* palm tree, which accumulated all of the ills of the people who stayed overnight in the motel. But, since this was my first palm tree sighting, I felt as if I was making progress.

Chapter 7


Someone claiming to be his daughter had called? As soon as his agent, Sidney Duckworth had told him, Martin had been overcome by a wave of anxiety, submerging him like a swimmer caught in an undercurrent. His panic was quickly replaced by a suffocating cloud of depression, which even now, more than an hour since he'd gotten off the phone with Sidney, smothered him. He buried his head in his hands and cursed the fact that denial was such a poor solution to real problems.

He did have a daughter. Not that he'd admitted that to Sidney when they'd spoken on the telephone during his periodic check-in with his agent, a check-in in which he'd again managed to disguise his whereabouts. His daughter was even legitimate, despite Sidney's insinuations. But it had been many years ago that he'd been married to Regina, her mother—years that resided in the back of his mind like an inquisitorial judgment, sentencing him to renewed torture every time he allowed himself to think about them.

Regina had been a beauty, a local Eugene girl working her way through the university, dreaming to become a teacher someday. She and Martin had met at a coffee house when she had shown up one night, hoping to sample the bohemian lifestyle, which in those days had thrived on the edges of the campus. He was an intense English major, older than she was by ten years and a hopeful writer who, in the spirit of the times, was experimenting with poetry, which he was reading that evening at the café where he worked as a waiter while finishing his degree in literature. He'd been there with Jeremy Slater, his best friend and fellow writer. Martin had been taken with Regina's fresh young look, her innocent curiosity. He had swept her off her feet with his puerile poetry and his pseudo-intellectual pronouncements about art and literature. It had all been bullshit...something he readily admitted now, but was not sure that he'd known back then.

Regina had put him on a pedestal and, like the self-centered chauvinist he had been at the time (and still? he wondered), he'd allowed her to do so... taken advantage of it, in fact. Not that he hadn't been attracted to her. He was, and even more so because his friend Jeremy had also been. In fact he'd always wondered whether, if he hadn't been so caught up in his rivalry with Jeremy, he would have ever married Regina. But the introverted Jeremy, whom Martin had secretly feared was a more talented writer than he, could not compete with Martin's social skills or good looks. Martin had emerged the triumphant suitor, and his friend had capitulated with grace, wishing the couple good luck and vowing that his enchantment with Regina would not come in the way of his continuing friendship with Martin. Regina and Martin had gotten married. Jeremy had been his gracious best man. Regina quit school to support her new husband so he wouldn't have to work and could devote himself to his writing and to completing the last year needed to earn his degree. Then she had gotten pregnant. Suddenly what had seemed like a comfortable arrangement, which had provided him both emotional and sexual support as well as a free ride through school, felt like an ominous responsibility. Always prone to bouts of anxiety, Martin was overcome by a debilitating attack of panic. He was unable to eat; he couldn't get out of bed to go to class. He drank to quiet his shattered nerves.

It was clear to Martin that he had to leave. Jeremy was appalled that his friend could even consider leaving the woman whom they both loved, especially with a child on the way. Martin's nerve faltered. Perhaps he should stay, ride out the anxiety attack until it went away of its own accord (it always did didn't it?), resume the course of his life as a father. Back and forth he struggled to decide. Then the baby came. By this time Martin had finished his degree, his anxiety had subsided to a constant background noise, which he kept at bay with modest amounts of alcohol, while he feverishly sent manuscripts to agents and publishers. Jeremy had reaffirmed his respect for Martin for having made the correct choice.

Then came the shock of Jeremy's death, which was a mystery to everyone but Martin. Regina had been devastated. Martin withdrew, his panic having returned tenfold. Everything in his life–Regina, the new baby–seemed tainted by its association with Jeremy's death. He could not force himself to attend Jeremy's funeral. While Regina was at the cemetery and the baby with a neighbor, Martin boarded a bus to New York, a change of clothing and his manuscripts jammed into the canvas pack on his back. He hadn't looked back, leaving a financially strapped young mother and six-month-old child behind him while he peddled his stories in the big city and started a new life.

He'd obscured the reasons for his leaving, even to himself, telling himself that his art had demanded what he had done. He'd invoked a higher justification for his behavior than simple family responsibility, the kind that constrained ordinary men. Somehow, he'd told himself, in the big scheme of things his writing would make up for everything. What a load of crap. He had been a shit and he knew it. But he had been powerless in the face of his overwhelming anxiety.

Now, according to Duckworth, Regina was dead, a piece of news that sobered him, figuratively, anyway. A chapter of his life was officially closed. The young wife who had remained alive in his memory would never grow any older. His daughter, or someone claiming to be his daughter, was looking for him. And he, the celebrated writer, gin bottle clutched to his chest like a child's chewed-on blanket, was hiding in this run-down marina in a third-word country.

His conscience nagged at him like a persistent voice. But conscience was one of those things that reared its head in moments of reflection rather than in moments of decision... at least it was that way with Martin. A momentary attraction, a fleeting opportunity for glory, a simple release from tension, these were what determined what he chose to do. And always his choices were based upon his personal satisfaction, not his concern for others, not upon a sagacious plan for his future. It was only when his latest quest was over—his glory achieved or his failure complete—that Martin thought about what he had done in terms of the kind of person he was. Only then was he haunted by that nagging voice of conscience.

He sat in his plush captain's chair, shirtless, wearing a pair of sun-bleached green shorts, his soft, sagging, middle-aged skin bronzed darker than that of the local population of Vietnamese. The humid temperature was already nearing one-hundred degrees. Only the mild, if pungent, breeze off the fetid river made sitting outside on his boat's deck bearable. The marina only held about 15 boats, half of them supporting permanent inhabitants: Americans, Australians or Canadians who, like himself, had migrated to this friendly, if still Communist, Southeast Asian country to drown their pasts in drink, in local women, and in anonymity. Just down the river was the ferry dock where passengers came by foot or motorcycle from the more populous other side of the river where the majority of the city lay. Behind him along the shore ran a road. Behind it were luxury condominiums and villas, the owners of which were a mixture of Chinese, Europeans, Australians and Americans. And along the rest of the river on both shores ran the city, teeming with life, a mixture of neighborhoods, a few of them wealthy, the majority crowded and poor.

Martin rarely frequented the tourist restaurants across the river or the wealthy expatriate neighborhoods near his moorage. Despite his loneliness, he was always afraid he might have to strike up a conversation with someone who would recognize him, ask him to explain what he was doing here in this dilapidated country, provide an update on the progress of his stalled career, divulge the depths to which his existence had sunk.

He was more likely to frequent the local bars in places such as *Cho Lon*, the Chinese district of the city or in the raunchy "backpacker district," where none of his academic or literary acquaintances was likely to show up, but where English was spoken almost as often as Vietnamese. The bars were populated by other lost souls, like him, and they were as good a place as any for trolling for local women, even if he often had to pay for them, and the gin was a hell of a lot cheaper.

And there was no one to confront him with his past. Damn! What in the hell could his daughter, if that was who it was, want with him? He'd never acted like a father nor did he harbor any suspicion that he would have been a successful one if he had. If she thought she could get any money from him, she was sure as hell wrong about that. Not that he didn't believe a daughter deserved something from him— she certainly did. But he didn't have anything to give her. He'd never had.

So why did he feel a deep and disquieting sense of guilt, a constant hint of nausea, as if peering into his past threatened a vertiginous collapse? He didn't have to work very hard to think of things he'd done wrong in his life, but what did broken relationships, unfulfilled promises of productivity, disappointed colleagues and literally hundreds of downright lies have to do with what he should be feeling, alone here on a boat on the Saigon River, with all of those bungled opportunities and dishonest relationships behind him? Everyone he'd disappointed or hurt had no doubt gone on and lived quite happily without him. As his autobiographical character in A *Dead Man's Tale* had discovered, there was no point in trying to go back and fix anything. Everybody had moved on, hadn't they?

Everyone except his daughter, apparently.

There was only one remedy for guilt, he reminded himself, and he took another long swig from the bottle of gin.

Chapter 8

Holy Moly, California never stops! If my boredom were any gauge, I should have been halfway across the country by now, but by noon I'd only reached Los Angeles. It took me more than an hour to get from one end of the city to the other, although how one would ever have known when the city started or ended, if there hadn't been signs to say so, was beyond me. Everything seemed to be in a state of deterioration—not like on TV or the movies—and the roads were cracked and potholed, many of them in the process of being repaired. I felt as if I had arrived in some devastated, post-Apocalyptic metropolis. I wouldn't have been surprised to find that apes now controlled the city.

Los Angeles became Orange County without any perceptible change in the scenery, except for the proliferation of signs for Disneyland and Knott's Berry Farm. I felt a wave of sadness. My mother had always promised that we would go to Disneyland, even when I had become too grown up, at least in my own mind, to want to go. As I passed one of the Disneyland exits I could see this dopey looking mountain, which appeared as if it were made from papier-mache with a bottle of white Elmer's glue spilled over its top. I was tempted to stop, but then I would have just missed my mother and felt guilty that I was experiencing Disneyland without her, when I'd promised her that I would be in college. Anyway, I didn't think I'd enjoy riding around in teacups or getting my picture snapped standing next to Goofy, and I reminded myself that, just like the *Blues Brothers*, I was on a mission, a probably misguided, ill-thought out chimerical mission, but a mission nonetheless.

When I finally hit San Diego, I could at last turn east. It was only mid-afternoon and I figured I could make it to Yuma, Arizona by early evening and stop there for the night.

When I entered Arizona and encountered my first Indian reservation, I remembered Taylor, the character in *The Bean Trees* who had stopped at a restaurant and been handed an Indian baby,

39

which she later adopted. Feeling like an abandoned child myself, I figured I didn't need to acquire another abandoned child, especially one needing feedings and diaper changes. I loved my mother, but I didn't want to *become* her by tending a baby at my age. I resolved to check my back seat for any stray packages, especially the kind that cried or peed, every time I stopped for food or gas.

I didn't find any Indian babies in the back seat, but I sure got a lot of stares at my spiked hair and tattoos when I stopped at the truck stops for gas and bathroom breaks. When I pulled into what my phone's Google Map said should be my last stop before Yuma, some yo-yo with a lot more tattoos than I had sidled up to me at the counter where I was buying a Snickers for the last leg of my day's journey.

"You and I look like a matched pair, little lady," he drawled in a hayseed twang, baring his lower arm and holding it up next to mine. Sure enough, a blue snake with red eyes was writhing up his forearm. Its tail held a rattle with little quotation mark-like dashes on either side of it, as if to imply that it was shaking its rattle.

Clever.

I went into my autistic spectrum mode and avoided eye contact with him. At the same time, I directed a serial killer stare toward the guy behind the counter, hoping to get him to get his butt in gear and take my money for the candy bar.

"You lookin' for a ride?' the geek with the tattoo asked, obviously unimpressed with my treatment of him as a subhuman, something he no doubt was used to. "I got my truck right outside. I got plenty of room. I even got a bed in it." He was leering over my shoulder and his breath smelled as if he'd been eating from garbage cans.

I moved a few feet away. "Can I pay for this?" I asked the idiot behind the counter. God knows what he was doing back there. He was probably zoned out on drugs. Everyone in the truck stop looked as if he'd recently been released from prison.

"Stuck-up bitch, huh?" the man's tone had become nasty. He moved over close enough that he was touching my shoulder. "Too good for a trucker, are you?"

I was starting to panic, but I was also getting angry. "Keep your hands in your own pants, mister," I said, without looking at him. I was ready to call him a shit-for-brains, even though I was scared to death of his reaction. Thank God the cretin at the cash register finally took my money. I told him to keep the change and turned and almost ran out the door. I didn't look back until I'd gotten outside.

"Fucking hippie!" I heard the man yell. He'd followed me outside. I looked back and he was walking toward me. "You think you can just walk away from me?"

I sure as heck did. I jumped into my car and slammed the door and locked it. Then I started the engine and backed out of my parking space, missing the dipshit trucker by less than a foot. As I headed back out on the highway I could see him in my rearview mirror giving me the finger.

I was shaking with fear and cursing myself for being a coward. I should have told the asshole to fuck himself, should have threatened to call the police if he didn't leave me alone. But despite my gutter mouth, I'm not really good at confronting people. I just want them to leave me alone.

I decided to turn on the car radio and try to take my mind off the idiot in the truck stop. I had to choose between country music and three stations with Christian preachers proclaiming that Jesus both loved me and wanted to condemn me to burn in hell. I chose the shitkicking music.

Except for a couple of Indian stores selling cigarettes, I saw no signs of human habitation. From one horizon to the other there was nothing but desert. I had visions of the car breaking down on the highway and me ending up like one of those dead reptiles I kept passing on the side of the road, baked by the sun into nothing but flattened skin. But I wasn't the only one on the highway. Every once in a while I passed or was passed by an eighteen-wheeler, or sometimes by a pickup hauling a trailer with horses. In less than an hour I would reach the outskirts of Yuma.

At some point I noticed a big white semi coming up behind me. It pulled up close and then just stayed there, sitting on my tail. Usually, especially on the long, straight stretches of highway, the big trucks floorboarded it and zipped right by me—me trying to keep within the speed limit for some unknown reason... probably fear. I tried to slow down to let this guy go around me, but he only slowed down himself. When he got close enough for me to see in his front window, I peered into my rearview mirror and saw that it was that shithead from the truck stop. Holy crap, the weirdocreep was following me!

I floored the gas pedal and tried to pull away, but it didn't take him long to catch up. He pulled to within a few feet of my rear bumper. I could feel the sweat running down my sides, and my hands were so slick with perspiration that I could barely hold onto the steering wheel. The jerk was following about ten feet behind me and I knew that if I tried anything wiseass, like putting on my brakes, it would be me who got the worst of things.

The houses and stores alongside the road were getting more numerous, a sign that I was getting close to Yuma. I was praying that I'd pass a cop of some kind and he'd see that the truck was following me too closely and arrest the bastard. But God wasn't listening, and the highway patrol must have taken the day off. I saw a sign saying that the *Wagon Wheel Motel* was only another mile down the road, and I realized this might be my only chance. When I saw a low building with a replica of a covered wagon sitting on top of its roof about 200 yards ahead, I slowed my speed enough that, when I was almost to the entrance to the motel, I could jam on my brakes, turn the steering wheel a hard right, and fishtail into the gravel driveway, nearly rolling the car in the process. I was lucky I didn't pee my pants. The white truck continued past, its tires smoking as the lamebrain behind the wheel applied the brakes.

I pulled up in front of the office and got out of the car. I could hear the truck out on the freeway. He was turning around. I couldn't believe he hadn't given up. The jerk was still stalking me.

When I entered the motel office, a blonde overweight woman with a pink complexion stared at me with a worried look on her face. "That was some entrance. Are you all right?"

I looked out the window and the truck was turning into the motel's driveway.

"That truck driver is after me. He followed me from the last truck stop and I haven't been able to get him off my tail. I need a room, but I don't want him staying in the same place with me." I hoped that she could sense my desperation.

She walked around from behind the counter and looked out the window. The dorkbrain was getting out of his truck. "Do you know him?" she asked me.

"I never saw him before the truck stop. I hardly even spoke to him, but he kept trying to talk to me, then he said I was being rude to him. I thought I'd gotten away from him, but he started following me on the highway." I'm sure I sounded as if I was a naïve teenager who needed a parent to protect her. That's exactly how I felt.

The woman opened the door and stepped outside. The truck driver was walking toward the office, a moronic smile on his face.

"I just called the county sheriff's office, mister," the woman said in a flat, calm voice. She was standing with her feet wide apart and her hands on her hips, looking like Melissa McCarthy in *The Heat*. "They're on their way here."

The birdbrain stopped, and his smile turned into a scowl. "Why would you call the sheriff? I'm just looking for a room for the night."

"Not in my motel, you're not. That young woman inside says you're hassling her. She's under age, and I'm going to see that you're arrested."

Even from where I was standing inside the office I could see the man's face blanch. "Hey, no need to call anybody, lady. I didn't know she was under age. I can get a room someplace else."

"You'd better do that before the sheriff gets here or you'll be spending the night in the county jail."

He held up both hands in protest. "OK, OK, I'm outa' here. No need to get upset." He turned around and walked back to his truck then climbed in and started it up.

The motel owner watched until the truck pulled onto the highway.

"You didn't call the sheriff," I said. "And I'm not underage."

She walked back behind the counter. She was smiling. "You look like you're underage, and he believed me about the sheriff. He won't be back, don't worry." She looked me over as if for the first time. I thought she was going to comment on my tattoos or face jewelry but all she said was, "you look as if you need some parents with you."

"Why? Do you rent parents along with the rooms?" I asked.

She threw back her head and laughed a full-throated laugh, which ended in a trail of giggles that shook her ample jowls as if they were bags of Jell-O. "That's a good one, honey," she finally managed to eke out between chortles. The fact that she'd saved me from the crazed trucker and her good-natured cheer made me want to confide in the woman, but my characteristic paranoia reasserted itself and I stopped myself, remembering that she might have saved me from one sexual predator, but for all I knew she was some kind of human trafficker and I'd wake up tomorrow morning handcuffed to the bed with a swarthy fat man injecting me with drugs so he could start me off in a life of prostitution.

"How far you going, honey?" she asked.

I figured it couldn't hurt to tell her my destination, at least vaguely, so I said, "The East Coast."

"Whewee!" she exclaimed, smiling broadly. "You've got a long trip ahead of you. How long have you been on the road so far?"

I told her this was my second day, that I'd begun my trip in Eugene.

She nodded and handed me my key. "I bet you've been eating nothing but fast food on the way. You want to have a real dinner with me? I've got plenty and I'm going to eat in about a half hour."

A real meal sounded good, but not if it was going to be laced with some kind of knockout drug. This could be the enticement that got me into her door and then became a kidnapping. On the other hand, she had saved me, and I could smell some fried chicken cooking, the aroma wafting like a beckoning hand a through the open door behind the desk. I guessed that was where she lived. "I don't want to bother you and your family," I said, trying to be cagey about finding out if she was alone or if there was a husband in the picture. If there was a man involved, there was no way I was going to sit down to dinner at her table. I'd seen enough movies about creepy motel owners to know that they always came in couples—the woman fat and friendly to sucker you in and the man gaunt, unshaven and wearing bib overalls, a Bible in one hand and a chainsaw in the other.

"I've got a daughter. She's out cleaning one of the units. She's about your age. She's a student at the junior college, but she helps me here in the afternoons and lives with me."

That did it. College students weren't often human traffickers, although I wasn't absolutely sure about those who attended junior college, but by then I was almost overwhelmed by the smell of the fried chicken, so I said yes. I hoped that her omission of any mention of a husband meant that she didn't have one.

## Chapter 9

I put my stuff in my room, which was made up in a western motif with a bedspread decorated with stitched lariats and window curtains with pictures of covered wagons on them, giving me the impression that I was staying in some kind of cut-rate theme park. I took a quick shower, this time with the shower curtain closed, and changed my clothes, brushed my hair and went back to the office. I was greeted by a girl about my age. She was a young version of her mother, short, plump—not yet obese, although I could see another fifty pounds headed her way like a friendly dog waiting to pounce all over her. Like her mother she was a blonde who looked as if she were ready to break into laughter at any moment.

"Wow, you're driving to the East Coast on your own?" she said, her animated expression making it look as if this were an unheard of idea. "My mother would never let me drive that far on my own." She laughed, although it was a pleasant, accepting laugh, so I guessed that she was just the giggly type. Her mother must not have told her about the crazyass trucker who'd chased me.

"My mother's dead," I answered, figuring that would take the edge off of her chirpiness.

Her expression changed from cheerfulness to horror. "Oh, my God! I'm sorry for being so insensitive. I was just trying to be friendly. Can you forgive me?"

I felt bad for making her feel bad. I'd gotten used to people mentioning my mother and it didn't bother me anymore, but I'd forgotten that telling them that she'd died might bother them. "Don't worry about it. My mother probably wouldn't have approved, if she was alive and knew about it. And the truth is, I'm a little scared about what I'm doing myself."

In spite of myself I had succeeded in making her even more intrigued. She introduced herself as Betsy and invited me into the apartment. The food—fried chicken, green beans and mashed potatoes—was already on the table, which was a heavy square oak affair with three plastic placemats and silverware and paper napkins already

46

in place. The whole layout was strategically placed in such a position that they could still see the front desk in case a customer came in. I was glad, because I still wasn't completely calmed down from the incident with the truck driver.

"Thanks for saving me from that crazy trucker," I told the mother, whose name turned out to be Candy, a name that fit perfectly with her bright yellow hair and pink complexion.

"What crazy trucker?" Betsy asked.

"Some truck driver was chasing Dillon down the road," Candy told her daughter. "When she turned in here he followed her. I had to chase him away by saying that I'd called the sheriff."

"Weren't you scared?" Betsy asked, her amazement evident in her voice.

"I was terrified," I said. "But your mom knew just how to handle him."

"Men are pathetic," Candy declared. "They try to show how powerful they are by taking advantage of women, especially young women." She looked across the table at me. "Not all men, of course. Maybe your father's a good man."

I didn't know how to answer her, so I just smiled and dug into the chicken, which had a Colonel Sanders-like golden crispy crust and tasted even more delicious than it had smelled when it was cooking. I began to relax in the warmth provided by these two friendly women, although their easy mother-daughter banter made me acutely aware how much I missed my mom. But their friendliness must have lowered my defenses, because as soon as I stopped licking my fingers, I began to tell them about my mother dying and my discovery that my father might be alive and might be a famous writer and that my road trip was actually a quest to find the answer to that question. I omitted telling them about my secret desire to be a writer myself and my hope that connecting with my father, if that was who Martin Bloom really was, would somehow solidify this identity for me. When I mentioned that the man who might be my father was Martin Bloom, Betsy sucked in her breath as if she had just received a jolt of electricity and then jumped up from the table and came back a minute later with one of Bloom's books, this one called, *The Fourth Season*.

"I'm reading it right now for my English Class," Betsy said. "I love it. I can't believe the writer might be your dad."

Hearing Martin Bloom referred to as my "dad" brought on a feeling of panic. Had I really dropped out of school, left everything I knew behind and risked my life on the road just because a man with my dead father's name resembled me in a nearly twenty year old photograph? No one named Martin Bloom had ever done anything to make me think he was my "dad." Suddenly I felt sick to my stomach.

"What's the matter?" Betsy asked. She and her mother were staring at me, anxiety on both of their faces.

"I'm an idiot," I said.

"Why?" the two women asked in unison.

"Martin Bloom is a famous writer. I'm reading him in my class at college, Betsy is reading him in hers, there's a Wikipedia page devoted to him. He's taught at Harvard. If he were my father, my mother would have told me. It doesn't make sense that she'd tell me that he was dead. She would have known that I'd find out if she had made that up."

"But you said your mother had hinted that he'd left her before he died," Candy said, her concern still evident on her face. "Maybe she thought she was sparing your feelings by telling you that he'd died rather than that he'd left and never tried to contact you."

She'd provided me another lifeline for my irrational dreams, even though believing my mother had lied to me all of those years was almost as devastating as believing that my hopes that my father was alive were doomed to failure. "I guess if she might have thought that she was doing the right thing," I answered, wondering if I were again lying to myself.

"I've read about mothers doing that before," Candy said, nodding her head in support of my resurrected, if tentative, hope.

So had I, but it was always in novels, although I didn't say that. Both women were looking at me with such solicitous gazes that I wanted to believe my father was alive for their sakes, if not my own.

"So you're going to surprise him?" Betsy asked, obviously trying to brighten my sagging mood.

I decided to go along with them. "I have to find him first. That's what this trip is about."

"Sounds as if you're going to have a story of your own to write," Candy added, looking as if she were about to break into giggles.

Betsy was reading the flyleaf of her book. "It says here that he's a professor of English at the University of Virginia."

*Why hadn't I thought to look at the rest of his books?* "Really? When was that book published?"

Betsy flipped to the front of the book. "2007"

"That was before he taught the class at Harvard. But it's another lead if I don't find out anything in Boston."

"So what are you going to say to him when you find him?" Betsy asked. She seemed to have faith that I would be successful in my venture.

If he really was my father and he'd never tried to contact either my mother or me, then what I'd like to say to him would be what I'd said to the cheerleader in high school who'd asked me why I was such a weirdo—*how come you're such an asshole?* But, actually, I was at a loss. I hadn't really thought about what I wanted to say when I met him, except to ask him if he was my father. If he was, then what I wondered was how much I was like him and how much of our likeness, if it existed, was related to why I yearned to be a writer. "I have no idea," I finally answered. "His agent said he's always broke so I won't be asking him for money. I think I just want to find out what he's like. I like to write myself, and my professors told me I had talent. Maybe I just want to find out what my father and I have in common."

"Have you read all of his books?" Candy asked.

"Only one. As soon as I found out he was alive and a writer, I took a leave from school and started off to find him. I just read the one book my professor gave me."

"Take this one," Betsy said, handing me her book.

"You're reading it for your class."

"I can get another."

"I'll pay you for it," I said.

Betsy's face lit up. "I've got a better idea. When you find your father, have him autograph it for me. Have him say, 'to my daughter's friend, Betsy.' "

I took the book. "How about to my daughter's best friend, Betsy?"

The two women beamed at me, then both of them collapsed into laughter.

The rest of the evening we spent reading parts of *The Fourth Season*, which, like A *Dead Man's Tale*, was about a man in his later years, this time a symphony conductor who had been working on his own composition for over fifty years and was trying to finish it before he died. Betsy had already looked up most of the *fustian* Martin Bloom had thrown into the story and we all made fun of the pomposity that characterized his use of language, although we had to admit that he was able to write in a way that read almost like poetry, especially when we read it aloud. Then Betsy and Candy began telling me funny stories about the motel business in Yuma. It turned out that Betsy's father had left Candy about the same time my father had left my mother. We joked that it was the same man, but her father had been a country western singer, who also felt he couldn't find his true calling tied down by a wife and daughter. And he was definitely still alive.

"Men are bastards," Candy said.

I wasn't ready to speak so harshly about a father when I didn't know whether he was alive or dead, and if he was alive, why he had left my mother and me. "My mother used to say that," I answered.

The next morning I left early, but with enough fried chicken, soft drinks and candy bars packed into an ice-filled cooler to start me down the road to the same figure as Betsy and her mom and probably a major attack of pimples to boot. We all hugged and I took a card with the motel's address and phone number and promised to be in touch.

I meant it.

## Chapter 10

He hadn't left his boat for three days. Finally, Linh came aboard to check on him and found him drunk in his bed below decks. After reviving him with strong coffee and a bowl of noodles, the latter of which made him throw up, she coaxed him out of the dark confines of his cabin and into the glaring sunlight of the deck above. When she had finally left him, sitting, crapulous, in his captain's chair on the boat's bridge so that he wouldn't tumble off the aft deck into the river, she promised to come back in another couple of hours to be sure he hadn't slipped back into a drunken stupor, or worse, off the edge of his boat. He appreciatively waved her goodbye and sat alone with only his own thoughts.

He'd dreamt last night. It was the same dream that had plagued him many times in the past. Martin was never able to identify the other character in the dream, although his reaction to the person whose image haunted his somnolent mind was as one of intimate familiarity. As always, he was being pursued; he felt it as a threat, enough to engender panic as he raced with leaden feet up a stairway, or a hillside—last night it was a pathway with a dizzying number of switchbacks. When he broke into the open, on the roof of a building, sometimes on a subway platform, or last night at the edge of a cliff, he turned to face his pursuer, his panic almost unbearable. The attacker moved toward him threateningly, hands outstretched, usually a knife, but last night, a pair of scissors held menacingly over Martin's head. Then, as always, Martin moved aside, his antagonist plunged past him over the rim of the precipice, and disappeared. Martin peered after him, seeing nothing but a vague fog. As he gazed into the fog his panic grew to a crescendo and he awoke, sweating, his heart pounding as if he'd had a hit of cocaine. He had no idea why the dream should cause him such anxiety or what it meant, and he could think of no solution but to put it out of his mind with a hurried and desperate swallow of gin. Sometimes, as today, when he awoke the next morning, he barely remembered the details of the dream. Only his anxiety remained.

He looked out over the water and thought about his daughter, if that was really who she was, searching for him back in the U.S., calling Sidney Duckworth to ask for help. Martin knew that Sidney wouldn't be able to help her. Even Sidney couldn't find him, safely ensconced here in Saigon. His agent couldn't find him, his fans couldn't find him, his publisher couldn't find him, his old girl friends, his academic colleagues couldn't find him, and neither could his daughter. He knew that he wasn't just buried here in Vietnam, he was decaying. He was sliding beneath the surface of life, and he no longer knew if he cared. The only thing that could rescue him before he submerged completely would be recovering the ability to write again.

He drank to quiet the anxiety that always accompanied him, like a faithful but vicious junkyard dog, and he suspected that he couldn't write because he drank. He had always drunk and, in the past, he'd been able to write at the same time. But he'd never drunk this much. Not all day. Not as a herald to each morning. The problem was that his thoughts only became clear enough to be useful to his writing when he was intoxicated, when his anxiety was subjugated by alcohol. For that he needed to be at least half-drunk. And when he was half-drunk, his first impulse was to become fully drunk.

So why not stop drinking? He knew the answer. When he was drunk his thoughts soared. If he ever wanted to write again, he needed his thoughts to soar. And when he was drunk, he became interested, once again, in life—at least until he became even drunker—and he always became drunker.

He picked up his well-worn notebook and his pen and looked out across the other boats, which were rocking gently in the warm, mild breeze. The marina was coming to life. The river that never slept was rousing itself to its full height of clamor and chaos with tourist boats, cargo ships, tiny vendors' boats laden with fruit, vegetables, or fish, houseboats draped with laundry and children, and a few pleasure boats plying the choppy waters. In his own marina the other residents who lived on their boats were emerging to greet the day. He wouldn't be the only one to toast the morning with a bottle of gin, or whiskey or even beer. That was who lived on boats in Vietnam.

He lived in the perfect setting to write, and he was watching the opportunity slip thorough his fingers like the water flowing past in the river. He put down his pen and notebook and picked up the gin bottle. He knew that he was on to something, but he couldn't grasp it well enough to capture it with words. He wanted to write about life, about what life felt like when it was ebbing away, not because of disease or death but from malaise, ennui.

He had begun a story about a professor, a brilliant poet and incisive critic, who was also a gifted administrator. As the professor had risen in academic rank, then to department head and finally to a deanship, his writing had gradually slackened. His poetic spark was dying, withering like a flame deprived of oxygen. He was caught between the conflicting modes of thought—the poetic that fed his writing and the analytic that was required to manage his academic career. Necessity was on the side of the analytic, the budget planning, the course assignments and tenure decisions, the recruiting strategies to find the most prestigious faculty and the most gifted students. His own prestige, his salary and his position, depended upon the sagacity of his decisions. Only youth and nostalgia were on the side of the poetic. And youth and nostalgia were losing the battle to budgets and curriculum.

When Martin confronted his hero's dilemma he provided him with the only option he had offered to himself. He made him drink. And now his hero's story and Martin's life were going in the same direction—nowhere.

He was aware that he was developing an obsession. In each of his novels he had tried to capture the experience of growing old, as if, by painting a picture in words of his struggle with age, he might fix it in place, like a moth inside a lepidopterist's glass box or a forever unborn fetus, mouth open as it silently voiced a perpetual scream inside a pathologist's jar. He had no illusions that such a description could halt the inexorable process. But despite the empty feeling of hopelessness that his realization provoked in him, it wasn't a cessation of aging that he was after; it was perspective. He hoped to gain enough perspective to understand—to understand how to cope with his failures, his misdeeds, the unforgiveable errors of his past. Must one suffer until the end? Was death just the closure of possibilities? Was that why he anticipated aging with such dread: because felt he was losing his chance to dig himself out of the abyss into which his life had fallen?

Malcolm Truong, his philosopher friend, had told him that his lack of perspective sprang from the emptiness of Western cultural constructions, which he had grown up believing were the meaningful paradigms for making sense of his life. Malcolm had counseled him to go to Vietnam, to explore Buddhism, to partake of the collectivist society in which an individual's life had meaning only in the context of his role within the family and the society around him.

Martin agreed that American society had become not just meaningless, but chokingly oppressive to him. Everywhere around him his colleagues and acquaintances seemed to be building their lives upon the pride they derived from following rules, from drinking in moderation, from paying bills on time, from recycling trash or giving up fats, and rising at dawn to jog the streets of their neighborhoods. And yet he knew that those same people, when they knew that their activities went unobserved by their contemporaries, spent hours perusing internet porn, or snorting cocaine, or cheating on their spouses, and most of all lobbying their god for the defeat of their competitors and friends, in business, in the research lab, in the pages of some refereed journal or literary review, or simply in the fast lane of the highway driving to work.

Despite Malcolm's promises, Martin had found the Vietnamese to be no different. The cultural practices of a collectivist society throttled nonconformist behavior like the shackles of a medieval dungeon. Competition for who could remember the details of ceremonial observances or the ingredients of traditional menus consumed the lives of the majority of the society's members. To follow the same habits as one's neighbors in diet, dress, religious practices and, most of all, in opinion about the larger issues in the world, represented the height of virtue. Everyone prayed, gave donations at the temple, lit incense for deceased relatives and repeated the name of the Buddha for protection and for greater success in the next life, while at the same time gossiping mercilessly about neighbors who failed to live up to the standards of the community. And beneath this monolithic societal exterior, wife beating, whoring, drunkenness, and cheating in business were as rampant as in the fabled cities of the plain.

He put the gin bottle to his lips, felt the cool mouth of the bottle, the smooth taste of the liquid, and imbibed deeply, waiting for the warm glow to suffuse his body. The sun was rising toward the apex of its trajectory across the hazy Asian sky, and the moist, hot air was already shimmering, like a diaphanous curtain, above the ripples on the mud-colored river. He felt the sweat rolling down his sides, pooling in the folds of fat above the waist of his shorts. He might not have found fulfillment, but, on the other hand, he was free as a bird here in Vietnam. So why, instead of feeling free, did he feel as if his every movement, literally or figuratively, was hampered by mysterious chains from his past? Tonight he could go down to the backpacker district and have a few drinks at one of the bars, maybe pick up a woman. He knew he'd sleep through the hottest part of the afternoon and wake up ready to do something for the evening.

He watched Linh coming toward his boat. He gave her a wave to let her know that he was all right. Her attention was thoughtful, and he felt guilty that she still believed in him. He knew that he wasn't the person she imagined him to be.

He took another long drink.

Would he ever write again? He didn't know. He hoped that, tonight, he wouldn't dream.

Chapter 11

I'd been worried about snow? I must have had the thought during one of my depressive fugues in which my non-stop, self-medicating intake of candy bars had overloaded my brain cells with enough extra glucose to cut their already challenged efficiency in half, or possibly further. Not only was there no snow, but the barren, sagebrush-strewn, wasteland of Texas and Oklahoma reminded me of the desolate, parched landscapes I'd seen on TV specials about the Middle East. No wonder the yahoos who lived here worshipped guns and primitive religions and married their first cousins. Earlier, the mountains around Albuquerque, New Mexico, had been reminiscent of Afghanistan. Except, if I had been in Afghanistan, I probably wouldn't have had to follow so many RVs driven up the mountain roads at half the speed limit by geriatric cases, their homes on wheels sporting corny names like "Mama's Moveable Kitchen," "Beauty's Beast," or my favorite, "No, YOU move the fuck over!"

At least there were no more strange sounds coming from my car's engine, even in the mountains.

The heat, as I continued farther east, was enough to melt my hair gel, and it lasted right up to the point at which I reached the outskirts of Boston. I pulled into a motel in some place called Braintree, which gave me visions of some kind of tree with pieces of brain tissue in the place of leaves and, to tell you the truth, sounded downright nauseating. But it was on the southern outskirts of Boston, and I was hotter than a baby in a microwave. I felt as tired as I had when my fascist high school P.E. teacher had made the whole class run for two miles and I'd had to take a break by ducking behind the gym to sit down and catch my breath ... and have a smoke. I had no inclination to tackle city traffic in my condition.

The next morning, I Googled Harvard University. The head of the English Department was a Professor Cox. I'd found his telephone number on the Department's website along with a description of its "preeminent place in American letters," which it attributed to its distinguished former students and faculty, including, to my surprise, Martin Bloom, whom they identified as a celebrated former member of their illustrious faculty. At least I was in the right place.

I called the English Department. When I requested an appointment with the department chair, his secretary asked me what it was about and if I was a student. I told her that I wasn't a student and my business was very important and confidential and had to do with one of their faculty. I must have ben convincing because she gave me an appointment that afternoon without even asking the identity of the faculty about whom I'd been inquiring.

I checked Google Maps and found out that there were about a million ways to get to Cambridge from where I was in Braintree, and of course I had no clue which one to take. I could have asked the motel clerk, but I hadn't wanted to look like a retard who didn't know what she was doing. Besides, he had been a pompous jerk who'd asked me all sorts of questions about why I didn't have a credit card, why I wanted to pay with cash, and then had acted as if he were doing me a favor by letting me stay in his fleabag motel. On top of that, I had barely been able to understand anything he'd said. He'd talked as if he were parodying the accents of Matt Damon and Ben Affleck in *Goodwill Hunting*. If everybody in Boston talked the way he did, I wouldn't have a clue what anyone was saying.

Finally, I decided that I might as well take the route through the city to get to Cambridge, since Google said that was the shortest way. The traffic in downtown Boston had thinned to only three times as many cars as I had ever seen on any Eugene street by the time I reached something called the Longfellow Bridge, which I crossed, then exited onto Cambridge Street and continued until I was in a neighborhood that looked as if it was populated by nothing but students. I figured I must be near Harvard, although the students didn't look any different than students in Eugene. Weren't Harvard students supposed to be more serious looking? Humorless? Grim? These students didn't even look *smart*. I didn't know what smart looked like, but I was pretty sure it didn't look like they did. Most of these kids were wearing grungier clothes than I was and were carrying ratty looking backpacks. Gathered around what looked like stairs heading underground in the middle of what I surmised was Harvard Square, were a bunch of metal studded, purple and green haired, black eye makeup, drop-out types, standing around, smoking, sitting cross-legged on the sidewalk strumming guitars or playing drums or harassing passersby. I'm sure their parents would have dropped dead if they'd seen what their progeny were doing. Mine had.

I parked my car, although finding a parking place that didn't require a pocketful of quarters had taken nearly a half an hour, and I ended up a good half mile from my destination, which was the Barker Center, a stately brick building, which was actually across the street from Harvard Yard. To get there I had to walk through the business district, which surrounded the university and bore some resemblance to the district around the University of Oregon, with lots of coffee shops and restaurants, low-cost noodle shops, and art galleries and bookstores. Passing one of the bookstores, I noticed a copy of Martin Bloom's *End of Passage,* a book I hadn't even been aware he'd written, sitting in the window. I couldn't stop myself from buying it. I must have looked conspicuously self-conscious when I made the purchase, because another female customer stared at me as if I were some kind of alien ... maybe it was my spiked hair. I guess people who frequented the local bookstores weren't used to the scummy types from the street buying books. I tried to give her my patented "screw you" stare, but she quickly turned away and left the store, looking more embarrassed than I felt.

When I got to Harvard Yard, my copy of Martin Bloom's book safely concealed in a plastic bag I'd been given by the bookstore, I couldn't resist peeking through the gate into the Yard, only to see that the students *inside* the school's walls were a different breed than those who were outside hanging around the subway station in the square. Those on the inside were more hurried, serious, well-dressed and, yes, smart looking.

I waited for the light in order to cross the street to the Barker Center, only to spy the same woman who had stared at me in the bookstore, standing less than a half block away and still eyeing me with a strange look. She looked as if she were about to approach me, but I had no interest in an assignation with someone who was probably a lesbian or something, despite the fact that she was beautiful, which was apparent even from that distance, so I stepped off the curb as soon as the light changed and marched directly to the Barker Center.

By the time I reached the steps leading up to the entrance of the building, I could no longer see the woman who I'd thought was following me, and I told myself that whoever she was and whatever her interest in me, it had nothing to do with my mission, which was to find Martin Bloom.... and perhaps the genesis of my personality. As I climbed the steps to the building, I paused for a moment, reassuring myself that at least some answers should be forthcoming from my meeting with Professor Cox inside of this building. I was feeling scared. Until now, Martin Bloom had been just an abstract idea in my head, a picture on the jacket of a book, not a real person. But he had actually been here, perhaps standing right here where I was standing, on the concrete steps of the building in front of its tall, imposing, colonial front doorway, possibly composing one of his novels within shouting distance of where I was standing, and he must have left some traces of his presence. Some traces other than, that is, a lost-looking stray young woman who felt even more out of place here than she had felt living the life she had lived before she had learned that her dead father might be alive and well and a famous, author, one who had even taught at Harvard University.

# Chapter 12

"I have to tell you up front, young lady, that Martin Bloom was not a regular employee of this University. He was an adjunct faculty member who was hired on a temporary basis to teach two seminars: one for graduate students and one for undergraduates. Whatever he did to you is not the responsibility of the university, but if you insist on pressing your case, you may speak to the university counsel." The Chair of the English Department looked down his nose at me through a pair of pince-nez glasses, reminding me of a picture I had once seen of William Butler Yeats. Maybe it was obligatory for an English Department chair to look like someone literary—or like an intellectual nitwit.

I wasn't going to be intimidated just because I was at Harvard. "Don't get your shorts bunched up, Professor Cox," I said. "I'm not pursuing any case against Martin Bloom. I never took his class. I've never even met him—at least not that I would remember."

"I'm sorry. I assumed that was why you were here."

"You must run an interesting department if you assume that every young woman who enters your office is here to sue you." I said.

He furrowed his eyebrows. "Professor Bloom had some, uh... difficulties with some of his students," he managed to say in a voice which sounded as if he were choking on a hairball.

"Really? I'm trying to find out if he's my father."

That startled the old fogey. Actually, Professor Cox wasn't that old. Probably only about forty or so, but his pince-nez glasses and his pin-striped suit and striped tie made him look the part of a stodgy old professor, which was probably the look he was trying to achieve. His hair wasn't even gray, and he wore it combed straight back, as if he were an actor in a 1930's or '40's movie.

"Whatever do you mean?" he asked, his eyes bulging from behind his small glasses. "I wasn't aware that Mr. Bloom was married, much less that he had a family. He certainly never acted as if he did." As soon as he said that he looked even more embarrassed. "Oh, forgive me. I didn't mean that the way it sounded."

I was sure that he *did* mean it the way it sounded. "My father's name was Martin Bloom; he was a writer who graduated from the University of Oregon about the same time that Martin Bloom the writer did. My mother always told me that my father had died, but I recently saw a picture of him on the back of one of his books, and he looks an awful lot like me. I decided to find out if he was my father. This university was one of the last places he was known to have been."

He looked skeptical. "What does your mother say? Surely she would know."

"My mother is dead."

"I'm sorry," he said, making an attempt at a sympathetic smile. But he still looked skeptical. "There are no records, anything like that to tell you who your father was?"

"My father was Martin Bloom. But I'm not sure if it's the same Martin Bloom who taught here and who is a writer."

"So you want to find him and ask him if he's your father."

"Exactly." I had been starting to think that English was this man's second language. "I'm trying to find out where he went after he left teaching here."

"I wasn't very close to Martin ... he being on contract and me simply approving his hire. He was good friends with one or two faculty members and some graduate students," Cox answered, looking uncomfortable, "... mostly female I'm afraid," his face colored as he said this. "Perhaps he's kept in touch with them."

Bingo! This was exactly the kind of information I was looking for. Now, how did I get this fartbrain to tell me the names of the faculty and students who knew Martin Bloom? "I'm just hoping to connect with him. Could you at least let me know their names?" I was acting as obsequious as I could without nauseating myself.

He seemed to be mulling it over. Probably weighing the rights of privacy of his faculty against his urge to avenge himself for whatever wrongs Bloom had dealt his department. Finally he spoke. "Sally Forkstone might be able to help you. Sally is a member of our faculty, and I believe she knew Professor Bloom quite well." A thin shadow of a smile crossed his lips as he spoke. I could sense that he was arranging retribution for whatever Martin Bloom had done to him and his precious Department of English. "I'll instruct Norma, out front, to give you her office address and telephone number. He also was friends with Professor Truong in Philosophy. I'm afraid I don't know Doctor Truong very well, but Norma can give you his campus address also."

I thanked him before his conscience had a chance to reassert itself. I left his office and stopped at the front desk to get the number and address from the secretary, Norma.

Norma was a thin, young, and pretty woman who had the look of a professional secretary–like my mother except for her slim build– certainly not a Harvard student working her way through school. She wore a lot of makeup and a very tight skirt. "You can talk to Professor Forkstone, if you like, but you won't find out anything useful." She leaned toward me, conspiratorially. "Professor Forkstone is a bitch who hated Professor Bloom." If you want to talk to someone who might be able to help you, talk to Elizabeth Roundtree. She used to be a student here, and she still lives in the area. If you give me your number, I'll try to find out where she lives and text you her address."

"Dr. Cox also mentioned a Professor Truong in the Philosophy Department. Do you know where his office is?"

She scanned a screen on her computer and told me the office number then showed me on a campus map where the office was located."

"This is great," I said. "But why are you helping me so much?"

"Don't listen to what old starchedpants says about Professor Bloom," she said, nodding in the direction of the chairman's door. "Professor Bloom was loved by a lot of students, and it was terrible that the university made him leave."

"You knew him?"

"Not as well as I wish that I had," she said, with a sly look on her face. "He had a way with words, that man, and he wasn't stuck up like the rest of the faculty. I thought he was great."

It sounded as if Norma might have been one of the women Martin Bloom had put his moves on, or at least she wished she'd been.

I thanked her for her advice and opinion and left the center feeling even more confused than when I'd arrived.

# Chapter 13

Professor Truong sounded as if he would be more helpful to me than Professor Forkstone, who was, to quote Norma, a "bitch." I followed my campus map to Emerson Hall, where the offices of the Philosophy faculty were located. The offices were on the second floor of the large, brick, boxlike building, which fronted on Harvard Yard. Unlike Barker Center, the floors of which had been highly polished and its main floor a large well-lit lobby with an open staircase leading to the second floor, Emerson Hall was dark, with well worn creaky wooden stairs, and little to see but closed doors on forbidding hallways. To my relief, Professor Truong's door was open wide.

Professor Truong, who I assumed from his name was Vietnamese, looked like an overgrown kid. He wore faded Levis, a red hoodie sweatshirt over a blue T-shirt, the latter which said, "New England Patriots," in red block letters, and a pair of ratty red tennis shoes. He was only about my height but at least three times my girth. He ushered me right into his office as soon as I knocked on the frame of his open door and he stood in front of me, surveying my face and hair and tattoos. "Finally I've found someone on this campus who looks like a philosophy student," he said. His face broke into a wide smile, as if had just told me a joke. "I hope you're here to tell me you want to enroll in one of my classes." He walked around behind his desk and sat down, directing an inquiring look in my direction and pointing to the chair in front of his desk, implying I should also sit.

I sat. He had been so friendly, I was tempted to sign up for school right on the spot, but instead I gave him a disappointed shrug and said, "I'm not here to sign up for a class."

""What's wrong? You don't dig philosophy?" he asked, his grin still stretching from ear to ear.

I was getting the feeling that I was talking to Yoda from Star Wars. As God no doubt said about his Son, I hated to bring him down to earth. "Philosophy's great. I think it's the favorite playground for great minds, but that's not why I'm here."

"You've got the look of a philosophy major," he insisted, still grinning, "that 'screw you, I'm into being my own person look. It's a rare look at Harvard, but one I welcome with open arms."

"I'm not a Harvard student," I said.

He narrowed his eyes and looked at me with his head cocked to one side. "So what *are* you doing here?"

"I'm trying to find Martin Bloom."

His face became serious. He stared at me even more closely than he had been, then his eyes widened in surprise. "You're Martin's daughter!"

I felt my heart racing. Was this the confirmation that I had been seeking? "He had a daughter?"

He nodded. "One he'd left when she was a baby... long before I had met him. I never knew his wife—he told me he had divorced her—nor met his daughter. I don't believe he had any contact with her." He began to grin again. "But she would have looked just like you."

I repeated my story about my father's name having been Martin Bloom and his having graduated from the University of Oregon. "But my mother always told me that my father was dead."

"And now you wonder if she was telling the truth."

"She died a year ago. I just made the discovery that the writer Martin Bloom fits the description of my father and, as you observed, looks like me."

He shook his head in wonder. "So here you are. You've decided to find him."

I nodded. "Why not?"

"That's not a good philosophical question. '*Why?*' would be the better one." He'd regained his humor. His eyes, which were like two black dots in long slits, had begun to crinkle at the edges in the beginning of another wide smile.

Something in his genial mood made me want to trust him. "It has to do with finding out who I am." I was embarrassed to say that I wanted to find out if I shared whatever it was that made him a writer.

"You'll have to figure that out for yourself. But knowing your past can help you in your definition. If Martin is your father you might find you have to give more than you'll receive in return. A lot of people who know Martin feel that way."

"Do you?"

He laughed and shook his head. "Just being around a man with Martin's mind was a gift for me. And he is a faithful friend, as much as he is capable of being."

"I don't plan to give him anything." I said. "If he is my father, then he never gave me anything, not to me, not to my mother."

He raised his eyebrows. "He gave you life. In my culture, that is regarded as the greatest gift of all. It is a gift that only two people in the world were able to create—you are who you are because of your mother and your father. A child must repay her parents in whatever way she can."

What Professor Truong said might be true in his culture, but it wasn't true in mine. As far as I was concerned, my father gave me half of my genes, but that was it. In terms of who owed whom, my father, if he really was alive, owed me, rather than I owed him; or in my most charitable frame of mind I might concede that we owed each other zilch. "I'm not concerned with who owes what to whom," I said. "I just want to find out if I do have a living father." I didn't mention my ambitions to become a writer and what it would mean to find that I was related to the *writer* Martin Bloom.

He nodded, still smiling. "And how do you intend to find him?"

"Well, I was planning on asking you where he was, but I guess you don't know. There's another professor whose name I was given and I want to talk to her."

He interrupted me, "You mean Sally Forkstone?"

I nodded.

"I'm afraid Professor Forkstone might give you a highly biased view of Martin. She and he did not part company as friends."

"Would she know where he is?"

"Not unless she hired a detective to find him. I'm sure that he and she do not communicate."

Great. I'd come all the way to Boston and I was no closer to finding Martin Bloom than before I'd started.

"Do you have any idea where he went after he left here?" I asked.

He nodded. "He made it as far as Stanford because he wrote me. He began teaching there, but I think he ran into some trouble. Martin wasn't very good at following university protocol."

Stanford? I was on the wrong side of the continent. "What do you mean?"

For the first time, Professor Truong frowned, an incongruous grimace that might have been a caricature of his usual cheerful smile. "Martin was haunted by something from his past. I never learned what it was. It stunted many of his relationships, filled him with such anxiety that he often had to drink to calm his fears. But he never followed anyone else's rules whether he was drinking or not."

I guess that was another trait I'd inherited from my father. "So how could you be best friends with someone like that?"

He'd regained his Cheshire Cat smile and now he leaned back in his chair, as if he enjoyed contemplating my question. "He helped me immensely. He could have been a philosopher if he hadn't been a novelist. In fact, most of his novels address philosophical issues—death, how to give one's life meaning. He's like those French existential philosophers of the last century, Sartre or Camus, who expressed their philosophies through their fiction. I was a writer myself when I met him—except I had no talent. Martin was gentle with me. He never likes to criticize someone else's work. But he told me my talent was in writing serious essays; I should pursue the search for truth instead of trying to make up stories. When he got a job at Virginia, he demanded that they admit me to the doctoral program in Philosophy as a condition of his taking the job. I struggled, not having a strong undergraduate preparation like the other grad students had, but Martin tutored me, encouraged me, and finally I could handle things on my own."

I felt a twinge of jealousy. How come Martin Bloom had extended himself for Professor Truong and completely ignored his own daughter? Or perhaps I was not that daughter.

The professor seemed to have sensed my thoughts. "Martin can be very generous with his time and his involvement. I'm sorry you missed having that experience with him."

I could feel the muscles at the sides of my mouth starting to quiver and I knew that in another second or two I wouldn't be able to keep myself from crying. But I wasn't going to do that. Besides, I *never* cried in public. I pursed my lips to stop any telltale shaking and said, in defiance, "he missed a lot by not knowing *me*." I wasn't sure that I believed it, though. I wasn't exactly a philosopher-in-the-making as Professor Truong had been.

His face softened. "I wish Martin *had* known you," he said, gently. Then he brightened. "But now he may get his chance."

I thanked the professor for his kindness and the information he had given me, meager as it was. Despite what he and Norma had said about Professor Forkstone, I figured I might as well try to talk to her and see if I could learn anything else before turning my whole trip around and heading back to California and Stanford.

"One last thing," the professor said before I left his office. "The last time Martin and I exchanged correspondence, before he left Stanford, I urged him to go to Vietnam—my country. I thought the change of culture might do him good. He chafed too irritably against the American fabric. I thought maybe some Eastern thought could help him find his way. He seemed to like the idea, but I don't know if he ever went. Maybe someone at Stanford would know."

Vietnam? Holy shit. What would I do if he'd gone there? To quote several thousand sixties-era, pot smoking, free-loving, draft-dodging American college students, going to Vietnam sucked the big one. I left Professor Truong's office feeling more confused about whom my father was and no more enlightened about where he was than I had been when I had arrived.

## Chapter 14

I started back across the campus to where Professor Forkstone's office was located, only to see the same young woman I'd seen before, lurking along the pathway outside of Emerson Hall. What was with this person? How could someone become fixated on me just by watching me make a purchase in a bookstore? Was this some kind of obsession at first sight? I decided to take the bull by the horns, or, to be more apt, the chick by the bra, and ask her what was up with the stalking routine. By the time I reached the place she had been standing, she was gone. Maybe my determined demeanor had scared her away. When I reached Robinson Hall, where Professor Forkstone's office was located, I stopped to brace myself for the encounter.

"I hope your not going to visit Professor Forkstone," a voice behind me said.

I almost jumped out of my skin. But then I turned and there she was, the woman who had been following me.

"Who are you?" I asked, leaning forward on the balls of my feet so that I could either kick her or take off running. It was a pose I'd seen in a YouTube video of how to handle an assault by a stranger.

Up close, the woman was one of the most beautiful females I had ever seen. Her face was un-made-up, but her eyebrows were perfectly shaped, and her dark hair, which hung in long waves down her back shone like that of someone in a shampoo ad. Her face was sharp, and her nose and forehead covered with barely perceptible freckles. To quote Brad about Angelina, she was beautiful. Nevertheless, I stayed poised on the balls of my feet, although it was killing my toes.

"My name is Elizabeth Roundtree, and I'm guessing that you are Martin Bloom's daughter."

To quote Archy McNally, my flabber was gasted. "You figured that out by watching me buy one of his books?"

"So you saw me," she said, an embarrassed smile clouding her beautiful features. "It was that and the fact that you look just like him."

"Really?" This was the second time in one day that I had been told that I resembled Martin Bloom. At least that meant that the resemblance I had detected wasn't something I had made up. "Norma, in the English department mentioned you. She said I should talk to you," I told her.

She looked puzzled. "About what?"

"I'm looking for Martin Bloom."

"You mean your father?"

"I'm trying to find out if he *is* my father."

"You don't know?"

I shook my head. "I know my father's name was Martin Bloom and that the author by that name looks like me. I'd always thought my father was dead."

Her face showed her puzzlement. "Do you want to come to my apartment and talk?"

She didn't look as if she was trying to seduce me and her expression was earnest, although filled with more pity than I cared for, but what could it hurt to talk to her? "Sure," I answered.

It was easier to walk to her address than to move my car. We reached her apartment in less than ten minutes. It was a modern-looking, metal-and-glass building on a lush, tree-lined street, looking more like the kind of residence in which a young stockbroker or advertising professional might live than one a student could afford. Her apartment was on the top floor. We took the elevator.

The apartment was spacious and gorgeous. The furniture, carpet, and wallpaper were all done in muted shades of brown and gray. One whole wall was a window, which afforded a vista across the tops of the nearby buildings to the Charles River in the distance. I could just see the buildings of the university off to the right. Her walls and shelves were adorned with numerous objects of abstract art.

She sat both of us down on her couch, which was low and leather and curved in an "L" shape, and drew her designer jeans clad legs up beneath her while I nervously clasped my hands together to keep them from shaking. She bent forward and took a cigarette out of a ceramic dish in front of her and lit up. Then she caught herself and offered me one. You bet I accepted.

"Martin mentioned that he had a daughter," she said, "But he never talked about her, and he acted as if he didn't want me to ask."

This was the second time that someone had told me that Martin Bloom had a daughter. I was encouraged. "My mother always told me that my father died when I was a baby."

"And now she's told you that he's alive?"

"My mother died a year ago. I was taking an English course, and one of Martin Bloom's books was assigned. I saw the picture on the back and started to wonder. My father's name was Martin Bloom."

"You're going to Harvard?" She couldn't conceal her look of disbelief. I knew I looked more like the street kids I'd seen in Harvard Square than the real students I'd seen in Harvard Yard.

"The University of Oregon."

I waited for her look of disdain, but she nodded as if she approved. "Martin's alma mater. Your father also attended Oregon?"

"And he was a writer...or wanted to be. That was nearly twenty years ago."

She nodded. "Everything fits. And believe me, your resemblance to Martin is striking."

"Norma said you might be able to help me. But you said you don't know where he is."

She shook her head. "I haven't heard from him since he left Cambridge. That was three years ago."

I felt my spirits, which had revived a little, start to sink again, as if as if they were tethered to an anchor. I had to blink back my tears.

Her brow creased in lines of sympathy. "He had a teaching position at Stanford, or at least they'd offered him one—as a guest faculty—for a year. I assumed that was where he went. Martin is no better at maintaining relationships now than he was when he left you and your mother, assuming that was what happened."

I was beginning to believe that, in fact, that was exactly what happened, although my mother, probably in a misguided attempt to protect me, had lied about it. "Professor Truong said that he taught at Stanford, but only for awhile. It sounded as if they fired him."

She nodded, as if she wasn't surprised.

"So what was your relationship with Martin Bloom?" I asked.

She pursed her lips and gazed at me as if she wasn't sure how much she wanted to tell me. "It feels odd talking to his daughter," she said. "He was old enough to be my own father."

"Don't worry, I won't be jealous. I never knew the man. The Martin Bloom you knew is a total stranger to me." I realized that I was starting to feel the same resentment my mother must have felt toward a man who turned his back on his family.

She smiled self-consciously, her sculpted eyebrows knitted in consternation. "You want all the gory details, don't you?"

I felt I was coming across as some sort of voyeur ... perhaps about my own father, which seemed kinky. "You don't have to tell me," I said, hoping that I wasn't blushing.

"We had an affair, which was why we both had to leave Harvard. I never complained, but several students did, and particularly one faculty member, who was jealous—Sally Forkstone, the one you were about to visit. The students thought he gave me unfair advantages because we were sleeping together. The truth was he gave everyone advantages they didn't deserve. He's a ruthless self-critic, but he's totally unable to say anything negative about anyone else's work, at least if they're his friend or his student. He gave out A's as if they were candy on trees. With my thesis, his constructive criticism was invaluable, but he refused to focus on its defects." She picked up her third cigarette and lit it. I turned down her offer of one for me. I was still trying to cut down.

"Martin is not just a great writer, he's a brilliant teacher. Like I said, he seems unable to criticize any of his students' work, and that handicaps his teaching. But other than that, his insights are brilliant, his knowledge of literature is voluminous, and he is a walking store of quotations. What he gave me as a teacher was priceless."

"And personally?"

She looked down at the carpet. "We began with lunches to talk about my work, then dinners and drinks, lots of drink—he drinks like a fish—then a full-fledged affair. But he never let up on pushing me to improve my writing." She blew smoke out of her nose. "It was the most intense, the most romantic, and the most intelligent year I've spent in my entire life. He took me to New York to meet his agent, he introduced me to every magazine editor he knew, and to other well-known writers. He was jealous, but he was also generous. All the time, we kept focusing on my novel, then my thesis, which was on Henry James, one of Martin's favorite writers. Martin didn't know why I was doing a thesis if I wanted to be a writer, but at that time I wanted a Ph.D. so I could teach. He went along with my ambition."

"So what happened that made you both leave?" I was becoming intrigued with her story... and amazed by what I was learning about Martin Bloom. How could I relate to such a man as a father?

She let her gaze wander around her apartment as if focusing upon some aspect of her décor might remind her of something. "It was really a number of things," she finally said. "I said he drank a lot and to tell you the truth, sometimes he was drunk when he was teaching. Mostly the students couldn't tell or they only suspected, but a couple of times it was obvious because he strayed so far off topic or he was staggering around the classroom. Then, I told you, some of the students complained that he was spending too much time with me and that it was because I was sleeping with him. I of course denied it, but one day when he was drunk, he bragged about it to the class. I was humiliated, and he was reported to the department chair. Since I wouldn't admit to anything or file any complaint against him, they couldn't just fire him, but I was so angry I broke off our relationship. The next thing I knew, he'd been offered a job at Stanford and he was gone."

"And they made you quit school?"

"They didn't make me. But I was very uncomfortable after he left. Everyone in the department—students and faculty—knew what had happened. Martin was gone, and I had to face people alone."

I thought I saw a tear in her eye. I was angry at how she had been treated. "Martin Bloom sounds like a jerk. Aren't you angry with him? Didn't he ruin your career?"

She bit her lower lip. "I was very angry at first, but then I realized that what we did was just as much my fault as his. Anyway, I want to be a novelist, and a master's or a Ph.D. isn't going to make a difference one way or another. And I can always go back to school if I decide to. I've got plenty of money ..." she looked around the room as if to prove her point. "My family is well-to-do, and they are willing to support me."

"But you must hate Martin Bloom." I was feeling horrified at the man she'd described to me...and I hadn't even met him.

She shook her head. "He's a unique individual—probably the smartest person I've ever met, and, having been at Harvard for a lot of years, that's saying something. But he's flawed—if not ruined. I hate to say this, since he's probably your father, but he's an alcoholic and emotionally, he's empty..." She looked at the picture window across the room. "Or maybe he's afraid. I could never tell. When it feels as if he's getting close, he pulls away ... as if he just shuts down. Then he drinks even more."

"Afraid of what?" Professor Truong had suggested something similar. Was I just curious or was I actually concerned about this man whom I'd wanted to be my father, but who now sounded as if he was a ruined individual?

She pursed her lips, as if in thought. "I have no idea. Something in his past that is painful to him. I tried to talk to him about it, but he said I was imagining things. He said there were lots of painful things in his past, but he wasn't afraid of them, even used them in his novels. When I said that using them in his novels might be a way of distancing himself from them rather than facing them emotionally, he got mad ... one of the few times he became really angry with me. He said I was prying, invading his privacy. So I dropped the topic."

"Have you tried to get in touch with him since he left?"

She shook her head. "I'm satisfied with the memories. I know Martin's limitations. I want to have a serious relationship with someone someday, and it won't be with him." She gazed at me, her face softening. "I'm sorry. That's not a very positive picture I've painted of someone you must be hoping is your father."

"Even when I thought he was dead I never had a positive picture of him. My mother called him a bastard, and it sounds as if she was right."

"So do you still want to find him?"

Did I? The Martin Bloom she had described was not someone I would ever be able to relate to as a father. Yet I sensed something about the man and his tortured life that felt familiar... something that reminded me of my self. "It's important to me," I answered. "I'm partly made up of his genes, and I want to know what that means."

She nodded as if she understood. "So where do you go from here?"

"What about Professor Forkstone? Professor Cox told me to contact her."

She shook her head, her exquisitely curved mouth formed into a grimace. "Sally Forkstone hates Martin. She hates me too. She was one of the ones who lobbied for Martin's termination." She lowered her head. "Martin had broken off an affair with her right before he became interested in me."

"She wouldn't know where he is?"

"If she did, she'd be pursuing him with a team of lawyers. She's out to get him, if she can find him."

What she said echoed both Professor Truong and Norma. "Then I guess I'll go to Stanford." Whatever was gnawing at me, causing me to want to connect with my father, was still feeding on my insides. I was determined to see things through to the end.

"I wish I could be of more help. I think it would be good for you to meet Martin, although you should prepare yourself to be disappointed. But I'm sure it would do him good to meet you."

I was pretty much blown away. Martin Bloom, who might or might not be my father, had deserted this gorgeous, bright lady, caused her to drop out of Harvard, and she was still worried about him. I thanked Elizabeth for talking to me. There didn't appear to be anything more I could gain from talking to her. When I left she gave me a hug.

Chapter 15

Martin felt good, better than he'd felt for some time, in fact. Miraculously, he'd gone the whole day drinking nothing more alcoholic than a couple of beers and, unusually for him, he had not been besieged by tremors or become paralyzed by anxiety. Although his momentary sobriety was as mystifying to him as it was undeserved, he'd taken the opportunity afforded by what he knew must be a transitory flight into health and eaten as many fruits and vegetables as his stomach could endure without pushing himself over the brink into nausea.

He also planned to take advantage of his momentary sense of wellbeing by risking his reclusiveness and visiting one of his favorite French restaurants in the tourist district, both for a steak dinner and because the particular restaurant, along with being tremendously expensive, was a great place for meeting women. The restaurant was located in *The Majestic*, Saigon's most historic hotel, dating from early in the last century, and its rooftop bar, overlooking the river, was a bountiful source of beautiful women, most of them young singles. Such women, mostly Vietnamese, were always looking for a rich American or European businessman whom they might entice into marriage or at least a brief round of lucrative dating, filled with presents of expensive clothing and jewelry. On more than one of his previous forays into the     jeopardous exposure furnished by the Majestic, he had been rewarded by scoring with just such a woman, although each time she had been understandably disappointed when the next morning she'd found that Martin was no more interested in marriage than he was in spending money he didn't have on jewels or dresses. But for him, such one-night encounters had been quite worthwhile.

He called Duc, the taxi driver who always took him into town and who knew which bars to cruise at closing time until he found Martin, always drunk, often passed out, and packed him into his cab and took him back to the marina, where he deposited him, safe and sound, in the cabin of his boat.

* * *

After polishing off a rare steak and a bottle of wine, along with two gin and tonics, Martin took one last look around *The Majestic's* opulent restaurant and decided it was time to go upstairs to the bar and look for some company for the evening. He stood, a little unsteadily, and headed for the elevator.

The dimly-lit and spacious bar was crowded, half the crowd being local--young and prosperous Vietnamese and other Asian nationalities, and the other half vacationing Americans, Canadians, Australians, and Europeans. Most of the latter were either guests at The Majestic or at one of the nearby hotels, having come to the luxury hotel's bar for the evening because of its location overlooking the river or for its somewhat risqué reputation, hoping for a little fun without having to encounter the notoriously raucous bar life which characterized the seedier establishments in the city. Along one side of the rooftop lounge was a long, mahogany bar, while the larger space nearer the river was devoted to individual tables, most of them occupied by couples or groups. He went straight to the bar and wedged himself between two young Vietnamese men, dressed in expensive looking slacks and silk shirts, both sitting on tall stools while he stood, and signaled for the bartender, Luan's, attention. Luan recognized his old, if occasional, customer on sight. Martin ordered a gin straight up. Once he had it in hand, basking in the aura of confidence he always gained by possessing a full drink, he turned to survey the crowd.

As always, the patrons at the hotel's bar, just like every other tourist bar in town, distributed themselves by ethnicity. The locals stuck to themselves or mixed with the vacationing Asians from China and Japan. At the other end of the bar were the Caucasians: Australians, Canadians, French, British, and, of course, Americans.

Martin knew better than to associate with the American tourists. The chances were too great that he would be recognized, and he didn't want anyone to know where he was or what he was doing at this moment in his life. Not only was his current state of affairs embarrassing, but he didn't want word to get back to his publishers, who were still demanding that he either finish his next novel or repay the advance they'd given him. He stayed at the Asian end of the bar, ready to signal his receptivity to one of the local young women he hoped would still be looking for an available older man.

He felt someone at his shoulder, smelled a vaguely familiar perfume. He turned and to his shock, found himself face to face with a tall, late-thirtyish blonde with a strikingly pretty, if severe, face. He recognized Sylvia Prentiss, his former Stanford colleague. His legs became weak, and he reached out to the bar for support. "Shit!" he said.

"It's wonderful to see you too," Sylvia said, drily. She appeared tipsy and threw her arm around his shoulder. "Martin Bloom, of all people. So this is where you hang out."

"Just passing through, Sylvia," he lied, his panic upon someone recognizing him still eating away at him like a hungry serpent gnawing at his gut. "What are you doing here?"

"I'm here at the Sheraton on a package vacation, and a group of us decided to come over here where we heard there was more action, at least for a hotel bar. I guess that's why you're here too. Are you on a tour?"

Regretfully, he noticed that a young Vietnamese woman, with a very short skirt and a provocatively revealing blouse, had been heading his way but veered off when she saw he was occupied. "How's the old farm?" he asked, avoiding her question and hoping to put her off with inanities. He could feel the sweat starting to flow beneath his arms.

"Competitive, as usual," Sylvia answered. "Say, what are you drinking? These Singapore Slings have got to be hell on a woman's figure."

"Try it without the liqueurs and juice."

"You mean straight gin?"

"Gin is the royalty of alcohol. The last remnant of the English speaking people's long history of domination over our poor Vietnamese friends who have been dominated by the Chinese, the

French, the British, the Americans, and the Russians at some point in their history. Drink it straight. It will give you perspective, especially the good Tanqueray they serve here."

"When did the English or the Americans dominate Vietnam?" she asked as she ordered a gin on the rocks.

He'd ordered another gin himself. He downed it in one gulp, then held his glass up for another. "Ok, so the Brits weren't actually here, but I blame them for the streak of imperialism that's endemic to the American nature. And the United States at least tried to control this country in the 1960's, if you recall. Of course it was in the guise of defending freedom. Well, we defended it until Uncle Ho and his legions of peasants in black p.j.'s kicked our butts and we turned tail and ran, leaving the helpless South Vietnam army to try to win a war against its own people. But we're winning now. Capitalism has taken over the country and the Commies who own the place are running scared. Why else would an establishment such as this be blessed with hordes of tourists like you and your friends invading it on a nightly basis?"

She looked at him with amazement. "You haven't lost your gift for bullshit, I see." Then her face broke into a grin. "What a treat to meet you here, Martin. We missed you when you disappeared, halfway through the semester. Dean Chappell particularly missed you. He said he'd see that you never worked in a decent university again."

He shrugged, relieved to accept a full glass of gin from Luan. "I'm not sure I've ever found anything decent about universities, Stanford being no exception, and Dean Chappell always was an asshole."

"Your assessment of each other appears to be mutual. Of course if you win a Pulitzer someday, even Chappell will be panting to have you back in his department."

He had had three gins just since arriving at the upstairs bar, and his anxiety had subsided enough to allow him to realize that he actually welcomed meeting someone familiar. And he was beginning to notice that Sylvia was better looking than he'd remembered. "Speaking of panting," he said, "you've got me a little hot, do you know that?"

She was also getting looped from her straight gins. "Really? You mean I can stir the great Martin Bloom?"

If she only knew how little it took, he thought to himself, while he looked across the  room at the young Vietnamese woman who'd been about to approach him earlier, and gave a shrug, as if to say, *what can I do?*

"Say, where are you staying, anyway?" Sylvia asked, lowering her eyelids seductively. He noticed that she had finished her last gin almost as soon as it had arrived. "This hotel?"

"I have a boat. I'm tied up in a marina on the river."

She looked impressed. "A boat? You mean like a yacht or something?"

He shrugged, as if not wanting to brag. "You want to visit?"

She looked down the bar at a small knot of tourists, who were laughing and talking. "I came with them, but they're just acquaintances who are on the tour with me. I'm out here alone. School starts next week, and this is my last fling of the summer." She looked as if she was weighing his suggestion. "Let me tell them I've met an old friend and I'll get my own ride back to the hotel."

He nodded. He wasn't exactly sober, but he was at least more sober than usual for this time of the evening or at this stage of a relationship. He stared at her swaying hips as she walked to the end of the bar and spoke to the group. He got out his cell phone and called Duc.

"So where are you teaching... or are you?" she asked as she snuggled up to him in the back of the taxi as it dodged its way between motorcycles, bicycles and the occasional car, all of which raced at headlong pace through streets clogged with traffic.

"I'm not. I'm living off my royalties and writing." He began to feel nervous about disclosing too much. "I'm sort of incognito over here. It's easier to write that way. Maybe you could keep it our little secret?."

She laughed. "Incognito... that's great. You were incognito even when you were supposed to be teaching. Who would I tell? Chappell? The only people who would be interested would be a few female students whom you left in the lurch after promising them A's for whatever services they might have offered." She smiled up at him, seductively.

"That's a lie. If any of those young women said I did that, they're lying," he answered. "Besides, I gave everyone A's. That was one of the reasons that Chappell was out to get me."

She snuggled closer. "Well, you don't have to promise me anything ... except maybe a little more gin. Have you got anything to drink on your boat?"

He pulled her closer. "It's the one thing I have in sufficient supply."

\* \* \*

The next morning he awoke with Sylvia's head on his arm and her body, warm and soft, next to his. It had been a great evening.

He started to ease himself out of the bunk. She turned her head toward him and smiled. "You provide a woman one hell of an evening, Martin. Why didn't we ever get together at Stanford?"

"Everything's easier in Vietnam," he answered, crawling over her and slipping on a pair of shorts and a t-shirt. "You were pretty intense at work, if I remember correctly."

"You mean, I actually worked... as opposed to you." She looked around for her clothes. "Have you got an extra toothbrush and some toothpaste? That gin was great last night, but it tastes like crap in the morning."

They each attended to their morning toilet, having to alternate in the boat's tiny head. Then he fixed them both coffee.

Sylvia sat down and looked around the boat. They were in the cabin where they had slept. "I didn't really see where you lived last night. I was too distracted. Don't you ever clean this place?"

He looked around at the stray clothes hanging off of every door handle and chair back and the pile of dishes in his small sink. "My cleaning lady quit."

"You need a woman in your life."

He hoped she wasn't thinking of herself as the woman to whom she was referring. She was surprisingly fun for a night, but he remembered the severity of her manner when they had taught in the same department in Palo Alto. She was ferociously competitive and shamelessly ambitious, as well as being a serious scholar—of Elizabethan poets, if he remembered correctly. Her writing consisted entirely of criticism and reviews in academic journals. She was a perfect fit for academia, and he hadn't forgotten her disdain for writers such as he, who never read the scholarly journals, much less wrote anything for them.

She was looking at the books arrayed along the wall above his berth. "Are you into Eastern religion? You've got a lot of books on the subject."

He shrugged. "That was part of the idea of coming here," he said, feeling self-conscious about admitting anything so personal. "I had a Vietnamese friend who told me that I had to come here to find myself. He was a Buddhist, and he thought that Buddhism would help me."

She raised an eyebrow skeptically. "And did it?"

"It's too paradoxical. It's all about searching for something but realizing that not only is there nothing to seek, but that the act of seeking is the antithesis of what one is hoping to find. So one must not search, but must do so diligently. It's hard work, that kind of passivity."

She laughed. "It sounds like it's made for you. But you gave up, I take it. I wonder if it occurred to you that it might only be you that never found anything—only you for whom there was no *there*, there?"

In fact, it *had* occurred to him that the act of looking inward might be futile for him because there was nothing within him to find ... or too much that he needed to avoid. "Bullshit," he answered. "I quit looking because I concluded that the whole damn Eastern religion thing was simply a sham. I quit looking for what didn't exist." His irritation surprised him.

She seemed amused by his anger. "The same way you always gave up on everything else, if I remember correctly. Other than your writing, have you ever completed anything at all?"

"I've got a daughter," he said belligerently, then immediately regretted his words. "Say, do you want to join me for a bit of the hair of the dog?" He reached for the bottle of Beefeater they had shared the night before.

"I can see you're coping with fatherhood quite well," she said, shaking her head in refusal of his offer of a drink. "What is your daughter like?"

"I have no idea, except she, or someone claiming to be her, is trying to find me." Now he really wondered why he had told her so much. She was sure to try to delve deeper.

"You don't even know if it's her?"

"We haven't kept in contact."

"And you're using the same mechanism to avoid her as you do to avoid everything else you don't care to deal with. You reach for a bottle."

Her comment angered him, mostly because he knew she was right. It also raised his anxiety. "Have you become an amateur psychologist as well as a literary critic?" He knew he was sounding defensive.

"Let's not fight so early in the day," she said, smiling as sweetly as she could.

"Sorry," he said. "This is my writing time. You're here on vacation, but this is where I work."

She looked stung. "Thanks for the evening and now get off my boat? You're pretty much a bastard, you know that, Martin?"

He shrugged. "I'm not a good morning person," he said, staring her in the face. He had no intention of sitting around over coffee with her and discussing either his daughter or his drinking habits. He was sitting on his bunk and, for no apparent reason, reached for his soiled captain's hat which hung from a peg at the end of the bunk and jammed it on his head, as if to emphasize his proprietary possession of his boat. He realized he looked idiotic, but he took a swig from the bottle of gin and stared at her in defiance.

She glowered back at him and then gulped down the rest of her coffee. "How do I get back to my hotel?"

"I'll call Duc," he said.

"Do that," she said, standing stiffly. Then her face softened. "You always were kind of a tortured soul, Martin. I guess you save all of your normal human emotions for your books. Anyway, I'm going to tuck this experience away and keep it to myself. I won't tell anyone unless you get a Nobel some day. Then all bets are off. It will be my 15 minutes of fame."

He sensed that she was trying to end their brief liaison on a friendlier note. He felt self-conscious. "You know the weird thing," he said, "... is that you really can be a fun person. But too quickly you fall back into that assistant professor striving for tenure, don't rock the boat, mode, which invariably includes judging anyone with even a tinge of creativity as something foreign, someone to be analyzed, but not taken seriously—even though analyzing him and his work is what earns you a living. You're a conformist, Sylvia, a cog in the academic wheel, sucking your energy from those who dare to struggle against the popular currents, while being afraid to jump into the torrent yourself."

"And you're not just a talented lush, you're a social philosopher?"

"I'm a chronically inebriated thorn in society's side. At least, I hope so."

"Well, if that's your ambition, you've achieved it ... or at least the first half of it," she said, her voice softening again. She leaned over and kissed him on the forehead.

He gave her a kiss on the cheek. "You're a good sport, Sylvia."

She frowned and shook her head. His comment had brought back her anger. "You have such a way with words, Martin. That's how I always wanted to be remembered the morning after ... as a 'good sport.'"

He shrugged and escorted her off the boat.

## Chapter 16

Travelling back to the West coast from the East coast seemed like a shorter trip, although it took just as many days as it had taken to drive in the opposite direction. Thankfully, the weather had cooled, and I could drive with the windows open most of the way. Even though I was trying to quit smoking, I had a lot on my mind, or at least that's what I told myself every time I lit up. But the truth was, all I'd really found out was that the quest for Martin Bloom was going to exact an emotional toll that I hadn't foreseen when I'd decided to embark upon it.

I stopped in Yuma to see Candy and Betsy and was treated to another blissfully delicious home cooked meal. They were both just as interested in what I had found out about Bloom as I imagined relatives would have been—if I'd had any relatives.

"Whewee, that Martin Bloom sounds like a wild one," Candy said, laughing. His escapades with students and colleagues and his drinking sounded more entertaining to her than they had to me. She saw that I was troubled by her obvious amusement. "I wouldn't want him as a father—or a husband, that's for sure—but you've got to admit that the old boy sounds as if he's a real character."

"But how can he write so sensitively when he behaves so shamefully?" Betsy asked. She was clearly mystified by what I'd told her about the author whose book she'd just finished reading. I'd asked myself the same question.

"I guess, to quote my favorite country-western song, he knows how people feel but he just doesn't give a shit."

"Well, that's not completely fair, honey," Candy objected. "From what you told me he was awfully good to that professor and, until he left, to Elizabeth what's-her-name. He just isn't consistent."

"He may have helped Professor Truong, but he hasn't kept contact with him—or with Elizabeth either. I just think he's like my mother described him ... a charmer who is too self-centered to stick it out with anyone... except he's not dead, which is also something she said about him."

Candy nodded. "He's a bastard," she said.

Betsy and I looked at each other. This time I agreed with her assessment of my father... if that was who Martin Bloom was. "Bastard," Betsy repeated. "Asshole bastard," I said. All three of us burst out laughing.

I left Yuma the next morning and made it as far as San Diego, and then the next day drove up the coast to Palo Alto. I didn't even have the name of anyone at Stanford. I only had Elizabeth's and Professor Truong's word that Martin Bloom had even taught there. I took a hotel on El Camino Real and, since it was still only mid-evening, I drove over to the campus, which was well illuminated in the deepening light of dusk—the *crepuscular* hours, to quote Martin Bloom. The university was populated by very few students, there still being a few days before the fall term on the West coast.

Stanford didn't have that insulated, historic feeling to it that Harvard did. It was embedded within an upper-middle class neighborhood of large, Spanish-style houses and had a wide, spacious campus of low adobe buildings connected by covered walkways, separated by large expanses of dry, yellow grass. But I knew that its professors constituted a who's who of the various fields in which they taught and the students were every bit as intelligent and industrious as those at Harvard, although, judging by the few of them that I passed along the sidewalk, with their backpacks, shorts and sandals, they cultivated a more laid-back persona than those on the East Coast. I entered a building labeled *Student Union* to see if anyone could tell me where the English Department was located.

The coffee shop in the Union was almost empty except for a few isolated clusters of students, talking or typing on laptops. Sitting at a table in one corner was a solitary male student, absorbed in a paperback novel, which I couldn't help but notice was Kingsley Amis' *The Old Devils*, which I had read during Doctor Hendrickson's summer class on the British novel. I figured he must have been an English major, since the novel had been written back in the nineteen-eighties and it wasn't a college student's typical summer reading fare.

"That's an interesting book," I said, having had to screw up all my courage just to speak to someone I didn't know. He looked up. He was a lot better-looking up close than I had imagined when I'd gazed, from some distance away, at his bent head engrossed in his book. He had curly black hair that fell almost to his shoulders and very dark, thick eyebrows and an equally dark but narrow mustache and a Mephistophelian goatee. He looked like a character from an Elizabethan drama. His face was narrow and his eyes large, dark, and piercing. He didn't smile. "Are you talking to me?" he asked, in a good imitation of Robert DeNiro in *Taxi Driver*.

I froze. I considered looking around innocently, as if it had been someone else who had made the comment. But if I was going to find out what happened to Martin Bloom here at Stanford I'd have to be more assertive than I usually was with people. "I was just commenting on the book your were reading. I read it myself last year."

He stared at me as if he was puzzled. "Are you in Professor Wiggins' grad seminar next term?"

I guessed his social IQ wasn't so hot since he'd mistaken me for a graduate student. "Do you mind if I sit down?" I asked.

Without looking at me, he nodded almost imperceptibly in the direction of one of the chairs.

*Don't sprain your neck being friendly, Stanford smart-tard.*

"I don't go to school here," I said, pulling out one of the chairs and sitting down. "I'm just visiting. You must be an English major if you're reading Kingsley Amis."

He still hadn't smiled. Up to now, he'd kept his head lowered so that he was looking up at me through the dark curls that fell over his forehead. He looked a little like Vince, the character from *Entourage*. "Kinglsey Amis is interesting, but nobody writes about aging like Martin Bloom," he said.

I couldn't believe I'd stumbled onto one of Bloom's fans. "Have you read much of Martin Bloom?" I asked.

It was as if a fire had been lit behind his smoldering eyes. "I've read everything he's written," he said, eagerly. "He's the only real genius in American letters today."

Holy moly, he wasn't just a fan, he was a groupie.

My face must have shown my reaction, because he immediately frowned and gave me a look of disdain. "I can see you don't agree. Don't they teach Bloom at wherever you *do* go to school?"

I guess I'd hurt his feelings, or his literary sensibility or his over-inflated Stanford ego. "I go to Oregon. They teach the graphic novel editions and omit the big words," I answered.

He didn't get my sarcasm. "But you don't enjoy him?" he asked.

"I'm biased. He may be my father."

His eyes widened. "You're kidding." Then his expression became skeptical. "What do you mean, he may be?"

I hesitated telling my whole story to a perfect stranger, but by now I'd gotten used to relating it to nearly everyone I'd met, so I told him.

"You do look like pictures of him," he said. "But he doesn't teach here, not anymore. I already checked. I'd read someplace that he was teaching here and that's one of the reasons I enrolled in this grad school. But everyone in the department either denies it or gets vague whenever I ask about him."

"If he left under the same circumstances that he left Harvard, which was where he was before he was here, then he probably embarrassed himself, the university, and several of his female students, and no one probably wants to admit that he was even on the faculty."

He looked skeptical. "What did he do at Harvard?"

"Had an affair with a student, taught class while he was drunk."

"He's a genius. He can do that."

This guy's adoration of Bloom was over the top. "Geniuses grow on trees at Harvard. They sent him packing. Probably Stanford did too."

He still looked puzzled. "So if he's not teaching here now, what are you doing here?"

Now who was going to sound lame? "I'm hoping someone knows where he went after he left here."

"It's a goddamn mystery. A literary mystery!" he said. His face had lit up as if I'd just offered to give him a blowjob. "Hey, do you want a cup of coffee?"

To quote my slut friends from high school, I'd do whatever it took. If he was a graduate student in English, he must know the various faculty members. "Can you introduce me to the faculty? Someone might know where he went after he left here. By the way, my name's Dillon. Dillon Bloom."

"Chris Fenner," he said. "How about that coffee?"

I nodded and he jumped up and headed toward the service bar. I noticed that he was tall, and slim, but not skinny. He walked with a sort of rolling slouch, as if he were gliding across the floor on a skateboard. He had on an oversize plaid flannel shirt, faded jeans, and a pair of ratty tennis shoes. He reminded me of the folk or blue grass singers I used to listen to at concerts in Oregon—minus the shitkicker accent.

"Are you a writer?" I asked him when he returned to our table, carrying two coffees. A graduate student in English must be some kind of writer. I remembered Elizabeth and her novel.

"I'm working on some things," he said, nodding. His look had become serious, almost somber. He stared at me with a fierce intensity. "I'm working on a novel and a play, but I refuse to talk about them."

He refused? Did he think I was going to threaten him with my coffee spoon until he told me the plots? "Why?" I asked.

He looked away, as if he were deciding whether to continue. Then, he took a long breath and looked back at me. "They're both being composed in my mind all the time. Like a background recording over which everything I'm experiencing is playing. I'm constantly moving the stories forward, almost at a subconscious level. I don't want to share them or write them down until I have them complete in my mind." He looked away again, as though it had taken a great effort for him to share so much.

Give me a fucking break. This guy acted like writing was some variety of religious experience. But didn't he also just say he hadn't actually written anything down? "Didn't you have to show some of your writing to get into graduate school here?"

"I would if I was officially admitted for a degree. I'm kind of a special student, like a guest writer that they allow to take classes."

A guest writer who hadn't written anything? This guy could float the Titanic with his ego. Anyway, he still hadn't answered my question about introducing me to the faculty. I asked him again.

"No problem. They're going to be blown away when they find out you're Martin Bloom's daughter."

"I might be. That's what I'm trying to find out."

"A goddamn literary mystery!" he repeated, still obviously excited. "Man, I'd love to meet Martin Bloom. He's one of my heroes." He sipped his coffee and kept staring at me.

I was having a hard time not staring back at him; he was so good-looking. He was what I imagined a struggling young writer ought to look like. I felt intimidated ... even if he did seem like kind of a flake.

"Are you a writer?" he asked, his voice becoming more intimate, as if he had broached a sacred topic.

Was I? That was still an open question in my mind. "I like to write," I answered, trying to avoid sounding as if I'd just nominated myself for sainthood. "But I'm not working on anything, and I haven't produced anything but term papers for my classes."

"A writer knows," he said, solemnly nodding his head, as if to confirm that it was a topic that had been settled long ago in his own mind. "You feel that need to write burning like a hot ember inside of you. You can't be satisfied unless you're doing it. That's why I always have my work in my head. I can't let it go."

"I love to put words together," I said. "But the only time I ever felt embers burning inside of me was when I ate some super hot salsa in Albuquerque. I haven't got a clue what I would write if I did write something."

"You'll know if it happens. Christ, if Martin Bloom is your father, then you've got the genes for it. I envy you."

Did I? I guess what I was hoping to find out was whether or not my father did share anything... like whatever the inner consciousness is that makes someone become a writer... perhaps the burning ember that Chris was talking about. I knew that I was in love with words—reading them and writing them—and maybe that was the essential factor. But I sure didn't have the gift for speaking words, which Chris seemed to have, or, from what my mother had told me, my father had. I wondered if you needed to have that flair for speech in order to write. Did writers just put on paper the same kind of things that they said aloud? If that was true, I'd better aim for writing haikus. I sipped my coffee and contented myself with staring at Chris's beautiful face. He was staring into his coffee, as if he was lost in thought. Maybe he was composing one of his stories in his head.

"Can I meet you someplace tomorrow?" I asked.

He looked up, as if I'd surprised him by speaking. "Where are you staying tonight?"

*Slow down, Romeo.* I remembered my mother's warnings. Chris seemed like a nice guy, and he certainly was attractive, but that didn't mean I was bringing him back to my hotel. "I've got a place," I said, being deliberately vague. "I can meet you here on campus in the morning. How about here in the Student Union building?"

His face fell. I guess I'd shattered his fantasies of ripping off my bra and panties. But then he nodded. "Maybe around nine-thirty. There aren't that many faculty around because it's still a few days before classes start, but those that are here don't arrive in their offices until about ten."

I was disappointed at the news that some of the faculty might be away, but since I didn't know if any of them knew anything about where Martin Bloom was, I would take my chances with what I could get. I finished my coffee and stood up. "OK, Chris. Good to meet you. I'll see you in the morning. Right here, at nine-thirty."

He nodded silently, then reached out and touched my hand. I guess it was some sort of sign that we'd made a connection, but I jumped. I don't let boys touch me.

He looked surprised at my reaction, but then he smiled. "Peace, Dillon."

Peace? Holy fucking shit, what had I gotten myself into?

Chapter 17

The next morning the Student Union Building looked more like a busy airline terminal than a college cafeteria. More students had arrived for the fall term, and a lot of them seemed to have gravitated to the Union building to hang out, drink coffee, share summer experiences, make drug deals, lie about their sexual conquests or whatever it was that socially normal students did when they were on campus. I'd never done more than buy a cup of coffee at my Union building at Oregon and then go find a corner where I hoped no one would bother me. Nevertheless, seeing all those students made me miss being in college. But looking around at the serious looks on the students' faces reminded me that, just as at Harvard, every student within my sight would have had to have a high school gpa that would have put mine to shame. I tried to salvage my self-esteem by reminding myself that, even at Oregon, I had gotten admitted because I'd aced the SAT, achieving a score that probably would have made even patrician Stanford think twice before turning me down. The thought made me feel better, but then I remembered that I wasn't here to enroll in school, but to find Martin Bloom.

Chris was at the same table, but he wasn't its only occupant. There were two Asian girls having an intense discussion about a math problem and a lone, older student with bad acne chuckling to himself over a book titled "Frontiers of Nanotechnology." *Uh... hello, freakheads.* I approached the table cautiously, as if I might have stumbled upon a coven of aliens. Then Chris stood up. He'd placed his backpack on a chair to save it for me and when he saw me coming he picked the backpack up, pointed to the chair, and set the backpack under the table.

"Do you want coffee?" he asked. He had a nearly empty cup in front of him.

"I had some earlier," I answered. "I'm ready to talk to the faculty before they get too busy with returning students and I have to make an appointment. To quote Sartre, 'let's make hay while the sun shines.' "

Chris looked at me as if I were speaking a foreign language. "Right," he nodded, grabbing his backpack and slinging it over his shoulder.

I was carrying a purse. In it I had a notebook and pen in case someone had something to tell me. I had also put on some makeup, which I always carried but rarely used. I even had on what I considered to be my best-looking outfit—a pair of black skinny jeans with string boots and a loose, white silk blouse. I imagined myself looking like Lindsay Lohan, but sober. Not too sexy—I had to talk to the faculty after all—but sexy enough that if I was ever going to catch someone's eye, this was the outfit in which I was going to do it. I knew that I had dressed for Chris, and it made me angry at myself when I thought about having done it. To quote Kim Kardashian, I didn't dress to impress anyone.

Chris was wearing a green-and-white checked cotton shirt, unbuttoned, with a gray t-shirt underneath that said, *White Horse Tavern, Greenwich Village.* Underneath the logo of a horse's head it said, *Est. 1880.* He had on a pair of skinny jeans himself, although his were badly faded and boasted gaping holes in the thighs and knees. He wore a pair of old black tennis shoes, also marked by holes. Either he was seriously into the ragged look, or his closet was a nesting place for moths.

"Interesting t-shirt," I said as we walked toward the door to the cafeteria. "Did you get it in Greenwich Village?" I was making conversation to overcome my nervousness. I'd never in my life imagined myself walking around a campus alongside a good-looking boy.

"The Whitehorse Tavern was the center of the New York literary scene for most of the middle of the last century. Kerouac used to hang out there. Dylan Thomas downed 18 straight whiskeys at the bar and collapsed and died. I used to hang out there myself when I lived in the Village."

*Thanks a lot, Mr. Guide to Modern Literature.* He'd obviously lived a lot more of the life of a writer than I had and he hadn't hesitated to show off his background. "Where do we go first?" I asked.

"Eric Chappell is the head of the English Department. He ought to be the one who knows the most about Bloom, since he's been running the department for several years."

"Super," I said. "Do you know Chappell?"

"Not well. He and I corresponded when I was working out how to take some classes. He had to give my application his blessing. He probably remembers me from our letters back and forth."

"No doubt," I said, making an effort to keep the sarcasm out of my voice. I suspected that Chris didn't know the department chair at all, but I resisted saying so. Anyway, I had my name and my tenuous identity as Martin Bloom's daughter. Chris, bless his bragging heart, was just an added chip in my favor.

We arrived at a building, which like most of the others had the look of a Spanish hacienda, with a covered porch wrapping around it and connecting it to the next, nearly identical building. This one was called *Margaret Jacks Hall* and the Chairperson's office was on the second floor.

"Let me handle this," Chris said, stepping in front of me as we entered the Chair's office.

I had been prepared to give my little speech to the department secretary about searching for Martin Bloom in order to determine if I was his daughter and wanting to talk to the Department Head. I hoped Chris knew what he was doing. He seemed a lot more confident than I felt.

"I'm Chris Fenner, a special student in the graduate department. Professor Chappell knows me. Martin Bloom's daughter is here to talk to Dr. Chappell about her father. Could you please let him know that we're here?" His imperative tone suggested that his directive shouldn't be questioned. From the look on the secretary's face it also suggested to her that he was an asshole.

"You will need to make an appointment," the secretary answered, as if Chris' attempt at a commanding attitude had both irritated and amused her.

"Excuse me," I said, acting as humble as I could manage without actually prostrating myself and begging. "I'm only here for a brief time and I'm desperately in need of some information about Martin Bloom, who taught here a couple of years ago. Could you please see if Dr. Chappell has any time he could spare to talk to me?"

She looked at me, then at Chris, then back at me. "Sure, honey. Let me ask him if he has a few minutes." She got up and went down a short corridor. I heard voices. Then she returned. "Dr. Chappell will see you now."

\* \* \*

"I'm afraid your Professor Bloom had a very short and, frankly, ignominious career here at Stanford," Professor Chappell said, looking over our two heads and out his window, which afforded a panoramic view of the campus quad. "We hired him to teach in our special program on the American novel, but it turned out to be a rather poor fit." Dr. Chappell was as pompous in his own way as Dr. Cox, at Harvard, had been. Chappell didn't look like a 1930's film star, as Cox had, but instead he looked as if he were an up-to-date but aging Hollywood leading man, like George Hamilton, that guy who had been on *Dancing with the Stars*. He had long gray hair, swept back and falling to his collar. His skin was tanned a deep copper color, and he had a pair of dark glasses perched on his head, as if they were a tiara. He wore an open collar, pink shirt beneath a lime-green sports coat. I couldn't see what he wore from the waist down as he was seated behind a massive oak desk, but I imagined that his slacks were as colorful as the rest of his attire. *Canary yellow?*

"Martin Bloom is one of the great American novelists of the last 50 years," Chris replied. "How could such a person not fit your program on the American Novel? I, for one, enrolled here because I'd heard he once taught in your department."

"And you are?" Professor Chappell asked, peering across his desk as if Chris were someone who had slipped into the room uninvited.

"Chris Fenner. You and I have carried on considerable correspondence with each other. I was admitted as a non-degree student in the graduate program."

Chris' description of his status when addressing the department chair was less imposing than when he'd described himself to me as a "guest author."

The professor smiled slightly and said nothing. Then he turned back to me. "Being a gifted writer and being a teacher are two very different things. Only a very few people can do well at both. I'm afraid Martin Bloom wasn't one of them. The rigor required of an academic career was beyond him." He smiled a pained, artificial smile. "Martin was somewhat of a free spirit. That isn't what's required of a teacher."

I was familiar with the story, and I wasn't dying to hear the Stanford version of it, especially coming from this arrogant asshole's mouth. "You can spare me the details, Professor Chappell. As the Persian king said to Scheherazade, I've already heard that story a thousand times. All I'm trying to find out is where Martin Bloom is right now. Some members of your faculty may have continued to have contact with him, and perhaps they could help me out."

He had a severe look on his face, which he alternately directed at me and at Chris. "Doesn't your mother know where your father is?" he finally asked.

She probably did by now, but unfortunately it was difficult for her to get messages to me from beyond the grave. "My mother died a year ago. That's why I'm trying to reconnect with my father. He's the only relative I've got left." I omitted saying that my claim to be Martin Bloom's offspring was an assumption, rather than a fact. Instead, I'd tried to make myself sound pathetic, hoping to provoke some well-concealed strain of sympathy in this man. Chris no doubt thought that I was a wimp.

Dr. Chappell stared at me for a long time, his lips pursed. I guess he was mulling something over. Did that mean he knew something? I hoped so and I hoped that he would tell me if he did. Maybe my 'poor little me,' act had worked.

"Martin left no forwarding address, except to his agent in New York. He wasn't really close to any faculty members that I am aware of." He hesitated, as if he were still weighing releasing some final kernel of information. "You might talk to Professor Prentiss, however. I don't believe she and Professor Bloom were close, but she did mention seeing him recently, although she didn't divulge where. Her office is right down the hall."

Whoopee! I could have kissed him if he weren't such a shithead. I thanked Professor Chappell profusely, and Chris and I left his office.

## Chapter 18

"I can't believe you said that thing about Scheherazade," Chris said. "I like to sprinkle my conversation with famous quotations."

"But you made that one up."

"Someday it might be famous. Anyway, you're the one who claimed that Martin Bloom was my father. I had to go along with you so we didn't come across as a pair of idiots."

"I'm convinced that you're Bloom's daughter."

"Really? What convinces you, since I'm still not sure myself?"

"I got out one of his books last night. You do look like him. Besides, what are the chances that two Martin Blooms both went to Oregon at the same time, both of them writers?" His expression suggested that he thought I was crazy for even questioning the idea. He didn't know how much I wanted to believe him... and was afraid to.

"Do you know Professor Prentiss?" I asked, changing the subject.

"She's supposed to be a bitch," Chris answered, loping along beside me with his skateboarder walk. "She teaches Elizabethan literature or something like that and the rumor is that it's impossible to get an A out of her. I've never met her."

"Super," I said. We had come upon her door, which was closed. There was a sign under her name on the door that said PLEASE KNOCK AND THEN WAIT.

I knocked and waited.

After a few seconds the door was opened by a tall, shapely female, who didn't look as old as I'd expected a professor to look. She had long blonde hair and a fantastic suntan. Her expression could have been cut from granite as she frowned at Chris and me. "Office hours don't start until the term begins," she said, not at all pleasantly. She looked me up and down. "Shouldn't you be in high school... or at a Lady Gaga concert or something?"

"I'm a Stanford graduate student," Chris objected.

She looked at him as if seeing him for the first time. "Not one who takes my classes, you're not." Her tone made her words sound like a reprimand. She started to close the door.

"Wait," I said. "I'm Martin Bloom's daughter, and we heard that you might have seen him recently." I'd decided that Chris' approach of acting with certainty made more sense than trying to explain myself with a series of doubts and questions.

She opened the door wider and stepped back from it to take another look at me. After a moment, she nodded. "You might very well be Martin's daughter. You look like him, and he told me he had a daughter somewhere looking for him."

"He did?" I said, feeling completely flabbergasted. "How did he know that?"

"How should I know?" she answered, looking irritated. She looked over at Chris. "And who is this? Martin's son?"

"He's a friend. He's helping me try to find my father."

She nodded again, but she no longer looked irritated. "You're trying to find him? Why don't you come in? Your little friend can come in, too."

Chris and I entered the office. In contrast to the department chair's office, this one was tiny, although much more orderly, the books and journals neatly placed on bookshelves and even her desk devoid of paper, except for a small stack in a box marked *incoming*. I got the feeling that Professor Prentiss was a no-nonsense type of academician. A small, high window behind her desk offered a view of the sky and a few clouds, in contrast to the picture window looking out on the campus, which had been in the chairperson's office. There were two straight-backed, wooden chairs in front of her desk and Chris and I each took one.

"How did you know that I saw your father?" she asked.

"Professor Chappell told us. He said he heard you talking about it."

She nodded. "Professor Chappell doesn't miss much. What else did he say?"

"He said you and Martin Bloom weren't really friends, but that you had run into him somewhere a little while ago. Professor Chappell said he didn't know where it was that you saw him."

"I'm glad to hear that he doesn't know everything," she said, drily. "And how long has it been since you've seen your father?"

"Eighteen years."

"What a wonderful father," she said in the same dry, tone. "Why in the world would you want to find someone who left you when you were a baby?"

That was a good question, but not one that I cared to address with this ogre. "My mother died a year ago, and I feel as if I need to make a connection with my only living relative." I was hoping that using the same story I'd told Professor Chappell might also wring some sympathy out of this dried prune.

She smirked. "If Martin is your only living relative, then I feel sorry for you, my dear. He must have been a selfish bastard when he left you, and I can vouch for the fact that he remains so."

Her language shocked me. "I'm not expecting much," I said, weakly.

"We're talking about one of the greatest writers alive," Chris chimed in. "I think anyone who is related to Martin Bloom would want to make some connection with him."

"What are you, a literary critic?" Professor Prentiss asked. She looked at Chris as if he were something she'd tracked in on the bottom of her shoe. "Of course Martin is one of our country's finest writers, but he's a poor excuse for a human being. You can take that from me, personally."

I didn't feel like debating her opinion, especially since she seemed quite adamant and, anyway, her description fit with much of what I'd learned from Elizabeth Roundtree. "Do you know where he is?"

She nodded again. "Yes, I do."

I looked over at Chris and, without thinking, grabbed his hand. I had prepared myself for another disappointment, and now I could hardly believe that, after two weeks of searching, I was finally going to find out where Martin Bloom—and perhaps my father—was.

She looked at Chris and me holding hands. "That's touching," she said, not even attempting to conceal her sarcasm.

"Where is he?" I asked, letting go of Chris' hand. I was growing afraid that Professor Prentiss wasn't going to tell us.

"Vietnam. He lives on a boat on the Saigon River. He's at a marina right downtown, across from all the fancy hotels."

On a boat on the Saigon River? She might as well have said he was in Outer Mongolia. "What is he doing there?" Even as I asked I remembered that Professor Truong had suggested that Bloom might have taken his advice and gone to Vietnam.

"The same thing he's done everywhere else," she answered, a sour look on her face, "hiding from everyone, including you."

I felt crushed. If Martin Bloom was my father, not only had he left me, but he was still trying to keep me out of his life. I sat there, dumbly, not knowing what to ask next.

Professor Prentiss' face softened for a moment. "I don't think you're the reason he's trying to stay hidden. He was hiding over there before he even knew you were looking for him. There are probably a lot of people who would like to know where he is—most of them not because they want to wish him well. Your father has disappointed a lot of people besides you."

I felt a little better. I wanted to ask her about her relationship with Bloom, but she was obviously one of those people who did not remember him kindly.

"What were you doing in Vietnam?" I asked her, not knowing what else to say.

"I was on a tour—Vietnam, Cambodia, Thailand." She looked as though she was becoming impatient. I guess she wasn't yearning to share her travel experiences.

"I've been there," Chris offered.

"You've been to Vietnam?" I was astounded.

"I spent almost six months in Southeast Asia last year."

"Doing what?" I asked.

"Backpacking, bumming around, gaining experiences." He acted as if it was no big deal. Traveling to Vietnam sounded like going to the moon to me, but I was the only one in the room who hadn't been there.

"Maybe you two can take this conversation outside," Professor Prentiss interrupted. She stood up and waited for us to do the same. Then she walked us to the door. "And good luck finding your father. If you do find him, tell him to fuck himself." She slammed the door behind us.

I guess I had a new quotation to offer to Martin Bloom if I ever found him.

"She's probably jealous," Chris offered.

"No. Martin Bloom sounds like a bastard," I said, using Candy and Betsy's favorite word for him. "She knows he is, and so do most of the other people who've met him."

"Martin Bloom doesn't have to be nice to every Tom, Dick or Harriet who thinks he or she knows literature ... or who wants a relationship with him, for that matter. He's a fucking genius, and geniuses don't have to be nice."

Chris seemed to be too enthralled by Bloom to be able to think straight about him. That was OK. Chris was an artist and artists probably had a right to extravagant opinions. I didn't put myself in his category, so my opinion was more mundane.

"Are you going to Vietnam?" Chris asked.

"Yes." I hadn't thought twice before I'd answered, although I'd never been out of the country and the thought of going to a foreign country where they didn't even speak English scared the shit out of me. But I'd come this far, so I wasn't going to give up now. Everything I'd learned so far pointed to the conclusion that Martin Bloom was my father. He also sounded like an asshole, but one who might be as tortured and as poor a fit to the society around him as I was. And perhaps that was part of why he was a writer. I felt like Alice diving down the rabbit hole.

"Good for you!" Chris said, smiling at me as if I'd accomplished some major feat instead of making what would probably turn out to be one of my all-time dumbass decisions. Then his face got serious "You have to get some shots first. The health conditions over there aren't what they are here."

Shots? Health conditions? I suddenly had visions of a bunch of creepy tropical diseases—malaria, Dengue fever, Ebola virus. What was I getting myself into? "What kind of shots?"

"Hepatitis, Tetanus, a few others. They've got a lot of diseases over there."

Perfect. I'd probably end up incapacitated for life, my body emaciated from lock jaw, yellow skin pockmarked by open sores, coughing up blood every time I tried to talk, but this was no time to be faint-hearted. To quote Isaac Newton, you've gotta sit where the apple lands. Or was that Steve Jobs? Anyway, for the first time I had definite information about Martin Bloom's whereabouts. Was I going to let the prospect of a few fatal diseases stop me from finding him? No way.

"Have you got a passport?"

I nodded and patted my purse.

"Good. That would be the main thing to hold you up. You can get the shots today or tomorrow. You're supposed to wait and get a second hepatitis shot, but they'll let you go without one. You can be ready to leave within a few days."

"Where do I do all this?" Chris seemed to know all the procedures; I had no clue where to get shots or even a ticket.

"A travel agent. They'll sell you tickets and arrange for you to see a doctor to get your immunizations."

"I guess I'll go look for a travel agent," I answered. I owed Chris a lot. I wasn't sure how to thank him.

"I'll go with you," Chris said. "I know an agent at one of the malls not far from here."

"Lead on, Macduff," I said as we headed for the parking lot.

## Chapter 19

Goddamn it, Martin thought, why couldn't he make his anxiety go away? The only thing that relieved his anxiety was alcohol. But the more he drank, the more insistent his anxiety became, rearing its head each morning as a feeling of dread, which sat like a slowly turning wheel in his belly, churning his entrails, sapping the power from his limbs, their strength slipping away like sand on a beach. When he felt like this, the way he felt now, he had no choice but to reach for the bottle.

But even with the bottle in hand, his anxiety never left him completely. He could feel it, like some insidious parasite, consuming his insides and leaving him powerless. It started with the worry that he would never be able to write again. Then his mind slid to the more chronic worries about the various diseases he might have. They were all illnesses of age and dissipation, any one of which he knew he deserved, if only because of the risks he'd failed to heed in a life lived through denial. Did he have to urinate so frequently because he drank so much or was it because his prostate had become enlarged? His own father had died of prostate cancer soon after Martin had graduated from college and, the danger of a similar fate had lurked in the back of his mind, hanging over him like the suspended blade of a guillotine since the moment he had turned middle-aged. And what about the occasional blood that appeared in his stool? Was it simply his irritated hemorrhoids or was it a sign that he had colon cancer? The thought of undergoing a colonoscopy terrified him. And his protruding gut; he told himself that it was what could be expected from his almost total lack of exercise, but he also knew that it could be a symptom of cirrhosis of the liver. His drinking was bound to ruin his liver sooner or later.

Despite his efforts at denial, he couldn't stop thinking that he was dying. He could get up right now and cross the river and see a doctor—there were many in the city who spoke English and were cheap—but he didn't move. Instead he lifted the bottle and took another drink. He was paralyzed by his fear of the doctor's verdict.

Casey Dorman

He carried in his head an image of a small animal, it might have been a cat or an opossum, it had been so long ago when he had seen it that he could no longer remember, and he had encountered countless replicas of the image in the years since. The animal had been run over on the road, its head squashed like a tomato, its brains extruding through its eye sockets and nose, and through a large fracture in the animal's flattened skull. The image had stuck in his mind, forming the prototype for his vision of sudden, violent destruction, what he imagined would be his fate. The image, frightening as he found it, was still part of his denial, because it was this image of an unavoidable catastrophe that he saw when he pictured his death, not the numbing heart attack, the blinding stroke or the apoplectic collapse into his own putrid vomit following a bout of drinking, which were, of course the more likely ways by which he would suffer a premature, if it could be called that, death.

He was fifty-two, not elderly by any means, but no longer young, and his body was worn out beyond his years. He knew that death was unavoidable, and he had no illusions about living to a ripe old age. Each day he ignored warning signs that his body was failing. He asked only that he have the time to reflect on his life as it slipped away from him. Death was frightening to him only because it meant leaving life without an opportunity to put things right or at least to sum things up. He had always harbored the intuition that behind the ravages of time there must lurk a *why*, a reason that the system failed while the captain of the vessel, still alert astride his storm battered bridge, could only watch as the ship he'd vowed to pilot crumbled beneath him. He had hoped for some poetry in the process, not simply the entropic descent into chaos, which he was growing to suspect was the real and whole truth of the matter. Maybe, after all, there was nothing to find. Maybe Sartre had been right: "Every existing thing is born without reason, prolongs itself out of weakness, and dies by chance." One just got old. It wasn't pretty, it wasn't poetic, and it didn't give any final sense of purpose to the years of life that preceded it.

Yet he still yearned for a perspective, a system of belief or theory, which could lend structure to his feeble attempts to make sense of his life and world.

He had come to Vietnam seeking that elusive perspective. What he had found was a third-world country, consumed by its own misery, its population trying to survive in any way they could. People, including children, roamed the city streets in all stages of dying, with missing limbs, with jaws and mouths eaten by cancer, with communicable diseases that could turn epidemic, if they had not already. It was rumored that parents sometimes severed their children's limbs to make them more pitiable and thus more remunerative as beggars. Whether or not such rumors were true, the number of maimed and malformed children grasping for alms on the street corners was astounding, despite the fact that the city had recently begun to crack down on beggary, pulling beggars off the street and putting them in temporary shelters, which became permanent, enforced "residences" for them if they were caught returning to their former trade.

The truth was that he could not shed the image of the flattened animal on the highway because it reminded him that he was only flesh and blood and that the trajectory of his life, just like the lives of all those poor souls around him, was guided by animal instinct, weakness of will, and blind fate. The musings he so desperately yearned to have time to entertain before his death were, in all likelihood, like his plans and hopes and aspirations, no more than mere epiphenomena, the random discharges of electrical energy created by a million synapses firing in sequences determined by the primitive reflexes of the hunter-gatherer wandering in confusion amidst the towering creations of a race whose quiddity consisted of always building and tinkering, with only the illusion of purpose. A million electrical impulses rumbling around inside of a human skull could, in the manner of quantum motion, produce the illusion of coherent thought. But in the end it meant nothing. The brain would finally slither from the skull's orifices into the earth from whence it had come, and all of the life behind it would disappear, devoid of meaning.

With great effort, he shook himself free of his obsessive ruminations. Right now he was more worried about somebody finding out where he lived than about how he would die. Why had he allowed himself to have a one-nighter, or whatever their brief fling should be called, with that bimbo, Sylvia Prentiss? She'd promised to keep the identity of his location secret, but she had left his boat pissed at him, and there was no doubt she would tell anyone and everyone where he was living. And that everyone could include his daughter if she ever found her way to Stanford in her quest to find her absent father.

It was noon. He had been sitting, drinking, and thinking for almost two hours. Even though September wasn't as hot as July or August, it was still almost 100 degrees. He was roasting, although dressed only in his swimming trunks and sandals, the loose, bare skin of his pudgy upper body exposed to the moist river air. He took a long swig of gin from the bottle in his hand and resolved that he needed to do something. Just drinking and thinking weren't ridding him of his anxiety.

He got up and crossed the deck of his boat, then stepped onto the dock and marched, as steadily as he could manage, toward the marina office.

When he arrived at the office he told Hinh, the marina manager, that he wanted to move his boat. The same company that managed the marina where his boat was docked managed several others up and down the Saigon River, private marinas, which served the luxury villas and condominium complexes that had grown up along the river bank over the last twenty or so years. Hinh volunteered that there was a slip available in front of the Riverview Condominiums, a newly-built community of expensive condominiums in three separate riverside towers well up the river, away from the downtown area. Two of the three towers were still under construction and only one was occupied, so the marina, which had been completed well before the rest of the complex, was mostly empty, except for the boats of the five or six owners who had already moved in, and those of a few other boat owners who were renting temporary docking space, as Martin would be.

Martin wasn't concerned about a long-term dock for his boat, since he could always come back to his current location in the future. But if he moved his boat to the Riverview marina, which was a private marina for the exclusive use of the condo residents, no one would think to look for him there. After a few months, Sylvia would forget that she had seen him, and his daughter would no doubt give up her search and hopefully forget her delinquent father as he had forgotten her all of these years, and he could safely return to his present location.

He handed over a wad of cash to cover his docking fees for the next several months, and the marina operator called over to the other marina and got a slip number. He could move the boat whenever he was ready.

What the hell, he thought, there was no time like the present.

His gaze wandered around the rundown marina that had been his home for the past two years. The only regret he felt in leaving was that he would no longer be able to see Linh each morning. He had grown fond of her and her honest, down-to-earth manner, not to mention the attractive antithesis she offered to his hangover-filled mornings.

He left the marina office and headed for Linh's café. The café was crowded with workmen: fishermen, construction workers, gardeners, all of them Vietnamese. Martin sat down on one of the plastic chairs and waited until he caught Linh's attention.

"I'm not hungry," he said, when she came to his table. Her pretty face brightened with the smile she always showed when she saw one of her favorite customers. "I'm leaving for awhile. Taking my boat up river for several weeks. I'll be back eventually."

"Why you leave?" Linh asked, not able to conceal her sadness as well as her surprise.

"Some personal stuff... nothing to worry about. I just wanted to say goodbye... and thank you for your friendship."

She touched his shoulder. "You good man, Ong Martin. Come back soon." She blinked back a tear, then turned and left to serve her other customers.

He walked slowly back to his boat, wondering if he was doing the right thing. But the thought of Sylvia Prentiss taking out her revenge on him by informing someone of his whereabouts renewed his determination. He had to master his anxiety.

After climbing aboard his boat and taking a few more swigs from the gin bottle, he cast off the lines and, slowly and a bit unsteadily, backed his boat out of his slip. The other marina was up the river about two miles, just around a sharp bend.

He drank steadily as he chugged up the river, hoping that his anxiety would subside enough that it wouldn't rear its ugly head again, as soon as he tied up at the next dock. He paid only minimal attention to the river and its constant flow of traffic, as he continued to ruminate about his foolishness at revealing his whereabouts to Sylvia Prentiss. The river traffic was heavy, but the farther away from the center of town he got, the less there was, although he still had to pay enough attention to dodge the deluge of floating refuse coming toward him from upstream. Soon he was passing a whole series of stately villas, sitting back from the river on wide lawns or nestled behind luxuriant green foliage, most of them sporting private docks with expensive yachts tied up to them. He doubted that there were any writers living in such splendor, even in a country such as this in which the cost of living was incredibly low. Not so inexpensive that he was living very high on the hog, he reminded himself, guzzling his bottle of gin to try to shore up his sagging ego.

By the time he pulled into the marina in front of the Riverview Condominiums, he was pretty well drunk. He remembered the slip number—it was 21—but he had no idea where it was located. Most of the slips were unoccupied, and he searched for markers on the docks and finally found that each one had a sign listing its slips' numbers. He found a dock labeled 20-29 and, with relief, gunned his boat in that direction.

He was going a lot faster than he should have been going, a fact which dawned on him only when he was nearly upon the dock. He fumbled with the throttle, hoping to put the engine in reverse in order to slow himself down, but he was too drunk and too confused and instead of reversing the engine he jammed the throttle and the boat shot forward, crashing into the dock, fortunately into his own slip and not into either of the two luxury yachts neighboring it. The impact catapulted him over the steering wheel and onto his boat's deck in front of the bridge. When he groggily clambered to his feet, he looked down and saw that the bow of his boat was shattered, and water was rushing in between the shards of fiberglass that made up the hull.

Goddamn it to hell! He said to himself. He took one of the lines, and stepped onto the dock and made the boat secure, but by this time it had sunk a good foot below the usual water line. "Shit and double shit!" he shouted, then sat down and watched helplessly as his boat slipped further and further below the surface.

In a minute he heard shouting in Vietnamese, and he looked up and saw four men rushing down the dock with gigantic white rubber floats hoisted over their shoulders. He watched as they fastened the floats to his boat and the sinking process finally came to a halt. The men continued to jabber to each other and stare at Martin with a mixture of amusement and pity. He had no idea what they were saying.

A smartly dressed young man wearing a shirt that said *Riverview Marina* hurried down the dock toward him. When he reached Martin's boat he shouted something to the other men in Vietnamese, then spoke to Martin in English. "Mister, your boat is badly damaged, and so is our dock."

"I guess I misjudged the distance... or my speed... or something," he answered, aware that his voice had trailed off into a mumble.

"We are going to have to charge you for the damage to our dock. Do you want us to repair your boat also?"

He couldn't very well live on a boat that, at any moment, might settle to the bottom of the river. "Do what you have to do," he said. "I guess I need to find somewhere else to stay for awhile."

The man who had spoken to him looked him over. Martin knew he didn't present a very impressive picture, a shirtless fat man dressed in shorts and flip-flops, sitting on the dock next to a sinking boat. "I have money," he said. "I'm an American. A rich American."

The man's eyes lit up, although the expression on his face was skeptical. "My cousin has a small hotel in town. Perhaps you would like to stay there. It is not a luxury hotel, but it is comfortable and his wife changes the linen every other day."

Even in his inebriated state, Martin recognized that this might be fate stepping in to rescue him. Anyone who'd heard he was living on a boat docked in a marina on the Saigon River would never think to look for him at a cheap hotel in the heart of the city. It was perfect. He felt his anxiety diminishing already. "I'll take it," he said. "Fix my boat and bring me the bill. And don't tell anyone where I'm staying."

The man nodded his head as if he understood. In Saigon, just like all other Southeast Asian cities, there were all sorts of people who wanted to keep their identities unknown. Most of them had money. "I'll call my cousin to come and pick you up on his motorcycle," he said.

## Chapter 20

We took my car to El Camino Real, and then Chris directed me south until we came to a vast Spanish-style mall, looking like something out of a travel brochure for Mexico and filled with one-story white stucco shops, all with identical red tile roofs. The parking lot was filled with Mercedese and Lexuses, and in one glance I saw enough middle-aged, blonde-coiffed, elegantly clad women to make me think we'd arrived at a garden club tea. I didn't recognize any of the stores' names, but that just meant that it wasn't the kind of mall that hosted a Wal-Mart or a Marshall's. Chris introduced me to an older woman named Sharon who owned the travel agency next to an optometrist's office and who knew both Chris and his parents. She was able to reserve an airline ticket to Ho Chi Minh City, which I found out was the proper name for Saigon, and arrange for me to have my immunizations at a local doctor's office. The cost was only $1100 for the round trip fare with an open return, which surprised me. I told Sharon that I'd need to go to the bank to get some cash. She told me she'd set up a doctor's appointment for me for that afternoon.

Chris and I left the travel agency, and I found a branch of my bank right there in the same mall. Chris pointed out that my particular bank had branches in Saigon, so I felt safe that I would have access to my funds in case something unplanned caused me to need more money.

"This is easier than I thought it would be," I said, as we sat in a Mexican restaurant waiting for our tacos and beans and rice. "Thanks for all of your help."

He smiled that killer smile at me, looking sort of shy as he gazed at me through the curls that had fallen over his forehead. "I've got a proposal for you," he said, his shyness replaced by a mischievous grin.

"What?" I could feel my stomach begin to tighten in the familiar feeling of discomfort I felt whenever someone acted as if he was about to confide in me.

"How about if I go with you to Vietnam?"

I almost chucked my lunch right there. "Why would you do that?"

"To meet Martin Bloom."

"That doesn't make sense," I said. "You're enrolled in graduate school."

"I'm just taking classes. They can wait. Meeting Martin Bloom would be a better education than anything I could learn here."

Now my stomach was tightening like a clenched fist. I'd never thought of traveling with someone else—especially a man. My first thought was that he was thinking that, by traveling together, he'd be able to get me into bed. Then I wondered what it meant about me that I was harboring such thoughts. I was coming unglued. "I'm not sleeping with you," I said, forcefully enough to confirm that I was hopelessly neurotic.

"Whoa, slow down. Who said anything about sleeping together? I just want to help you find your father and meet him myself. C'mon, I know Saigon. I've been there, and I know a lot of people there. Anyway, you're a young woman, and it's not safe for you to travel there by yourself."

He had a point. Several of them, in fact.

"I'm no hippie," I said.

"There haven't been any hippies since 1975," he answered. He looked as if he were laughing at me.

"You were one. You lived in Greenwich Village and went backpacking to Vietnam and all those other Asian countries, like the Dharma Bums or something."

"I'm a writer. So are you. We have to follow our muses."

"To quote Hemingway, that's a bunch of crap. I'm not following a muse anyway; I'm trying to find Martin Bloom. Besides, I bet you were taking drugs and having group sex or whatever, most of the time you were over there." I didn't even know that Chris used drugs or anything about his sexual proclivities, but that was my vision of American students backpacking in foreign countries.

He shrugged. "I wouldn't use drugs in Vietnam. It's too dangerous if you get caught. They have a death penalty for anything more serious than marijuana."

Great, I was going to a country that put tourists to death. "I can't pay for you," I said, although I was beginning to hope that he would come with me. It did seem safer to travel with a companion, although I noticed that he hadn't denied my group sex accusation.

He shrugged again. "I've got money. You saw how little the plane fare cost. Once you're there everything is dirt cheap."

"Really?" I was starting to feel more and more positive about the idea. But then I wondered if it really made sense. "Don't you have to file a leave of absence from school or something?" I sounded like Randolph Fuller, my nerdy neighbor in Eugene.

"They never really admitted me anyway ... just let me take classes. Fuck 'em. We're going off to meet the real guru."

How could I argue with Chris' reason for wanting to meet Martin Bloom? After all, I was seeking to meet him for the same reason—except I was hoping that I'd find the answer to my questions about whether he really was my father and why I felt so different from everyone else and whether I was destined to become a writer. "What about your parents? That travel lady knows your parents. Don't you have to ask them or something?"

He laughed. "My parents don't care what I do. They've let me travel all over the world. They travel all the time themselves. That's why Sharon, the travel agent knows them and why I knew about her agency."

Did I really want to do this? I mean, when I'd started looking for Martin Bloom I'd never planned on leaving the country, particularly not with a young man I hardly knew. Chris was crazy for wanting to come with me just because he admired Martin Bloom—or so he said. I was still suspicious of his motives, but I had to admit I was relieved not to have to go to Vietnam alone.

\* \* \*

The plane trip to Saigon was uneventful. Chris and I sat next to each other and, because the plane was only half full, we each had room to stretch out across several seats and sleep. When we were awake we both read. I was working my way through *End of Passage,* which I had bought in Cambridge while exposing my heritage to Elizabeth Roundtree. It was a story about a man who'd tried to satisfy his lifelong ambition of sailing around the world solo but found that being alone with his own thoughts was an unbearable torture. It was a familiar enough feeling that I found myself identifying with one of Martin Bloom's fictional characters. The poor sailor finally gave up and turned back home to try to put his life together back on land.

I, meanwhile, was sailing on ... but not alone.

"It must be weird, knowing that the author of the book you're reading could be your father," Chris said.

He was right, but I wasn't going to admit it. "Most authors are probably someone's father," I answered, feeling self-conscious about having his attention focused on me.

"I wonder if you can read him objectively."

"I don't read anyone objectively."

"Whatever," he said, looking mildly irritated. But then he recovered. "You'll love some of his other books, *A Memorial to Time, A Parting of the Ways,* and *Rebecca,*" he answered. All of a sudden he seemed to have dropped his Stanford grad student pose, and his tone was more cordial.

"*Rebecca* sounds as if it's about a woman," I said.

"It's his only book in which the main character is female," Chris said. "It saved him from the critics who were starting to say that Bloom was a misogynist ... although a few still accused him of being anti-women."

"Why?"

"Rebecca's not entirely an appealing character."

"Really?"

"She's sort of a Becky Sharp type, if you remember Thackeray's *Vanity Fair.*"

I did, although I thought Chris was throwing in the literary reference to show off. "What does she do?"

"She lies to her best friend to get her to break off her engagement, then marries the fiancé herself. But she remains so jealous of the friend that she fails to see her husband really does love her, and she ends up ruining their marriage. Only when she is elderly and her husband has died, does she try to reconcile things with her friend, but by then it's too late."

"Sounds as if he's misogynistic, or at least sexist," I said. I wasn't surprised, given what I'd already learned about Bloom.

"Nonsense," Chris shot back, an offended look on his face. "The protagonist could have as easily been a man as a woman. He was just telling a story."

"What's *A Memorial to Time* about?" I asked. I sensed it was better to avoid challenging Chris' apparently fragile ego by engaging in a debate.

"This middle-aged multimillionaire, Phineas Butler, decides to go back to his home town and rebuild his family house exactly as it was when he was growing up. He even tries to use the same builders who had built the original house. His idea is that he will live just as his family did when he was a child. Except that now he will be so rich and powerful that he can control everything in the town and get revenge on all of those who treated his family poorly."

"Really? Sounds like a dream a lot of people probably have." It *did* sound interesting—paranoid and spiteful—but interesting

"Except his plan fails," Chris continued. "He plans to run roughshod over everyone else, but it doesn't work. He finds that he has to get to know all of those people all over again. What he finds out is that they're completely different than he thought they were. Everything he'd thought he'd known about them all of his life had been wrong."

"His plots all sound as if they have share a certain theme. Always about aging and trying to set things right, then finding out that it's not possible."

Chris smiled, smoothing his goatee with one hand. "You know Freud had a concept of a *repetition compulsion*, where an action or experience is repeated over and over in an attempt to finally gain mastery over it."

"Do you think that is what Bloom is doing?" I asked, recognizing the aptness of Chris' description to Martin Bloom's writing.

"If he is, Freud's idea was that the true reason for the fixation on that experience is subconscious. The person feels a drive to repeat the behavior, but he doesn't know why—or the reasons he makes up are spurious; they serve to misdirect his awareness of his motives."

"That's interesting," I said, and I meant it. "You should be a teacher." I meant that, too.

"I'm a writer. I don't mind explaining literature to others who need help understanding it, but I wouldn't want to do it as a living."

He didn't mind *explaining* literature to someone who needed help understanding it ... someone like me? What an arrogant asshole. "What *do* you do for a living?"

He looked at me as if he couldn't believe I'd asked the question. "I'm a writer. I do whatever I have to do to support my writing. I've worked in a cannery, washed dishes, worked on a fishing boat, tended bar, you name it."

"What did you do in Vietnam?"

"I told you I was backpacking. I didn't need much money. You'll find out how cheaply you can live in Saigon when we get there. I didn't really work there. I sort of bummed around, seeing friends, learning about the culture, drinking a lot."

"You must have had some source of income while you were there."

This time it was his turn to look self-conscious. "My parents gave me an allowance." His admission made him look even more sheepish.

"How old are you?"

"Twenty-six."

"And you lived off your parents' money?" I didn't shout "loser" and point a finger at him, but I hoped the condemnation was evident in my voice.

"That wasn't where I got all of my money, he said, his irritation evident. "I'd just finished working at a cannery in Alaska, and I'd saved a bundle. In Saigon it went a long way. Besides, I made a little money on the side." He had a smug look on his face.

"Doing what?"

"You'll see when we get there. Like I said, I had some money from working in the canneries in Alaska, and I was able to loan a few people some money and get it back with interest."

He was a loan shark? I couldn't tell if he was telling the truth or making up a story. Anyway, whatever he had done in Vietnam before, it didn't sound very substantial and maybe not even legal. But so what? Whatever he'd done in Vietnam before didn't have anything to do with what we were doing now. In a few hours we would be there, and we were there not to earn money, but to find Martin Bloom. I turned away and went back to sleep.

Chapter 21


My God, everyone in the Saigon Airport was Asian! Duh. All of a sudden it dawned on me what a ginormous step I'd taken by traipsing off to a foreign country. All around me people were jabbering in a language I couldn't understand, as if I'd just sat down to watch a foreign movie and found that it had no subtitles. I felt as if everyone were staring at me and wondering what I was doing in their land. Hadn't we been at war with these people at one time? Why hadn't I paid more attention during my AP history class? I looked up at the entrance to the airport and saw a flag with a single star hanging next to a second flag with a hammer and sickle. I guess we hadn't won the war; these people were communists. Holy fucking shit, what had I done?

Chris must have sensed my discomfort because he reached out and took my hand. "Calm down, Dillon; they love Americans over here. They think we're all rich—or suckers. You'll see when we get out of the airport. Everyone will try to sell you something."

I was glad he'd taken my hand, but I disengaged myself almost immediately, not wanting to give him the idea that I was dependent upon him. "You speak Vietnamese, right?"

He shook his head. "No need to. Most people in Saigon know at least some English."

We had retrieved our luggage, and we were approaching the customs counter.

"If they ask you for money, just act as though you don't understand them," Chris said. He acted nonchalant, as if refusing a request for a bribe from a government official in a strange country was a natural thing to do.

*How about acting as if I was scared shitless?*

But Chris turned out to be right. I acted dumb, and the only question I was asked by the skinny customs agent was how long I planned to stay in Vietnam and why I was there. I told him I was planning to stay two weeks and that I was on a vacation. He opened my suitcase and poked around. He pulled out a pack of cigarettes, opened it and sniffed inside. After giving me a hard stare, he closed the suitcase, pushed it back to me and waved me through. He kept the pack of cigarettes.

"What were they checking for in our suitcases?" I asked Chris when we got far enough away that the agent couldn't hear me.

"Drugs. They do that to all young people, especially those with beards, like me or tattoos, like you."

"He kept my pack of cigarettes."

Chris shrugged. "They do that."

"Assholes," I muttered.

Chris laughed. "Hey, there are some countries where they'd plant drugs in your bag and then throw you in jail so they could make your parents pay a lot of money to get you out. It's been heard of even here. Consider a pack of cigarettes a cheap bribe for getting into the country."

It may have been cheap, but I was still irked that someone could just take something of mine like that, as if he had the right. I wanted to go back and make a fuss. To quote the typical NASCAR fan, didn't they know they were messing with a goddamned American? But Chris' words had frightened me. Who would pay if I got thrown into jail here? A supposed father who denied he even had a daughter? My dead mother? I'd rot for years behind bars, surviving on nothing but rice and water. "What do we do now?" I asked Chris, trying not to let my fear show.

"Find a hotel."

Chris hailed a cab and named a street that the driver seemed to know, and we headed into town. If I'd thought the highways driving into Boston or LA were crowded, I hadn't seen anything. It was morning, and all around our cab were what seemed like thousands of motorcycles, their riders often having their mouths and noses covered with masks, making them look like outlaws in a Western movie ... or like terrorists. But how many terrorists rode around with tiny babies sitting in front of them, older children sitting behind and a grandmother behind the kids? People here often rode three, sometimes four people to a motorcycle—as many people as fit in an

SUV in America. Mixed in among the motorcycles were bicycles, many of them also with multiple passengers or anything from chicken coops to mattresses piled on top of them. And down the edges of each street there were motorcycles and bicycles traveling in the opposite direction! Even worse, pedestrians made their way through this chaotic mix of vehicles with no regard for crosswalks, stoplights or anything else. People crossed the street at corners and in the middle of the block. The traffic never stopped for them; it just went around them. I held my breath, waiting for someone to get hit, but they always seemed to make it across.

"This is crazy," I said to Chris. "You could get killed just crossing the street here."

He nodded. "It takes a while to get used to it. When we get to the backpacker district the traffic doesn't move quite so fast, and there are more pedestrians."

"There's a district just for backpackers?"

"That's what it's called, unofficially. Almost every large Asian city has one, but Saigon's is especially good for people like us. There are a lot of cheap hotels and restaurants and lots of Americans and Australians and Europeans. It's easy to get by on English and we won't go broke if we have to stay awhile looking for your father. That's where I stayed when I was here a year ago. I still have some contacts there."

"Shouldn't we stay somewhere near the river? He lives on a boat."

"Everywhere is near the river. It runs through the middle of the city. Trust me, the backpacker district is the best place for us to stay."

What could I say? Chris had been here before, and I hadn't. Anyway, after using a third of my cash for the plane fare, I was glad to hear that we would be able to find a cheap hotel. I was also glad that I'd see other Americans, not that I planned on making any friends, but seeing people who looked like me would be reassuring—especially if they spoke English. I wondered what kind of people came to a foreign country with just a backpack. People like Chris, I guess.

Chris was right about the cost of the hotel. We found one that cost us $12 a night. Chris wanted to share a room. He said he needed to save his cash, but I figured it was just a scheme to get me into bed with him, and I told him to forget about it. At twelve bucks a night there was no way he couldn't afford his own room. Anyway, each room was so small that there was barely enough room for one person to move about, much less two, and if we were both in the same room I'd never have any privacy. I didn't feel like having someone else listen to my bathroom sounds or share a soggy bath towel, and I wasn't convinced that Chris was a person who had the same distaste for human closeness that I did. I wasn't sure anyone was.

Unbelievably, the room was air-conditioned, which was good because it must have been a hundred degrees outside. And the hotel advertised a free breakfast in its postage-stamp size restaurant on the ground floor. It was located down what I'd have called an alley, but which seemed to pass for a major thoroughfare in this area of town. The taxi had barely fit into the street and the driver had driven relentlessly between the buildings, honking his horn to clear the way of motorcycles and pedestrians. All along the sides of the street had been vendors, squatting next to little carts of cigarettes, juices, beer, coffee, and noodles. Many of the doorways opened up into small shops or cafes. I'd never imagined there could be so much activity in such a small space.

We each checked into our own room and I was beginning to unpack when Chris knocked on my door. "I'll be back in about an hour or two," he said. "I just wanted you to know."

Back in an hour or two? I began to panic. This shithead was planning to leave me by myself. "Where are you going?"

"I need to look someone up. Let him know I'm in town. It won't take long; then we can go look for Bloom."

"Looking for Bloom is why we're here. You said you'd help me." Was I whining? I knew that I was whining. Goddammit! Goddamn him! Goddamn me!

"Hey, you can go out on the street, get used to the neighborhood. Just remember the name of the hotel and meet me back here in a couple of hours. I'm going to ask my friend if he knows your father. He knows a lot of expatriates. I'll be back soon. Enjoy Saigon."

123

He had a shit-eating grin on his face, as though I should be so pleased with his cuteness that I'd be happy with anything he did. No doubt he was used to charming people with his smile. I wasn't charmed. But I wasn't going to whine any more, either. "Go," I said. "I'll just make myself comfortable in the middle of this Jackie Chan movie set and meet you here in two hours." *If I'm not raped or mugged*, I thought to myself. What a bastard he was for leaving me alone.

I closed the door and sat down on my bed. I could hear the traffic sounds through the wall. I took a peek out the window and decided that it really did look like a scene from a Jackie Chan movie. Every doorway seemed to contain a shop and people sat on stools selling their wares or eating or just staring at the traffic. I'd never seen so many living creatures packed together since I'd kicked over an ant's nest in our back yard. There were motorcycles moving in every direction at once. Thankfully, a fair number of the people on the street looked like Caucasian tourists, hopefully Americans, the kind of people I would have avoided as if they were freaks and misfits back home, but who now looked to me as if they were my long-lost siblings. I sat back down on the bed and tried to work up my courage to leave the room.

After living for nineteen years with the only significant man in my life being an absent father who I had presumed was dead, here I was, more than halfway around the world, searching for the aforementioned parent, who might not even be my parent, hoping that finding him would somehow help me find myself. And now here I was lamenting my abandonment by Chris, whom I'd only met a week ago and knew almost nothing about other than that he was an irresponsible, bragging, flake who idolized the man I'd spent my life despising. As my dead mother was no doubt saying up in heaven, why was her only child such a fucking idiot?

My quest for Martin Bloom had made sense to me when I'd begun it—I wanted to find out if he was my father and, if he was, to see if I could learn something about myself by getting to know the genetic half of me with whom I'd never shared any experience–or at least that's what I had told myself. Until I'd read *A Dead Man's Tale*, it had never occurred to me that there might be someone in the world with whom I had something in common. But so far my quest had shown me that, in addition to writing prose in the magical way in which I hoped to write someday, Martin Bloom faced the world in many of the same ways that I did. He kept everyone at a distance while waving a big "fuck you" sign in their faces.

Maybe I just hoped that if he was my father, that would fill up some of that void I'd always felt when I tried to figure out who I was. But Professor Truong had told me that I'd learn who I was from myself, not from someone else, even if he was my father. Well, I was finding out things about myself that I'd rather not have found out. Like that I could become dependent upon a man, for instance, and that as soon as I did, he would walk off and leave me stranded in some God-forsaken Asian hellhole. The feeling was as bad as a swarm of bumblebees up my ass.

But did I really need Chris? I wasn't sure. Right now I thought he was an asshole, but I also wished I was more like him. He didn't seem to be afraid of anything. He'd traveled all over the world by himself. He seemed as comfortable in Vietnam as he was in the U.S. And look at me. Until a few weeks ago I'd never even left Oregon. Now here I was in another country, cowering inside my tiny hotel room like a lost puppy finding herself abandoned in the dog pound, waiting for my master to come and rescue me.

I hated Chris. What if he didn't come back? That was stupid; he'd paid for his room already. But what if he was meeting an old girlfriend? What if he needed a break from me? My mother had left the house more than once saying that I was driving her crazy. And why was it bothering me to think that he had an agenda of his own? Was this what it was like when you got attached to someone–that you were suddenly filled with fears, worries, paranoia? I wished my mother were around so I could talk to her about it. Even a telephone call would have helped. She'd bawl me out and tell me I was making a mistake by looking for my father and making an even bigger mistake by doing it with Chris—a young man upon whom, she would tell me, I shouldn't depend and who was probably just trying to use me. Use me for what? As a way to meet Martin Bloom? So what?

Screw all of this rumination. I was probably just delaying having to face the world outside of my hotel room. It was time to gather up my skirts, so to speak, and hit the street.

The street, even my little alley, was a circus. I no sooner emerged from the lobby of my hotel than I was accosted by a vendor offering me a tour—of the city itself, the villages outside of the city, the river, the Viet Cong tunnels, you name it—he could take me there. I shook my head and said no, backing away from him as fast as I could, but my reluctance only added to his enthusiasm to make a sale. The only thing that saved me was a waif-like woman with a lined, tired face and dirty hair, who was carrying a baby and who, with the deftness of a politician grabbing the spotlight from her rival, pushed the vendor aside to lobby for a donation for her ailing child. I gave her a dollar, but she didn't go away. She just kept nodding toward her child, who looked as if he hadn't had a bath in days and had snot running out of his nose and into his mouth. His mother kept repeating, "sick, hungry," so finally I gave her a five, then remembered *The Bean Trees* and had a panicky fear that I might have just bought her baby. But she just kept jabbering at me so I walked away as fast as I could. She continued to follow me, one arm around the sniffling baby and the other extended toward me grasping for more money, like a deserted wife chasing her errant husband. I began to panic.

Looking around desperately, I ducked into a coffee shop that had outside tables, or more accurately, plastic footstools surrounded by miniature plastic chairs on the sidewalk in front of it. Inside were bigger tables and chairs of the same plastic. Customers were drinking coffee or eating what appeared to be noodle soup, ladled up from a big pot in front of the shop, tended by an old woman sitting next to it on a chair who, when she wasn't ladling soup, was chopping up raw chickens with this humongous knife. I sat just inside the door and ordered a coffee. A young girl brought me a tiny cup with some kind of metal pot thing filled with water stuck on top of it. When I checked the cup after about three minutes, it had filled only about an eighth of an inch. The pot must have been dripping at the rate of a hospital IV. I waited patiently until I couldn't hear it dripping anymore, and then removed the metal pot and took a sip. It had taken so long that the coffee was barely warmer than the air outside. I drank it anyway, thinking that at least, surrounded as I was by five or six other patrons, all but one of them Vietnamese, drinking coffee or eating their noodles and chatting with each other, I was rid of the beggars and vendors for awhile. Since several of the other customers were smoking; I lit a cigarette. How bad could a country be that allowed you to smoke in a restaurant?

The street traffic in front of me could only be described as controlled chaos. Even my use of the word controlled was a charitable concession to the fact that I hadn't witnessed any outright collisions as I sat watching the eclectic mix of taxis, motorcycles, and bicycles. The motorcycles were so numerous they reminded me of invading hordes of cavalry, like a motorized Mongol army. And a large number of the drivers were wearing facemasks, which I assumed they wore to protect themselves from the pollution rather than to conceal their identities. Bicycles and pedestrians moved past me with no discernible pattern. There was a traffic light at one of the intersections, but no one seemed to pay any attention to it. A block away no less than five streets emptied into an intersection that had no traffic light at all.

Although the majority of the faces passing me belonged to Vietnamese, a not inconsiderable number of Caucasians, some young and some old, were on the street, most of them walking, the young dressed in shorts and T-shirts and sporting backpacks, many of their packs bigger than my suitcase, while the older ones dressed in long pants, proper walking shoes, and gaudy shirts. Invariably, the oldsters, men and women alike, were wearing hats. Directly across from me was what looked as if it was a real restaurant, advertising Pizza, beer and something named Pho, with a large number of young people sitting outside on plastic chairs eating and drinking. The sight of a bunch of people my age and of my complexion reassured me with the probably illusory and no doubt racist thought that I was not completely adrift by myself in an alien world.

I sipped my coffee and smoked while my thoughts returned to the question of what I was doing here in this strange land. In some ways, finding myself in the midst of someone else's culture, feeling alienated and isolated, different from nearly everyone around me, was a feeling with which I was familiar. This was how I had always felt, at least since I'd reached adolescence, even in Eugene. But at least when I was in Eugene the scenery around me had been familiar. I'd looked different from everyone else because I had made myself look that way. And the bottom line was that, until a year ago, despite my façade of independence, which I desperately displayed like a sandwich board announcing my pugnacious identity to the world, I had always had my mother's presence to fall back on if I found myself too frightened by my self-imposed isolation. Even since she'd died she had remained present in spirit, in the condominium which we both had shared and in which I continued to live, even in the hearse-like presence of her Honda, lurking in the shadows of the garage and ready for me to use whenever I overcame my reluctance to expunge the ghost of its last passenger. Now I had no one.

Not even Chris, the asshole.

My anger was returning. He really was a bastard for leaving me. But before I could amplify that thought, here came the asshole, ambling up the street as though he were just as much at home here as on Palo Alto Boulevard. When he saw me he looked startled, and, for just a moment, I thought I saw a tinge of guilt in his eyes, but then a broad grin creased his face. It was everything I could do to keep from crying in relief but I'd be damned if I was going to let him know that I had missed him.

"OK," he said. "I found my friend. I'm ready to go."

Out of spite I didn't answer him. I just thumbed through the Vietnamese bills in my wallet, having no idea how much a cup of coffee cost. All the bills were in astronomical denominations, 10,000, 50,000, 200,000, 500,000. The Vietnamese currency was the *Dong* and it was apparently inflated as much as the Goodyear blimp.

Chris reached over and pulled out a 20,000 bill from my wad. "That's a little less than a dollar," he said.

I looked at his beaming face and nodded a perfunctory thank you, while I felt this sudden wave of self-consciousness, a fear that my hair was a mess, that I'd been perspiring profusely and probably smelled like a locker room, that the coffee had made my mouth taste sour and I was emitting invisible clouds of bad breath, like a small sulfur factory belching pollutants into the atmosphere. Realizing that it was Chris who had prompted my self-consciousness, I had a sinking feeling that I'd just crossed over into that la-la land of mindlessness inhabited by prom queens, cheerleaders and lovesick teenagers. I hated myself.

"Who is your friend?" I asked, and was immediately angry with myself for not being able to stop myself from asking.

"Just a guy I used to know. He's a local, but he keeps tabs on most of the Americans who come and go through the city."

A guy and not a girl? Was he lying to me? Was there an old girlfriend who'd been waiting for his return to Saigon so they could resume their romance? A slinky Vietnamese bar girl he'd been sending money to each month to support their love child? I'd seen that once in a movie. Or maybe one of these blonde backpacking amazons who was taking a break from her wealthy family back in England or Australia? My imagination was torturing me. "Did your friend know anything about Martin Bloom?"

"He's seen him around. Said he thought that he'd been here for a couple of years, but he didn't know where he lived."

"You seemed pretty anxious to meet this friend." Oh man, there I went again. I hated this!

He looked at me suspiciously. "I wasn't particularly anxious to meet him. Besides, I thought that he might know something about Bloom."

"But you wanted to meet him alone."

He looked angry. "What is this, the third degree?"

"Sorry. Let's go down to the river and look for that marina that Professor Prentiss mentioned." I was really blowing it. I had to forget about Chris's friend and concentrate on why I was here—to find out if Martin Bloom was my father.

## Chapter 22

Chris and I walked through the crowded narrow streets of the backpacker district, where at least one out of every ten persons was obviously a tourist and maybe even more than that, since I couldn't tell who might be Asian tourists from who were the native population. After a mile or so of trudging through shoulder-to-shoulder crowds and dodging hundreds of motorcycles to make it across streets, we arrived at the hotel district, which fronted the river. Chris pointed out the massive *Hotel Majestic*, dating from the time of the French occupation, and the newer *Renaissance Riverside*, both of them proudly displaying their five-star ratings on placards mounted on the walls next to their entrances. The people leaving and entering were mostly older Caucasian couples or well-dressed Asian families. I didn't respond to any of Chris's tour-guide chatter, although I had the feeling that he was trying to make up for his earlier show of temper. As we neared the river he reached over and took my hand. "Sorry to be so mysterious about whom I was talking to. I was just frustrated because I thought my friend might have known where Bloom is right now, and he didn't. You'll meet my friend later tonight. He's gonna drop by our hotel."

I was still suspicious about whether his friend was really not a female, but I guess if whoever it was, was going to come by our hotel later, I'd find out.

"This is the river," Chris announced, as we stood on a broad sidewalk looking out at an expanse of water only about a quarter of a mile across. I had been thinking it would be wider, like the Columbia at Portland, but it was more like the smaller Willamette. Except this river looked like the water in my kitchen sink when the garbage disposal had gotten stopped up by the salad I'd tried to wash down (I'd forgotten to remove the olive pits). It was strewn with vegetation, leafy, luxurious vegetation, obviously attached to nothing and moving with the speed of a fast-moving boat. Some of the patches of plant life were larger than the back yard of my mother's townhouse. The river itself was a yellowish-brown color, like the mud in one of the street gutters in Eugene after a heavy spring rain. Besides the vegetation, every imaginable kind of garbage came floating past, making me think that I had been right about the river being used as a refuse receptacle. In less than five minutes I saw plastic utensils, sandals, a rubber tire, every size of Styrofoam container imaginable, clear plastic garbage bags stuffed with paper, and coconuts—tons of coconuts—most of them with one end cut off, so I concluded that they too had been discarded into the river. It wouldn't have surprised me to have seen a bloated cow or buffalo float past, or a family of six clinging to the roof of a house. I figured that if I'd been closer to the water I'd have been able to see a constant stream of condoms and cigarette butts so thick that it would have looked like an infestation of algae during a red tide.

Amidst all of this flotsam and jetsam was a steady stream of river traffic. There were barges, all going down river, long metal rafts loaded with containers piled two or three high on their decks. Several small, odd-shaped boats with sharp prows and tiny cabins hanging out over their sterns, like miniature Chinese Junks, putt-putted steadily down stream. Chris pointed out the fish symbols on their prows indicating, not that they were born-again Christians, but fishermen, probably headed down to the sea. I saw larger imitation Chinese Junks, which announced that they were available for hire, some advertising that they were floating restaurants. A beat-up ferry crossed back and forth from one side of the river to the other, carrying foot passengers and motorcyclists. I couldn't see any bridges crossing the river at all, although Chris said that there were several in the city. There were two or three ocean-going vessels docked farther up the river and, to my joy, a small marina directly across from where we were standing, exactly as Professor Prentiss had described it.

"There it is!" I shouted, grabbing Chris by the shoulder and pointing to the other side of the river. I couldn't believe that I was this close to finding the man who could be my father.

"You're right, that's it! " Chris said. He seemed as excited as I was. "We can take the ferry. " We were only a few hundred yards from the terminal where the small ferry took off from our side of the river. It looked as if it landed just a few hundred yards downstream from the marina.

We hurried over and purchased tickets, then waited for five minutes while the ferry returned from its trip to the other side. This ferry, which was one of two that seemed to be operating, was a one-story boat, painted white but covered in soot and grime; it took only motorcycles, which were parked in the open space on its deck, and foot passengers, who sat both inside and atop the thing. Chris and I crowded aboard with about a hundred others, all, from what I could tell, Vietnamese. The boat took off with a lurch, then, with a thump, thump, thump of its engine, steadily threaded its way among the floating river garbage until we reached the other side.

We walked from the ferry dock, and, within minutes, we arrived at the section of riverbank above the marina. It was across the road from a row of massive houses, all of which stood behind high walls and gates. A long wooden walkway led down the riverbank to a wharf on which sat an office and a café. From the wharf, three docks jutted into the river, each with four or five boats tied up on either side of it. I felt my stomach tighten. Martin Bloom was on one of those boats.

"Let's ask at the office," Chris said, starting down the walkway. I followed him, scanning the different boats to try to see if I could identify any unique feature that might tell me that it belonged to Martin Bloom. None of them looked very new or very clean, although several of them were at least 45 or 50 feet long and must have been expensive. I saw laundry hanging from the railings of several of the boats, suggesting that their owners lived aboard.

We reached the main dock, but the office was closed and locked. There was no sign saying when anyone would be back. In the café next to the office a woman was serving noodles to a couple of Vietnamese men who looked like workmen.

"Let's ask at the café," I told Chris.

"I'll ask," he said, stepping in front of me before I even got to the café's entrance.

"Do you speak English?" he asked the woman.

"I speak English, yes," the woman answered. She was a strikingly pretty woman with an even more striking body, which she displayed with a low-cut blouse and tight fitting pants. Her smile toward us was friendly. "You want lunch? Coffee?"

"We're looking for Martin Bloom," Chris said. "Is one of these boats his?"

She shook her head, causing my excitement to plummet like a rock.

"Ong Martin go," she said, still smiling. "Take boat and go up river to fancy marina. He gone one week ago."

At least we had found the place he'd been ... until a week ago.

"What's the name of the marina?" Chris asked.

She shrugged. "Don't know. You are friends of Ong Martin?"

"This is his daughter," Chris said, gesturing in my direction.

The woman looked surprised. "Daughter? From United States? Ong Martin never say he have a daughter. He act like he's not married." She was staring at me with intense interest. "He know you coming?"

I shook my head. "He didn't know," I answered, although I wondered if I was wrong and that was why he had left.

The woman's look of curiosity had been replaced by one of smiling benevolence. "You will be good for him. Ong Martin is lonely. He just drink and write. He is good person but he drink too much."

Unbelievably, this Vietnamese café owner was worried about Bloom. I again marveled at how he managed to collect valuable people around him, despite his obvious defects as a human being.

"How far upriver are the marinas?" Chris asked her.

"Around corner of river." She pointed upriver "Big buildings, rich people. Marinas next to buildings."

"He probably went to one of the marinas attached to the new luxury condos along the river bank over on this side of the river," Chris said, looking at me. "We can get a taxi and ask the driver to take us."

I thanked the woman, who reached out and took my hand, squeezing it and repeating "Ong Martin's daughter," several times, as if the fact of my existence amazed her.

Chapter 23

We climbed back up the walkway to the road above. There were lots of motorcycles whizzing by us but no taxis. We headed back toward the ferry port.

"You've got money for a taxi, right?" Chris asked as we trudged along the road.

"Of course. Why, don't you?"

He looked guilty. "I'm running a little short."

"You mean you're broke," I said. He was over here running around doing God knows what, and he wanted to do it on my money. "Whatever," I said. We had arrived at the intersection where our road connected with the road coming up from the ferry dock. There were two taxis sitting at the curb. "Let's get a cab."

The cab driver, who spoke good English, told us that the marinas were only a few miles upriver. They belonged to the high-priced condominiums and villa compounds that lined this side of the river. "Foreigners live there," the cab driver told us, "... rich foreigners. Pay big rents, have boats. Paid for by big companies."

"How would someone who didn't live in one of the houses or condos get to put his boat in one of the marinas?" I asked the cab driver.

The driver shrugged. "Sometimes they rent out space while still building condo. When condo finished no private boats allowed."

"Take us to one that's not finished yet," I told him.

We arrived at a building site, which was surrounded by a high fence on which were posted pictures of three tall high rise apartment towers and several repetitions of the name *Riverview*, which was apparently the name of the condominium complex, the half-built outlines of which could be seen from the road. The driver turned the taxi down a narrow road that ran along the side of the fence toward the river, then ended at a sizeable parking lot just off to the left of a tall building that was still under construction. Below us was a marina, consisting of mostly barren docks with about two dozen sleek-looking boats tied up to two of them. A wood and glass office sat on a main dock from which several other docks fanned out into the river.

I could feel my stomach tightening again. Was this finally to be the moment I had been waiting for?

We walked down a winding concrete stairway to the dock. Inside the building that said it was the office a man wearing a shirt that had *Riverview Marina* stitched across the pocket addressed us in English. His crisp white shorts and short-sleeved shirt gave him the appearance of what I imagined a yacht club employee must look like. "Welcome to Riverview Marina. How may I help you?" he asked, an ingratiating smile on his face.

"Were looking for Martin Bloom's boat," Chris said.

The man stared back at us with a blank expression. "Who?"

"Martin Bloom," Chris repeated.

He still looked as if he'd never heard the name before.

"Is there another marina?" I asked.

He shook his head again. "Two other marinas but they're only for residents of the villas. Does this person own a condominium here at Riverview?"

I shook my head, although I was uncertain whether he did or didn't. "We heard you took other boats besides those of the condo owners," I said.

He nodded. "Do you have a boat?"

"We're looking for Martin Bloom's boat," Chris said, irritably. "He was supposed to have moved it here."

The man shrugged his shoulders. "Sorry. It's not here."

"Do you mind if we look at the boats tied up here?" I asked.

"Go ahead," he said smiling and gesturing toward the docks where the several boats were tied up.

"I don't know what we're looking for unless we see him sitting on the deck of one of the boats," I told Chris as we headed down to the docks. "We have no idea what his boat looks like or what its name is."

"Let's just walk around," Chris answered. "Maybe there will be someone on one of the boats and we can ask him if he knows Bloom."

None of the boats seemed occupied. Unlike the small marina where Bloom's boat had been before, at this one people didn't seem to use their vessels for residences. None of the boats had any telltale signs that would have identified it as belonging to Martin Bloom. I noticed that just visible on the other side of an outgrowth of trees was what appeared to be a small boat repair operation. A single boat sat on a concrete dock, supported by some kind of wooden cradle and two men were working on the bottom of the boat near its front end. I could just make out the name on the back of the boat. "Rebecca." I remembered Bloom's novel by the same name.

I hurried back to the marina office. "Is that boat repair operation part of your marina?" I asked the man in the office.

He nodded cautiously. "It belongs to Riverview Marina, yes."

"Who owns the boat that's being repaired?"

He shrugged his shoulders. "Until the marina is fully open we repair anyone's boat. I don't recall the owner."

"What's up?" Chris asked, walking up to us.

"The boat being worked on over there is named Rebecca. Isn't that the name of one of Bloom's novels?"

"Does that boat belong to Martin Bloom?" Chris asked, his tone more aggressive than mine had been.

"Not Martin Bloom," the office man answered.

"Whose is it then?" Chris demanded.

The man shrugged again. "I not remember." I noticed that his English skills had deteriorated.

"He must have left his name," I said, taking my cue from Chris' forceful attitude, although it didn't seem to be working.

"Not leave name," the man said.

"Come on," Chris said. "You must know whose boat it is."

He shrugged again. "Not know." He looked like he was losing his interest in the conversation along with his linguistic abilities.

"Screw this," I finally said and walked back up the steps far enough to be able to skirt the trees and then to scramble across the grassy hillside until I was above the boat repair shop. When I set foot on the dock, one of the men sanding the bottom of the boat looked up, startled. He looked at me, and then he looked over at the marina manager, who could just be seen through the trees.

"Never mind him," I said. "Whose boat is this?"

The man looked back at me blankly.

"Boat," I repeated. "Who boat?" I was trying Pidgin English. I had to try something.

The man just shook his head.

I walked to the stern of the boat and read the name again. It said *Rebecca* and below that was the name *Ho Chi Minh City*. I debated asking if I could go aboard, but, given that I had no way of talking to these men or of getting any assistance from the marina manager, I decided there was no point. Anyway, I was convinced that this was Martin Bloom's boat.

I clambered back across the bank and descended to the main dock of the marina. "Let's go," I told Chris.

"Did you find out anything?" he asked, looking at me with what I thought was new respect.

"I'm sure it's Bloom's boat. They couldn't tell me anything." Chris nodded. "Let's take a cab back to the hotel and have dinner or something. My friend will be over later and I can ask him to keep looking."

"We could wait here. If it's Bloom's boat he's bound to come back to get it when its repaired."

"That could be days or a week."

He was right. We couldn't just camp out on the dock and wait for him to show up. "At least we should check back every few days."

"We can do that. But let's go back now. I don't want to miss my friend."

"Why does he have to meet with you tonight? I thought you already asked him to find Bloom."

Chris looked sheepish. "I told him I'd give him the cover off of one of your books. One with Bloom's picture on it. That way he can show it to his friends."

It made sense. A lot more sense than waiting around until Martin Bloom's boat was fixed and he came back to retrieve it.

We crossed back across the river, then headed for our hotel. As soon as we arrived in front of the hotel I felt overwhelmingly hungry. Chris suggested a little Italian restaurant that was hardly more than a hole in the wall but was just down the street.

Chris ordered a beer and asked if I wanted to share a pizza. We were sitting at one of the tables at the front of the restaurant near the sidewalk.

"We'd better share something, since you're broke," I said, and ordered myself a coke.

"I told you, I'll have some money soon. I just need to find these people I loaned money to last time I was here."

"You know this city pretty well," I said. "Does your novel take place in Saigon?"

He stared at me as if he couldn't believe I'd asked such a naïve question. "No. I was just meeting different kinds of people, finding out what it was like to live in a different culture, how I felt inside. I wasn't interested in Saigon, as a location."

"So where does your novel take place?"

He got this dreamy look in his eyes and stared off into space. "I'm not quite sure yet. I haven't pinned it down."

I wondered if he'd give me the same answer if I had asked for the novel's plot. I was starting to think that he didn't have anything in his head but the idea that he was going to write something some day. It was becoming clearer and clearer to me that, when it came to writing, Chris talked a lot better game than he actually played. Or to quote the designer of the first blimp, the whole thing was just a bunch of hot air.

"I hope your friend has better luck finding Bloom than we've had," I said, trying to get back to our purpose for being here.

"Trust me; Lee—that's his name, he's Chinese—he knows everyone and every place that Americans hang out—from the ritzy to the sleazy."

"I doubt that Professor Prentiss was in someplace sleazy when she ran into him. She didn't look the type."

His face lit up. "You're right! Don't worry, Lee knows his way around those fancy hotels as well as around the backpacker district."

"Lee seems to know everything." I was being sarcastic, but he didn't seem to get it.

"Yeah. I told you he grew up in Saigon, but he hangs out more with the tourists."

"What does he do?"

"Lee's into lots of things." He looked uncomfortable.

"Lots of things, like what?"

"He can find anything a tourist wants. He's sort of an arranger. He arranges stuff for people."

"That sounds kind of shady."

Chris shrugged. "The lines between legitimate and shady are pretty fuzzy here in Saigon."

Great, I thought to myself. That was all I needed—to get mixed up with some underworld character. "Shady like how? Does he deal drugs, run prostitutes—what?"

He shrugged. "I never knew exactly. He's just involved in a lot of things and he knows everyone, even the police. He's never been arrested himself for anything, so whatever he does can't be too bad. I just heard rumors."

I was supposed to be happy that he didn't have any *hard* evidence that his friend was a criminal? "I thought you and he were close friends."

"We are. That's why he's willing to help us find your father. And he wants to meet you. I told him about you."

"You told him what about me?"

Chris looked at me with those deep, dark eyes. He smiled, almost shyly. "I told him you were with me, that we were a couple. I didn't want him fixing me up with someone else. He does that too... finds women for people who are visiting."

*Isn't there a name for men who supply women to other men?* "Lee sounds like a pimp to me. A pimp and who knows what else."

"Hey," he answered, "we have to use every tool at our disposal. We can't stay here in Saigon forever."

Despite my suspicion about his friend, I liked what Chris had said about us being a couple. Of course I immediately hated myself for liking it. But I didn't get angry with Chris. In fact, it was all I could do to resist reaching across the table and taking his hand. I guess I was feeling lonelier than I'd thought.

Anyway, Chris was right. Lee was probably just the kind of guy who would know the type of people Bloom hung out with. I paid, and we headed back to our hotel. As we passed a street corner, a well-dressed man, who had been talking to two uniformed policeman who were sitting on their parked motorcycles, turned and smiled at us. He held up a hand as if for us to halt. "You are American tourists, is that right?" he asked, in reasonable English.

"Who are you" I asked. Chris had gotten quiet and was looking around with the furtive look of cornered rat.

"I am Detective Nguyen." He pulled out a card that identified him as a policeman. "I am just checking to be sure that both of you are enjoying a safe vacation in our city."

Chris mumbled something and continued to look away. I was no cop, but to me, his behavior had "guilty of something" written all over it. And this was my traveling companion. I thought of asking the detective if he had a gun so I could shoot myself. Instead I asked him, "Do you stop everyone who comes here and ask them if they're enjoying themselves?"

"We do ask a lot of people that question," the detective answered. He seemed very confident of himself. "But we mostly ask young Americans. We want you to be especially happy in our country." He smiled a fake, ingratiating smile. "Where are you staying in the city?"

I gave him the name of our hotel. At least he didn't write it down.

"Well, have a good vacation. We don't want you to get into any trouble," he said, looking down the street as if he was preparing to go.

"Don't worry, we will," I answered, staring straight at him.

He smiled again and walked away.

"What was that about?" I asked Chris. "And what was up with you? You looked as if you'd just been caught cheating on an exam. Is there something you're not telling me?"

He shook his head, "It's just that I don't like cops. He was warning us that we're being watched."

"Watched? Why would the police watch us?"

"They watch everyone. Remember, it's not a free country. This is Communism. They target young foreigners, particularly Americans but also Austalians and Europeans, who might be buying drugs. It's their way of telling us that if we do something wrong, they will know about it."

"But we're not doing anything wrong! We're not buying drugs or anything else."

"They don't know that. Anyway, don't worry. My friend Lee can handle the police if they start to hassle us."

"Hassle us? Why would they hassle us?"

"You have to admit you look like a druggie."

"You do more than I do. And around that cop you looked like you'd just been found plotting an act of terror or something."

"They don't have terrorism over here."

Sometimes Chris was incredibly concrete. Were my analogies really that difficult to appreciate? "You'd just better not be doing anything to get us into trouble."

He looked sheepish. "I'm not. That's just normal hassling. Anyway, Lee can fix things with the police. Don't worry."

I hope my frown conveyed my skepticism.

Chapter 24

I have to admit that getting hassled by the Saigon police had unsettled me. And I still wondered why Chris had acted so strangely. Neither of us had anything to hide, at least of which I was aware. I tried to put the whole episode out of my mind. When we got to the hotel I took a shower, then I lay down on the bed and started reading *A Memorial to Time*, which I'd found, almost miraculously, at a tiny, closet-sized book exchange next to the hotel. It was a well-worn, used paperback copy, and I'd had some reservations about what diseases the last person who'd owned it might have been carrying, but then I'd reassured myself that since the previous owner was obviously interested in good literature, at least they would be *sophisticated* diseases.

Someone knocked on my door and, when I opened it a crack to peek out, Chris pushed it open and walked into the room. He was wearing only a towel wrapped around his waist. His hair was still wet. He walked all the way into my room without turning around. Even though I was pissed that he would just come barging in like that, I couldn't help but stare at his back, which was well-muscled and smooth. Every time he moved, his shoulder muscles rippled as if he had ropes knotted beneath his skin.

"Have you got a comb?" He asked. "I can't find mine."

"You came into my room half naked, just to ask for a comb?"

"Sure. I figured it was OK. You seemed to like me calling us a couple," he said, turning around and looking directly at me. His hair hung in wet strands over his forehead and down to his shoulders. His chest was smooth and as well muscled as his back had been. I had to admit that just looking at him made my stomach feel as if it were inhabited by hundreds of furiously swarming butterflies. "Maybe we should act more like we really are a couple." He locked into eye contact with me with a look that would have been described in a romance novel as "smoldering."

Sure, let's hop into bed and screw like rabbits, I thought to myself, not, I admit, without feeling some temptation. But I could hear my mother's voice in my head, warning me about men who would try to get me into bed. She'd told me how persuasive they could be and that I would have to fight my own feelings to say no. But I was also afraid of coming across as a naïve prude to Chris. He was older than I was, had probably had tons of girls already, and I was trying to keep up with him in the role of burgeoning writer traveling to exotic lands. Being a virgin didn't fit the role very well. Then I remembered my panic when he'd left me to go meet his friend, Lee. To quote some big-boobed, over-madeup country singer I'd heard once, I wasn't going to be anyone's bitch. Probably the actual words were, "I ain't gonna be nobody's bitch." Whatever the words were, I was sticking to them.

I looked Chris right in the eye and said, "We're not a couple, and we're not having sex, if that's what you're implying we should be doing." I hoped he couldn't hear that my voice was shaking. I'd come to a decision, but it had been a close call.

"You're not as adventuresome as you act," he said, still standing in front of me in his towel and displaying his bare chest. I was almost praying that he wouldn't drop the towel. I had made up my mind. but I felt better not having to rely completely on my tenuous resolve.

"I'm just stronger than you think I am," I said, surprised at the pride I felt when I heard myself say it. I gave the spirit of my mother a wink with my mind's eye. I went into the bathroom and picked up the comb I'd left next to the sink, and then handed it to him. "Now go back to your own room and put your clothes on and quit parading around like Channing Tatum. I'm busy reading my book. Your friend is supposed to be here anytime."

I could see that I'd hurt his feelings, but he just gave me a petulant frown, then grabbed the comb and went back to his room. I felt as if I'd just won a moral victory, but I knew that the margin of victory had been pretty slim. I breathed deeply and tried to relax. I went to the window and looked out on the street below. Even though it was evening, it was still light outside, partly because the sun was just setting and partly because nearly every shop had lights, sometimes whole strings of them across its doorway. I looked at the noodle shop across the street. Whom should I see there but Detective Nguyen. He was dipping a pair of chopsticks into a bowl of something and didn't appear interested in our hotel, but his presence right across the street from us seemed awfully coincidental. Was I getting paranoid or were Chris and I really under some kind of surveillance? I tried to calm myself by lying down on the bed and resuming my reading, although I couldn't help but get up to look out the window every two minutes or so. After about five minutes, I didn't see the detective any longer, and I began to relax.

After a while I heard a knock on Chris' door, which was right across the hall from mine. I could hear a pair of low voices but I couldn't make out what they were saying. When someone knocked on my door, I opened it and Chris stepped in, leading a tall, Asian man.

"Lee, this is Dillon," Chris said. "Dillon, this is my friend, Lee Cheung."

Chris had already told me that his friend was Chinese. But this was a Chinese guy who must have been fed more than rice and fish when he was growing up. Either that or he was a cousin of Yao Ming. He was easily more than six feet tall, had long black hair pulled back into a ponytail, and was wearing aviator sunglasses. He sported a mustache, but, unlike Chris, no goatee. He wore an expensive looking short-sleeved silk shirt, unbuttoned at the neck, and cargo shorts and sandals. He looked as if he hadn't been able to make up his mind whether he was trying to look sinister or casual. His legs were very tan.

He nodded, then strode forward and stuck out his hand. "Good to meet you, Dillon." He pumped my hand a little too enthusiastically. I wondered if he was high on something. It was hard to tell behind the reflective glasses.

"Lee says he thinks he can help us," Chris said. He was also looking agitated, rocking back and forth from one foot to the other like a toddler who had to pee. "Oh, yeah," he said, as if he'd just remembered something, "... let me get that book cover with Martin Bloom's picture." He immediately turned and went over to the nightstand next to my bed and pulled the dust jacket off of Betsy's copy of *The Fourth Season*. He pulled on it so hard he almost tore it.

"Jeez, Chris, take it easy," I said.

"Sorry," he answered. "I'm just excited that Lee may know your father."

"I recognized his name," Lee said. "I've seen him around, but it's hard to describe him to anyone else. The picture will help." He took the dust jacket from Chris. "Yeah, I *do* know this guy," he said. "I never talked to him, but he hangs out in some of the local bars. I know a guy who drives him around."

I was excited. "Really?"

Instead of answering, Lee gave a knowing look toward Chris. "Have you told her?" he asked.

"Told me what?" Whatever was going on between the two of them, I didn't like it. I didn't particularly like Lee. He gave the impression that he and Chris had something going on that didn't include me, except maybe as a patsy.

"Lee says that it's gonna take some money to find your father," Chris said, a sheepish look on his face.

"Ya gotta grease a few palms, y'know?" Lee said, "That's how things work over here." His laid back California beach drawl sounded odd coming from a six-foot-two Chinese man with a ponytail who, except for the shorts and sandals, looked like a character out of *Big Trouble in Little China*. I wasn't all that surprised that he'd asked for money.

"I thought you said you knew someone who drives Martin Bloom around," I said to Lee, trying not to let the anger rule my voice—or my judgment—and resisting falling into Chris' habit of referring to Bloom as my "father." I still wasn't completely sure that it was true.

"That driver's not gonna talk unless we make it worth his while. Especially if your Dad is trying to lay low and doesn't want anyone to know where he is. And if your father is in hiding, then he won't go to his usual hangouts."

"How much money?" I asked.

"A couple hundred bucks," Chris said. "I'd pay him, but..." he gave his signature shoulder shrug and sheepish grin, "... you know my financial situation."

I looked at him with a look that I hoped conveyed my disgust. "And you think I'm an unlimited source of money?"

"You've got an ATM card. I've seen you use it. Your HSBC bank account, remember?"

I stared at Chris. Thanks for letting your money-hungry gangsta friend know that I've got access to cash, I thought. I was doing my best to try to trust Chris, but this deal with Lee was putting my trust to the test. I had the $200 in my purse, but it was the principle of the thing. I didn't want to get suckered into something just because they thought I was a naïve girl. On the other hand, I wanted to find Martin Bloom, and this was the closest I had come to him so far.

"OK," I said. "Do I get my money back if you don't find him?"

"No problem," Lee said. "Results guaranteed."

Did I look like a complete shit-for-brains? "I'm completely reassured," I said, making no attempt to conceal my sarcasm.

"He'll find him," Chris said, looking apologetically at his friend. "Trust me. Lee knows how to find people here in Saigon." He was rocking back and forth on his feet as if he were prepping for an Olympic event. "Do you want to go the ATM right now?" He looked as if he were ready to race me down the stairs.

"I don't need to," I said, giving him the iciest stare I could muster. "I have the money in my purse." I rummaged around in my purse, separating ten $20 bills from the others, while trying to avoid showing either of them how much money I actually had, which was still nearly fifteen hundred dollars. I handed Chris the $200 and he handed it to Lee, then they did some sort of goofy ghetto handshake thing, which must have signaled that they had completed their deal, whatever kind of pimp, drug-dealer deal Chris' friend might have gotten him to agree to.

"I'll start looking around. I'll find that driver, first thing," Lee said to me, looking over at the door as if, now that he had his money, he was eager to get out of the room.

148

"That detective who talked to us was across the street, eating at the restaurant," I told Chris. I was trying to remind him that he had said that his friend Lee could fix things with the police.

"You must mean Detective Nguyen," Lee said, smiling, barracuda-like. Why did everyone always look as if he knew something I didn't know?

"You know him?"

"I asked him to keep an eye on you for me," Lee said, still smiling. "Chris is an old friend, and you are a young woman who is new to the city. I wanted you both to be safe."

"Safe from what?"

"Just safe," he chuckled as he said it. "Don't worry. There is much less violence in Saigon than in American cities. But it is easy to have things stolen. And sometimes there are people who want to sell you things that will get you into trouble."

"If you mean drugs, I don't use them," I said.

He nodded. "That is very good. Then you shouldn't have any trouble." He looked over at Chris, his smile absent from his face. "But I will still have my friend the detective look in on you. It makes me feel better."

I thought that Chris looked frightened, but he managed a smile. "Good idea. Thanks, we both feel better, don't we, Dillon?"

I didn't answer. There was something going on between the two of them that I didn't know about and I didn't think they wanted me to know about.

"I'd better go," Lee said. "Don't forget our deal," he said, giving Chris a look that was anything but friendly.

Chris' eyes widened. "No problem, bro. We're cool."

Lee left and I turned to Chris. "I don't like that guy. The whole thing with the detective sounds fishy to me. And what deal was he talking about?"

Chris shook his head. "Nothin'. He was just reminding me of something we had going when I lived over here."

I couldn't tell if he was lying or telling the truth, although I suspected he was lying. Anyway, it didn't matter. Whatever he and Lee had going had nothing to do with me. "I still don't like him."

"He's a bit of a shady character, but I told you that already. And anyway, that's what it takes to make it over here. He's not some kind of criminal or anything. He'll find Bloom; I have absolute faith in that."

"For 200 bucks," I said.

"Hey, it's not for him. He's right. Everyone here expects to get paid, even if they just give you the time of day."

That hadn't been my experience so far, but Chris knew Vietnam better than I did.

"I just want my money's worth," I said.

I decided it was time to go to bed. Chris said he couldn't sleep, and he was still pacing around the room as if his underwear were giving him a wedgie. He said he was going out to look for some of his old acquaintances. He didn't seem displeased that I didn't ask to come along and I was too tired to even want to. And this time I didn't mind seeing him go.

## Chapter 25

The marina manager's cousin's hotel was in the backpacker district of Saigon, a location familiar to Martin from his prowls around the city and a part of the city he enjoyed because of the cheap food and drinks and the fact that nearly everyone who worked in the area spoke English. The hotel room itself wasn't large, but the walking around space was titanic compared to what he'd had available below deck on his boat. There was even a little kitchenette. He made coffee for himself in the mornings, but he wasn't about to start fixing his own meals. Anyway, the district was filled with small restaurants, most of them Vietnamese, with a sprinkling of faux Italian and French cafes, which still served mostly Vietnamese food, but at which you could find a pretty good pizza or crepe for a couple of dollars

Now that he didn't have his boat, the problem with drinking was that he had to go out. Being a solitary drinker, when that had meant sitting on the deck of his boat in the middle of a well-populated marina, hadn't seemed so, what?—well, frankly, so alcoholic—as did sitting on the bed in his motel room and slamming down shots of gin.

Of course he could drink less, but, especially coming off of the binge he'd begun when he'd landed his boat like a beached whale on top of the dock in the high-class condo marina, there was no way he was going to sit in his room and cope with a reduced regimen of alcohol. Whenever he made a half-hearted effort to cut down his daily consumption of gin he was overcome with anxiety. Not just everyday butterflies in the stomach anxiety, but life-questioning, existential, self-hating, society-chastising, backbone-shimmying anxiety, the kind that made him want to crawl into his bed and pull the covers over his head and curse God, the universe, and mostly himself, while he fought waves of nausea and a skull-shattering pain in the back of his head. The only thing that would relieve his anxiety was alcohol. Alcohol allowed him to float above his self, cognizant of the grime and filth of his life, but untouched by its grasping tentacles of despair. The problem was that, in order to reach that level of invulnerability, he had to drink more and more. The nagging thought that he had done something wrong, committed acts which could not be remedied and would be found out by everyone who knew him, grew like a malignant tumor in his brain, lurking just below the level of his consciousness, threatening to overwhelm his very sense of self. He could quell this sense of foreboding, which emerged in lock-step with each hour of his sobriety, only by a desperate and headlong dash back to his bottle of gin. And so to keep up the pretense that he wasn't just a hotel room invalid, he went out to the cafes and bars.

But even as he sat, downing gin after gin in a sidewalk café or in a dark and quiet bar, he remained alone, fading into the anonymity of the middle-aged expatriate drinker, losing himself as he became lost to the world that might want to find him.

So, given his confidence that he was now sufficiently ensconced in obscurity to be invulnerable to intrusion from anyone from his past, he was completely thrown off stride to be told by Duc, his cab driver, that someone was looking for him. He received Duc's news while in the middle of a half-hearted, drunken pursuit of one of the thinly clad bar girls at the *Mekong Bar*, one of the livelier establishments over in District Five, known as *Cho Lon*, the Chinese area of the city. It was also known as the center of activities for the so-called *Cho Lon Mafia*, reputedly a branch of the notorious "Triad" gang from Hong Kong and Macau, which dated from the Qing dynasty in China. Still operating after nearly four hundred years, the *Triad* had branches all over the world, including Saigon. Martin liked the area because the tourists who frequented it were almost all Chinese and not American, and the local police, being in the pay of the Chinese gangs, allowed prostitution to run rampant and pretty much out in the open. The police cooperated with the gangs in extorting local businesses and had almost no interest in the few Americans who ventured into their area, unless they became bar or restaurant owners, which they almost never did in Cho Lon.

"Who's looking?" he asked the taxi driver, who had tracked him down in the bar in order to check whether he was doing OK and whether he was inebriated enough yet to require a ride back to his hotel.

"You know that tall Chinese who runs whores in the Chinese tourist bars around here? A guy named Lee. I think he's involved in gambling. Maybe drug selling."

Martin searched his memory. He knew a lot of whores, but none of their pimps, and he never gambled or used drugs. He knew that there was a big market for marijuana, mostly among the young white tourists in the backpacker district. Selling or even possessing "harder' drugs, such as cocaine or heroin, could bring the death penalty, so even the mafia didn't sell it to tourists or locals, although they were known to facilitate its shipment from such points of origin as Myanmar to destinations in Europe, Australia, and the United States.

He had a vague recollection of a tall Chinese guy he'd seen in a few bars, including the *Mekong*, and who had enough of a reputation for engaging in unsavory activities that Martin knew to stay clear of him, but other than that, he'd never really paid much attention to him. "I may have seen him, but I don't know the guy. Why is he looking for me?"

Duc shrugged. "I don't know, but he knew I drove you. He showed me your picture."

He couldn't suppress a shudder. If the man had his picture, he was serious about finding him. "What did you tell him?" He heard the anxiety in his own voice.

"I said you'd moved your boat and I didn't know where you went."

"Shit!" Martin swore. He ordered another gin, even though he was already three sheets to the wind, but Duc's news had threatened to sober him. "That Goddamned Sylvia. I bet she told my publisher where I am—or my agent. They're pissed because I spent my advance and haven't come up with a new book yet."

"This Chinese, he has some rough friends. If he finds out I lied, he's liable to come after me."

The fear in Duc's voice caught Martin's attention. He looked over at the cab driver. Duc was a skinny, middle-aged man—probably no more than forty years old—with a wife and five children and he had been Martin's most faithful friend since he'd arrived in Saigon. Martin didn't want to put him in danger. "Go ahead and tell him where I am. Say I contacted you and told you I was in a hotel in the backpacker district. If this Chinese guy is looking for me, it probably means that whoever asked him to find me is still in the States. I can talk to the guy directly and pay him a little something to keep quiet."

"Thank you, Ong Martin. I don't like to get involved with these gangsters from Cho Lon."

"I don't blame you," Martin said. He gave one last look of longing in the direction of the fetching bar girl, who gave him a polite smile back but then went on to sidle up to another customer. "Take me home, Duc, while I can still walk." It was only midafternoon but he knew he'd be back later. Maybe he'd have better luck with the bar girl at that time.

The next day, Duc showed up at his room just as Martin was about to go out and walk the few blocks to his favorite café for his first drink of the day. His head was still throbbing from the previous evening's debauchery, but he knew that several cups of coffee and a few gin sunrises would have him back in peak condition within an hour or so.

"I'll give you a ride, Ong Martin," Duc offered.

Martin gladly accepted, knowing that relief for his hangover would come that much sooner if he didn't need to walk to the restaurant. "Just passing by?" he asked the cab driver.

"I talked to the Chinese last night. He said no one is after you. But he wants to meet you at the Mekong Bar tonight to talk about who is looking for you."

Martin had almost forgotten their conversation from the afternoon before. Whatever uneasiness it had engendered had been obscured by the nausea, the headache and the anxiety that went along with recovering from a night of heavy drinking. Now it all came back to him. "The Mekong sounds safe enough. That must mean that whoever is looking for me isn't over here or he would have picked an American bar. This Chinese guy must be acting as a go-between."

Duc continued to drive, blithely ignoring the innumerable motorcycles as if they were a swarm of gnats to be swatted away if they ventured too close. "He said to be there around 8:00."

"Can you drive me?"

"No problem, Ong Martin."

They'd arrived at the cafe. Martin got out of the car. "Pick me up at the hotel around 7:30. I'll try to be more or less sober."

Duc nodded and drove off.

Martin took a deep breath and entered the cafe. This morning he ordered his gin sunrises before he ordered coffee.

## Chapter 26

Chris was still acting weird. I could hear him going in and out of his hotel room every hour or so, and even when he was in the room he was so agitated he couldn't sleep and kept knocking on my door to see if I was awake, which, thanks to him, I was. In between his excursions, he paced; I heard him showering three times in less than four hours. When I opened my door and asked him what he was doing, he just said that he had some unfinished business from when he'd been here before that he had to attend to. He'd be done with everything by tomorrow, he told me. Then he went out again. Around 2:00 a.m. he finally came back to his room to stay.

We went to a late breakfast at the hotel, then we went back to the river where we could sit and have coffee. Across from us on the other shore, I could see the marina where Professor Prentiss had told us that Martin Bloom's boat had been docked. I kept thinking that I might see him at any moment, even though I knew that made no sense, since he'd moved his boat from this run-down marina to the fancier one up the river a week ago. Chris was so hyper that his head was bouncing around like a bobble-head doll's, and he kept naming people he was going to meet to question about Bloom.

"I thought we paid your criminal friend, Lee, to do that," I said. "Correct that; I thought that *I* paid your criminal friend to do that."

He frowned at me. "Lee will come through, but he's got his contacts and I've got mine. I know a few people who might know something."

"Do you want me to come with you?"

His face showed his alarm. "These people freak out when they meet new people. Why don't you go shopping or something?"

Shopping? Whom did he think he was talking to—his mother, his sister? My mother? "That's bullshit, Chris. I'm the one looking for Martin Bloom. Now you and Lee are running around acting all mysterious and you want me to become a tourist. What's going on?

What the hell kind of people freak out when they meet someone they don't know? In a foreign country, for God's sake?" I knew that I was that kind of person, but I, of course, was exceptional.

He visibly calmed himself, letting his shoulders sag, then stretching out his hands, palm upward, as if he were doing some kind of Buddhist or Hare Krishna thing. "Sorry, Dillon. It's not that mysterious. These people are mostly artists and writers. We hung together when I lived over here. Almost every one of them is here because he or she is a recluse, just like Bloom. They don't like to be around people. I thought they might know Martin Bloom, though. Even though all of them are social isolates, the expatriate artist community here all know each other and he's the most famous artist of any of them, by far."

His explanation made sense—maybe. Which still didn't mean that it was true. But he wasn't that pleasant to be around in his agitated state, anyway. And I was feeling better and better every time I was able to do something without him. "Fine, then I'll go shop," I said, quoting Paris Hilton, although I had no intention of actually shopping.

Chris headed off in his direction and I stayed at our table and had another cup of coffee, enjoying the cool breeze that blew in off the river. The wind-rippled water, muddy and filled with garbage as it was, sparkled in the bright sun. The buzz of thousands of motorcycles punctuated by the staccato accompaniment of car horns, provided an almost musical background to the morning that I found stimulating, even as I became drowsy in the morning sun. I could see why Martin Bloom might have chosen this spot to do his writing.

Eventually, pleasant as the weather made me feel, I began to feel uneasy, fearing that I was being lulled into some kind of tropical torpor instead of actively taking up the search the author who might be my father. I knew that Lee was supposed to be doing the looking for me, and that Chris was meeting with the local expatriate literary community, or at least so he said, but I didn't have much faith in either one of them. For all I knew, I would never see Lee or my $200 again, and Chris was out there somewhere partying with his old friends.

I paid the meager bill for the coffee and braved the life-threatening traffic to wend my way back along the streets to the backpacker area. I didn't think I'd find Martin Bloom anywhere near the hotel where Chris and I were staying, but I didn't want to wander too far from the neighborhood with which I was becoming familiar until I'd gotten more used to finding my way around Saigon. I decided to walk the streets of the backpacker district and at least get used to exploring a strange city and overcoming my fear of the unknown.

I wasn't the only college-age Caucasian strolling along the narrow streets of the district. About every twentieth person was someone who looked just like the university students I had left behind in Eugene. It made me wonder if I had overestimated the conservativeness of my fellow college students back home. I guess not everyone who was college age spent his or her weekends getting blitzed at a frat party, balling in a dorm room, tailgating at football games or, like me, holed up in the library. There were lots of couples, but also some single males and females my age, most of them tanned, the girls all seeming to be large, big-boned, and slightly overweight in an athletic, Amazonian way and with hair that had been bleached by the sun, as if they must have recently been hiking in the mountain jungles and just come into the city for some R & R. The males were equally strapping and healthy, even though they looked a little scruffy and unwashed. Every one of the young people, males and females alike, looked as if they were more comfortable than I was, chatting with shopkeepers or sitting on plastic chairs in doorways or along the edge of the street, eating everything from noodles to fresh fruit sold by street vendors, and drinking tea or beer. When I overheard any of their conversation, they were usually speaking some northern European tongue like German or Swedish, or occasionally English, more often than not with a British or Australian accent. Most of them looked as if they felt they belonged there, which I guess they did, since the district catered to their crowd. Their self-possession made me feel isolated, although not enough that I wanted to approach any of them and strike up a conversation. But their numbers and their relaxed attitudes made me feel more confident that I wasn't risking my life wandering through the streets of a foreign city.

The backpacker district fit the definition of a "warren" about as well as any human habitat I had ever visited. The closest thing I could relate it to were the scenes of urban deterioration in the movies that had been made of Philip K. Dick stories, such as the Martian city in the Schwarzenegger version of *Total Recall* or future Earth in *Blade Runner*. The main streets were just wide enough for two cars to pass each other, although the pedestrians, who tended to walk in the middle of the street, had to move out of the way for them to do so. Despite there being less traffic, the traffic pattern, with cars, motorcycles, bicycles and people on foot, was even more chaotic than on the main streets, since there were no stop signs or traffic lights and apparently no rules about which side of the street to drive on. It reminded me of the way ants scurry in apparent confusion around the entrance to their nests and, just like among the ants, there seemed to be very few collisions.

Off of the main streets were alleys, some of them wide enough for one car, many of them too narrow for anything but motorcycles and pedestrians. I shied away from these alleys, they being darker and more forbidding than the main streets, which were filled with sunlight, traffic, and the babble of people, but then I saw enough young people emerging from the narrow alleyways that I finally ventured down one. I was surprised to find a mixture of houses and businesses, most of the former being open to the alley, their inhabitants, seemingly oblivious to my passing presence, eating or doing washing in plastic basins while children played just inside the door. The air, which was hot and thick with humidity, despite the shade, was rife with the pungent smells of cooking food, especially the strong odor of what Chris had told me was Vietnamese *fish sauce*, a condiment used to flavor nearly all of their dishes. The businesses included tiny shops with clothing hanging in the doorway for sale, all sorts of food shops, and even restaurants and hotels. It didn't seem to matter how narrow the alley was, it would invariably house one or two hotels or simply doorways with large signs above them offering rooms for rent. Occasionally, these hotels were modern, if not elegant, even though they advertised rates of less than $20 per night. Discovering them in these dark alleys was like finding a pearl beneath the gray, clammy body of an oyster. And the traffic, both foot traffic and motorcycles, using these alleys

Casey Dorman

was voluminous. On more than one occasion I was forced to flatten myself against a wall or step inside a doorway to avoid being run down by a motorcycle zipping at nearly full speed through the narrow passageway. I felt like a cockroach scurrying into a crack to avoid being stepped on.

As I emerged from my first alleyway adventure I was brought up short by the presence of the always smiling, Detective Nguyen, lounging with his legs crossed and his back against the wall of one of the buildings, a bottle of water in one hand as he aimed his attention in my direction. I was less shocked than when he'd accosted me the day before.

"Miss Bloom, you see I've learned your name," he said. "Out for a morning stroll?"

"Haven't you got any real crimes to be investigating?" I asked. I assumed that Lee Cheung had told him my name.

"I'm actually doing that," he answered, his face becoming serious. "Today I am not here to watch you."

"Really? You investigate crime by leaning against a building?"

"It's fascinating what can be observed. You are aware that I am a policeman, but most of the other young people are not."

"I thought you didn't usually arrest tourists over here."

"Only when they abuse our hospitality." His smile had returned.

"I'll remember that," I said, as I turned around and headed up the street.

I didn't trust Detective Nguyen, and I wasn't sure that he wasn't still keeping me under surveillance, although I couldn't think why he would, but knowing that there was a police presence in the area emboldened me to explore the rest of the streets and alleys in the district until I felt just as comfortable walking about as did all the other young foreigners who inhabited the area. Once I stopped focusing my attention on whether I was being followed by a rapist or about to be accosted by a pickpocket, or just run over by a crazyassed motorcycle driver, I noticed that there were an awful lot of places to drink in the neighborhood and a lot of people drinking. Many of them were older

160

men, at least Martin Bloom's age. My mood brightened. Maybe I would find my father here after all.

The drinking establishments were a mix of simple street vendors who, along with the fruit, candy and soft drinks they offered, sold beer and with it, if one chose to sit and enjoy such fare, they offered a small plastic chair, resulting in people sitting and drinking almost anywhere, from the openings of alleys and doorways to right out into the street. There were also more formal, if that wasn't too much of a misuse of the word, open air cafes, similar to the one in which Chris and I had eaten the night before, spilling their tables and chairs into the sidewalk and forcing people to walk in the street, as if the boundaries of their properties extended as far as they could place furniture. Their fare invariably included pizzas, and several kinds of beer as well as, in some cases, hard liquors. I also noticed some genuine bars, dimly lit or hidden behind closed doors, with exotic names like *The Lido*, *Asian Girl*, and *Saigon Night*. At the end of one street, sitting at a busy intersection was the *Crazy Buffalo*, with a forty foot neon picture of a buffalo's head on the side of the building, making it look like it belonged in Disneyland instead of in the center of Saigon. It had a sidewalk café on the street and advertised a nightclub on the second floor.

None of the ubiquitous older men drinking in cafes, often with young Vietnamese women next to them, resembled Martin Bloom. Most of them looked as if they were chronic alcoholics, with pot bellies and red faces. The girls with them were invariably young, pretty and dressed like the Dragon Lady. Maybe they were being paid by the hour to keep the old men company. I tried to build up my courage to go inside the darkened bars but, poking my head inside one and seeing nothing but sinister looking clouds of smoke with shadowy figures of men and a few scantily clad women slouching next to them, I imagined all sorts of obscene activities going on in the dark corners of such places, and decided I'd wait until I had Chris with me. Instead, I headed for more of the alleys, which had less chance of offering a glimpse of Martin Bloom but also tested my adventurousness and, if I could get used to navigating them, might embolden me to try the even more ominous-looking establishments I wasn't yet ready to visit.

I started down one of the alleys, bigger than some others and just wide enough to allow an occasional car, so long as no one was coming in the opposite direction. As with the other alleys I had explored, once I was a little way into this one, it didn't seem as threatening as it had appeared at its entrance. It was crowded with the usual assortment of residences, shops and hotels. The three and four-story buildings on either side enclosed the street in dark shadows, but ahead I could see that there was bright sunlight, so I guessed that, like most of the other alleys, it connected at its other end with one of the major streets in the district. As I neared the end of the alley, I could see that there was a sidewalk café with a cluster of tables at the junction of the alley and the street into which it emptied. Most of the chairs at the café were taken by young Caucasians, and I could see that several of the young people were crowded around one table, listening to one of their group addressing them. With a start, I realized that the object of their attention was Chris. I quickened my steps and was about to call Chris' name, when I saw that he was taking money from some of the young people and handing them something in return.

## Chapter 27

My bottom-feeding, slime-sucking friend was dealing drugs! But would he do it this openly? Chris obviously had no idea that Detective Nguyen was only a few streets away. I backed away and retreated into the shadows of the alley. I kept watching what Chris was doing, hoping that I would detect some other explanation for what I saw than the obvious one that had leapt into my mind, causing my previously buoyant spirit to come crashing to the ground. As I stared at him I brushed the tears from my eyes and tried to ignore the empty feeling that was beginning to inhabit my whole body.

The more I watched, the less disappointed and the more angry I became. Was this the "deal" Chris and Lee had with each other? Even if the people Chris was talking to were the artists he had mentioned, it was clear to me that he wasn't just asking them about Martin Bloom. He was selling them drugs—no doubt drugs he had gotten from his sleazy friend, Lee. Probably that was why he didn't feel any fear of the detective finding him out, since Detective Nguyen seemed to be in cahoots with Lee Cheung. I felt like an idiot. What had I gotten myself into? Drug dealers were the slime of the earth. Suddenly I felt like my brains had been reshuffled and I'd been left with only half a deck. I could hear my mother saying, "I told you so." I felt more alone than I had felt at any time since the day I had buried her.

I headed back to the hotel. I had to decide if I was simply going to walk out on Chris, or if I should stay. I mean I had put out 200 bucks so that his douchebag friend would find Martin Bloom, and if I walked off I would not only never see my 200 dollars again, I'd also probably never find out if Bloom was my father. I just had to figure out how I was going to take advantage of whatever help Chris or his lowlife friend could provide without becoming any more involved with them than I had to be.

The first thing I did when I got back to the hotel was pack my things back into my suitcase, grabbing things from drawers and throwing them into my suitcase like Jennifer Aniston probably did after she found out about Brad and Angelina. I wanted to be ready to split at a moment's notice if that looked like the smartest thing to do. Then I just sat. I was still dependent upon Chris and his friend for any help I needed to find Martin Bloom. Or was I?

The dockmaster at the condo marina had been lying when he said he'd never seen Bloom. There was no doubt that the man was a dishonest sleaze. That meant I'd probably be able to bribe him. Lee and Chris had said that that was the way things were done here and just about the only things I had going for me right now were cash and an ATM card.

Screw you, Chris, I said to myself as I grabbed my purse and then stood in the middle of the motel room debating whether to take my suitcase with me. If I could get the dockmaster to tell me where Martin Bloom was, I wouldn't need Chris anymore and if I didn't need him to help me find Bloom, I didn't want him around me. I had a fleeting thought that maybe I was being unfair, jumping to a conclusion about him dealing drugs, but then I remembered what I'd witnessed. There was no question in my mind that that was what I had seen going on. Still... maybe I should give him a chance to explain. While I stood, as paralyzed by my indecision as a frozen laptop, there was a knock on the door. I heard Chris calling my name.

I opened the door.

Chris strode into the room. He looked startled to see me standing in the middle of the room with my purse in my hand and my suitcase on the bed. "What are you doing?" he asked.

*Getting as far away from you as possible.* "Nothing," I said. "I was just thinking. Trying to figure out what I was going to do this afternoon."

He stared at the suitcase. "Are you packing your things?"

"I hadn't unpacked everything yet," I lied, hoping he hadn't noticed that I actually had unpacked completely when we'd first arrived. "I was debating how much to leave in the suitcase and how much to put in the drawers."

"Put it all in the drawers," he said. He had a wide grin on his face, as if he'd been privy to a priceless joke and was dying to reveal the punch line. "We're not leaving here soon. Lee has found Martin Bloom."

I sat down on the bed. "You're kidding me." All of a sudden Chris' disreputable activities and my imminent departure flew out of my mind.

He sat down next to me—too close, if you asked me—but I was too eager to hear his news to complain. "Bloom is going to meet Lee tonight at a bar. Lee wants us to be there. Bloom doesn't know that you're even here."

"So we're going to surprise him?" It wasn't the kind of reunion I'd had in mind.

"You don't want him running away, do you?" Chris asked. "Oh..." he added, digging into his pants pocket, "...here's your 200 dollars back. Lee didn't need it after all."

His scumsucking, drug-dealing, pimp friend was giving me my money back? All of a sudden I felt ridiculous. Chris' friend had actually found Martin Bloom, and he was even returning my money. And in my mind I'd accused Lee of being a criminal psychopath and Chris of dealing drugs for him. I'd even thought they'd stolen my money.

I threw my arms around Chris and gave him a kiss on the cheek. He turned and wrapped his arms around me. I guess he thought that I'd finally given in to his charms, but the truth is, I was just feeling grateful... and guilty. I still wasn't going to let him take advantage of me and I hadn't forgotten how lost I'd felt when I thought he was the only one I could depend upon and he'd violated that trust. I pulled away. "I saw you with your friends," I said.

"What?" He had a momentary look of panic on his face. "What do you mean?"

"I was walking around and I saw you and a group of people at this café at the end of an alley." Some of my suspicion was returning as I remembered what I'd seen. "You looked as if you were selling something to them."

He stood up and faced me. He looked angry. "So you were spying on me?"

"I wasn't spying. But you said your friends were reclusive so I didn't want to just walk up to you and ask you to introduce me. I turned around and left." I had lied but he seemed to believe me. "Why were they giving you money?" I asked. I held my breath waiting for his answer.

He shrugged his shoulders. "A few of them owed me money from when I was here before. I had a lot more money than any of them did back then, because I'd just come from the cannery job in Alaska. I loaned several of them money at different times. Now they're doing better so they were paying me back."

He seemed so casual about telling me the story that I decided it must be the truth. He hadn't even had to stop to think before he'd said it. "Did any of them know Martin Bloom?" I asked, hoping that by asking, he'd see that I wasn't questioning him any longer.

"They all know who Bloom is, and one or two had heard that he was in Saigon, but none of them knew him personally. They're probably too young to hang out with someone his age. Anyway, it doesn't matter now. We're gonna meet Bloom tonight." He looked excited. "Your search will be over, and I'll get to meet the greatest living American writer."

I still felt like a shit for having doubted Chris, and I was glad that I hadn't come right out and said that I'd thought he was selling drugs. Now my anxiety was about meeting Martin Bloom. I decided to unpack my things from my suitcase and take a nap. After that, I'd take a shower, and then it would be time for us to go. I just hoped that this time the promise of seeing the man who might be my father wouldn't turn out to be an empty one, as it had been each time in the past.

## Chapter 28

Chris appeared to be as excited and anxious about the meeting as I was. He locked himself in his room and then spent at least a half hour in the shower. I knew this because after his shower, he knocked on my door and again asked if he could borrow my comb. His hair was still wet, and of course he wasn't wearing a shirt, which made me think that he was using his need for a comb as an excuse to try to seduce me. Did I look that desperate? Probably. But this time I made him stand in the hall while I handed him the comb instead of letting him into my room where he could parade around like a character from *Magic Mike* as he had before. He said he'd give the comb right back, but he must have spent an inordinate amount of time doing something to his hair, although I couldn't tell what, since, when he finally knocked again and handed me back the comb, his hair had the same shaggy look it always had.

After I finished my own preparations I invited Chris into my room. "So what's the plan?" I asked him. "And how did Lee get Bloom to agree to meet him?"

"Apparently Bloom found out through a cab driver that Lee was looking for him and he contacted Lee. I think he thinks it's his publisher or someone who is trying to get money from him."

That Martin Bloom would reach out to Lee was bizarre, but I wasn't about to quibble. The main thing was that I was going to get to meet him.

I still didn't have a clue what I would say to him. I wasn't going to talk to Chris about it, because I knew he'd be full of advice and most of it would be bad. Anyway, he was too busy thinking about what *he* was going to say to his favorite author.

"Do you think I should bring along one of his books?" Chris asked. "You know, just to let him know how much I appreciate his work? That could be an entrée into us discussing some of his writing... or maybe even my own."

"I told Betsy I'd get his autograph on her copy of *The Fourth Season*" I said. "One of us needs to bring the book along in case we never see him again after tonight."

Chris stared at me as if I were out of my mind. "That's so juvenile, asking for an autograph, like we're groupies and he's a rock star or a baseball player. I'm not going to do that. Besides, what do you mean, in case we never see him again? I'm sure he's your father. He's gonna want to reunite with you."

I felt my stomach tense with anger. Reunite with me? Martin Bloom might be a famous author and someone whom I admired for his writing, but he had never shown a scrap of interest in me as his daughter... a daughter he even knew was looking for him, according to Professor Prentiss. Chris may have thought that Martin Bloom was some sort of literary god, but I knew that, as a human being, he was a failure. "If he wanted to reunite with me, he wouldn't have made zero effort all of these years," I said. "And you heard Professor Prentiss. She said Bloom knew that his daughter was looking for him and he made no attempt to even contact her." Just listening to myself say the truth extinguished most of the excitement I had been feeling about our upcoming meeting. The truth was obvious. If Martin Bloom was my father, I was on his—to quote Nikki Minaj's opinion of Mariah Carey— "drop dead list."

I sat back down on the bed and tried to calm the turmoil building inside my body. I had to think about what I was doing. Was there any point in meeting Martin Bloom? If he was my father, he was nothing but a selfish bastard who hadn't wanted to be a husband or a parent, and I was going to force myself on him, whether he wanted it or not. What did I plan to do? Ask him if he'd give me a hug? I'd told myself I just wanted to find out the truth. I didn't need anything from him. But that wasn't true. I needed to find out how much of him was part of me. And I knew that I wanted him to be my father. Despite his unadulterated egoism, Martin Bloom's writing expressed the yearnings of a soul that was similar to mine. Knowing that he and I were related would tell me that I was not alone in the world. But even if he rejected me? My depression returned.

"Don't chicken out now," Chris said, looking down at me. I guess my thoughts were written all over my face.

"What's the point?" I asked, not even looking up at him.

"The point is that we're going to meet one of the world's greatest writers. It doesn't matter whether he's your father—that's beside the point. He's a fucking literary genius and we've tracked him down and now we're going to get to talk to him. If you're scared because he might be your father and that he's been a piss poor excuse for a father all these years, then just think of him as the kind of writer we'd both like to be. We've got to learn something valuable just by talking to him."

His words gave me some relief. I breathed easier, and, for just a moment, anyway, I could glimpse a different perspective. "You're either one of the most insightful or one of the most manipulative people I've ever met," I told Chris. "Probably you're both." For a second I had the feeling that Chris had more in common with Martin Bloom than I did. "Let's go meet the bastard."

Casey Dorman

Chapter 29

Martin awoke from his afternoon nap with three hours
remaining before Duc was scheduled to collect him and drive him to
the Mekong Bar. He was still drunk. *Why not?* The day had to come
when someone would find out where he'd been living, despite the low
profile he'd been able to manage for the last two years, and he might
just as well be drunk when he faced it. It was probably his publisher,
that shrew Marilyn Reams. She was the one who'd finally, albeit
reluctantly, signed off on his advance for the book that he was
supposed to have completed two years ago. According to his agent,
Sidney Duckworth, Reams had been trying to cut off Martin's royalty
payments from his earlier books until he'd either paid back the
advance or delivered the book. Duckworth had managed to work with
the publisher's accounting department so that they just took a
percentage out of Martin's royalties each month. It left barely enough
to sustain Martin's meager life style, but Reams was, reportedly, still
pissed.

He reached for the gin bottle next to his bed. So what if
Marilyn Reams had found him? What could she do? Nothing. Except it
worried him that she'd allied herself with a gangster to track him
down. In fact, it seemed to him to defy logic. How would she have
known about a Chinese underworld figure in Saigon? But stranger
things had happened, and, in Vietnam, anything was possible. For all
he knew she had contacted the police to track him down and they had
contacted this Lee fellow. The mafia in Saigon often worked with the
police and they knew ways to make people cooperate that frightened
the shit out of him. What's more they seemed to operate with
impunity. But that was just against local Vietnamese, wasn't it? They
didn't usually go after foreigners, especially Americans.

He tried to concentrate on what he remembered about the
Chinese guy, Lee, whom he was supposed to meet. He'd seen him
around, but he'd never had anything to do with him. There were
rumors that some of the women Martin had hooked up with at places

like the Mekong Bar worked for the Asian, but Martin never asked and he always dealt directly with the women. And there was that one time that he'd seen Lee at the marina, coming aboard a newly arrived boat with his entourage of muscle and making a scene with the couple from Australia who had just tied up on their sixty-foot sloop. He'd heard scuttlebutt about the couple having welshed on some drug delivery they were supposed to have brought in from Myanmar, and the next day the sloop was gone. A few days later, the papers reported the couple's bodies having been found in the river downstream from Saigon. The authorities claimed that their boat had capsized in rough weather on the river and they had been unable to swim to shore, but Martin knew that that was just a story that was designed to allay the fears of the tourists.

He took another drink and pulled the bed covers up to his chin. Marilyn Reams was a bitch, but she wouldn't put a hit out on him, would she? That was ridiculous. But Lee whatever-his-name-was, the Chinese, as Duc called him, might have promised her he could either get Martin to start writing or get him to send back his royalty checks. Martin had visions of himself imprisoned in an underground torture chamber, locked in a Vietnamese tiger cage, being forced to produce a page of writing a day or he'd start losing toes and fingers or God knows what else. He pulled the blanket down far enough to reach for the bottle and pull it under the covers with him.

When Duc knocked on the door, Martin awoke, his head under the covers and an empty gin bottle next to his face, its odor like the sweet breath of an intimate lover. He staggered out of bed and opened the door. "Be ready in a minute," he told the cab driver.

He looked in the mirror. The face staring out at him was unshaven with dark bags under its eyes. His hair stood out in every possible direction. He reminded himself of Mickey Rourke in *Barfly*. He grabbed his toothbrush and toothpaste and turned on the shower with ice-cold water and stepped inside. He felt a momentary flutter of his heart, and for a second he worried that he might have a coronary right then and there, but it went away almost immediately. He brushed his teeth and scrubbed his body as rapidly as he could manage, then stepped out, pulled on a set of underwear, combed his hair and shaved, put on some long pants and a Hawaiian shirt and sandals and stepped back out the door to a placidly waiting Duc. He felt better but he was still definitely drunk.

"Be careful, Ong Martin," Duc told him on the drive to the Cho Lon district. "The Chinese, he's not a nice guy. Don't make him any promises. He never forgets what anyone owes him."

The cabbie's words weren't reassuring. He felt as if he needed another drink, but he knew that Duc didn't carry any gin in his cab. They arrived at the Mekong Bar and he walked in, feeling unsteady on his feet. The restaurant section was located in the back of the establishment and the bar was in the front near the street. He looked around and didn't see any Chinese hoodlum so he went to the bar and ordered two gins. He downed the first one on the spot, although he hardly felt its effects, then carried the second into the restaurant. He could see a tall, vaguely familiar person sitting alone at a table. The Chinese man, who sported a ponytail and dark glasses, waved a hand to signal Martin to join him.

"It's an honor, Mister Bloom," the man said, standing up to shake Martin's hand. "You are a very well-known American writer. I had no idea we had such a celebrity living right here among us. My name is Lee Cheung."

Martin shifted the drink to his left hand and reached out and shook the man's hand. He sat down heavily in one of the chairs. He could feel the room starting to spin around him. "I can't pay anyone anything," he said, although he felt as if his mouth wasn't working right when he talked. The words came out all run together, as if they'd been poured from a pitcher.

Lee laughed. He had a wide smile and shiny, white teeth, which reminded Martin of the fangs he'd once seen on a wolf when he'd visited a zoo. "Nobody wants any money from you, Mr. Bloom, at least not that I know of. Not me, certainly. I just wanted to meet you. I've never met a famous writer before."

Martin had finished his second drink and he held up his glass to the waiter, who seemed to be ignoring him.

Lee snapped his fingers and two waiters appeared at his shoulder. "Mr. Bloom would like another drink," he said. "I'll have a beer."

The drinks arrived and Lee picked up a menu. Martin had noticed that he had been scanning the room as if looking for someone. Was this when the kidnappers appeared, he wondered. "Would you like dinner, Mr. Bloom?" Lee asked. "It's on me, of course."

Martin looked around to see whom Lee was looking for. He couldn't see anyone whom he recognized, but half of the clientele looked to him as though they were probably Chinese Mafia. He knew he was being paranoid, but he also was developing the feeling that he had walked into some kind of set up. He gulped down his drink. "Maybe just a bowl of pho," he said. The thought of food made him nauseous, but he didn't want to offend the Chinese. "And one more drink."

He got his drink and asked the waiter to bring the bottle to the table. The waiter looked at Lee, who nodded, and the waiter brought a half full bottle of gin and set it on the table. Martin wolfed down a quick one, then poured himself another but let it sit, more as a good-luck talisman than anything else. How bad could things get with a half bottle of gin on the table? When he looked across at Lee, he had a hard time bringing him into focus. Either Martin was weaving back and forth or the Chinese was.

"Are you all right, Mr. Bloom?" Lee asked. "Perhaps you should slow down on the drinks. This is a good restaurant. You must surely want more than a bowl of noodles."

"What?" Martin asked. The man's voice sounded as if it were echoing down a long tunnel.

"I asked if you were all right and whether you didn't want more to eat," Lee said. He was still scanning the room. Suddenly he smiled broadly. "I have a surprise for you, Mr. Bloom," he said.

Martin froze. Marilyn Reams couldn't be here, could she? No way, he thought. Then what did the Chinese mean? Was this the hit man coming after him? Did they just walk up to your table and shoot you in front of all of these people? He slowly turned around, expecting to see the barrel of a gun pointed at his head. Maybe he'd just hear the bang and not feel anything. He could still hear Lee talking. His voice still sounded as if it were coming from a distance.

"Mr. Bloom, this is your daughter," Lee said.

He looked up and saw a young woman with flashing metal hanging from her face and with jet black hair, spiked on top and hanging in shaggy clumps down the back of her neck. She had his face or what his face had looked like when he was 20 years old. "Jesus fucking Christ," he said.

"Father?" Dillon asked, looking at him expectantly.

"Jesus fucking Christ," Martin repeated. Then he passed out.

## Chapter 30

Every person I'd met in the last month had told me that Martin Bloom was a drunk, so why had I been surprised that he was drunk when I'd met him? I'd seen college friends get so drunk that they'd passed out, but I'd never seen an adult that way. So Martin Bloom had been able to expand my experience already—and he hadn't even needed to be conscious to do it.

Lee had called a cab driver, apparently the same one who had told him where Bloom was living, and the driver had come and collected the author— gently, I thought, so maybe this driver was a friend of Bloom's—and taken him out of the restaurant. When I'd told the driver I thought that I was the man's daughter, he had given me the name and address of the hotel where Bloom was staying. It turned out to be only two blocks from where Chris and I were staying. So here I was, the next morning, the abandoned daughter come to call.

Chris and I had come together and we'd come early—8:00 a.m.—just because I hadn't trusted that Bloom wouldn't bolt, once he woke up and realized that someone claiming to be his daughter was in town looking for him. Once again I had overestimated him. We had to pound on the door and when it finally opened, it was clear that we had wakened him and that he was seriously hung over. He didn't recognize me.

"Hello, Mr. Bloom," I said. "It's me again. Last night wasn't a nightmare."

He stared at me. He was still dressed in the clothes he had worn the night before and it was obvious he had slept in them. His hair was mussed and he was unshaven and he looked at me with a squint as if the light was painful on his eyes. "Jesus fucking Christ," he said. For a famous writer, he seemed to have a very limited vocabulary.

He just stood there in the door without inviting us in. I figured he was preparing to say "Jesus fucking Christ," one more time. Before he could repeat his incantation, I asked if we could come in.

"I'm still asleep," he said, not moving aside.

This man's ability to cope with reality was seriously challenged. "You just wish you were," I answered. "But you're standing at your door talking to me, and you're not inviting me in."

He looked at me as if he was assessing whom he was dealing with. Then he breathed a long sigh, lowered his head, turned around, and walked back into the room, leaving the door open behind him. I glanced at Chris and then entered. Chris followed me. There were two chairs sitting next to the window. We both sat down.

"So you're Dillon," he said, casting his gaze around the room until he finally fastened on the gin bottle on top of the dresser and then got up and walked over to it, unscrewing the top and taking a drink directly from the bottle.

"You know my name?" I was in shock, realizing that he'd just confirmed that he was my father.

"Of course I know your name. I named you." He took another drink from the bottle. "I heard Regina's dead."

"Mom died a year ago," I said, still reeling from finding that my question about him being my father had been answered. "She'd always told me that you were dead."

"Really?" He smiled. "I wonder why she said that?"

"Maybe she knew how you looked in the morning."

He frowned. "She must have been really angry with me. You must be too." He stared at me for a moment. "She had a right to be. So do you. I was no husband and no father." I was becoming aware how old and worn he actually looked...and unhealthy. He took another swallow. "If you thought I was dead, how come you're here?"

"I was assigned your book to read in a college class. Your picture was on the back and it looked a lot like me. My professor said that you had graduated from Oregon, and so everything fit, the name, the face... everything." Now that I said it, I wondered why I had ever doubted that Martin Bloom was my father.

He was still staring at me. "You do look like me... when I was young." He smiled again. "That must have irked Regina." He shook his head. "So now you're here. I'm actually glad... even though I was frightened to meet you."

"Frightened?"

"You ought to hate me." He looked down at the floor.

"I'd like to get to know you."

He took a deep breath and looked at me. "Then let's go somewhere and talk. "I need some coffee and breakfast. Let me take a shower, change my clothes and then we can all go to breakfast. How does that sound?"

*Not so fast, you crafty old bastard.* "You have a tendency to disappear," I said, looking him straight in the eye, amazing myself with my own temerity.

He laughed again. "Wait downstairs. You can watch the front door. When I'm ready to go, I'll come down and we can all walk to a cafe. Don't worry, there's no back way out of this place, and I'm too old to go out the window." He shook his head and laughed again, as if he found my suspicions funny.

Chris and I stood and then said goodbye. We walked back down the stairs and sat in the tiny lobby of the hotel.

"He's kind of an asshole," Chris said. He looked as though he was depressed.

"A lot of people agree with you," I answered. Martin Bloom did seem like an asshole, but there was something likeable about him, too. I wasn't sure what it was, and I wasn't even sure it wasn't just that I wanted him to be likeable. Or maybe I saw some of myself in him.

We didn't say much more. I was thinking about what my mother would think if she knew what I was doing right now. Probably that I'd done the thing she hoped I'd never do. I knew that she'd be afraid that I would get hurt. The thought made me miss her.

177

Chapter 31

After about fifteen minutes, my father came down the stairs. He was shaved and had on different clothes and his hair was combed. He didn't look all that bad, except he still had dark circles under both eyes.

"I guess you weren't a figment of my imagination," he said as we left the hotel.

"You probably thought so last night," I said.

"I don't even remember last night."

He directed us to a café a few blocks away. It was one of those hole-in-the-wall places, but it advertised pizza, hamburgers, and breakfast, as well as beer and cocktails. My father greeted the waitress as if he knew her. "The English Breakfast is good here," he said, "or they'll make you an omelet if you want. They also have noodles, which the locals eat for breakfast lunch and dinner."

My father ordered an omelet, coffee and a something called a *gin sunrise*. He referred to it as a "healthy breakfast drink." Chris and I each ordered coffee and the English breakfast, which consisted of sausage, an egg and a slice of tomato.

The waitress brought the three coffees and my father's gin sunrise at the same time. The drink looked like orange juice with a trace of something red in it. When I asked, he admitted it had, "a touch of gin," in it, to "give it a little life." He downed half of the drink before he even took a sip of his coffee. "How did you find me?" he asked.

"I followed your trail from one university to another. I talked to Malcolm Truong and Elizabeth Roundtree, but neither of them had a clue. Finally Professor Prentiss at Stanford told me where you were."

He shook his head. "She must have been pissed at me."

"She said if I found you to tell you to fuck yourself."

178

He laughed, but then he began coughing so hard that I thought he might throw up. When he finally stopped coughing he looked at me. "Were Malcolm and Elizabeth pissed at me, too?"

I shook my head. "They both said very nice things about you. Professor Truong is worried because he hasn't heard from you, but Elizabeth has no desire to see you again, although she isn't mad at you."

He seemed to think about what I'd said. "Who are you?" he finally asked, looking at Chris.

Chris was smiling. He straightened up as if he were attending a job interview. "Chris Fenner. I'm a writer and a friend of your daughter's. And one of your greatest admirers." He pulled the copy of *The Fourth Season* from out of his backpack and showed it to my father.

"I hope you don't carry that everywhere you go," my father said. He looked at Chris as if he might have something wrong with him.

"Actually, it's your daughter's," Chris said, embarrassed.

"A friend of mine wanted your autograph," I said. I wasn't embarrassed at all. If I got nothing else from my father, I was going to get him to autograph Betsy's book.

"You came all the way here to get my autograph?" he asked. I could hear a trace of humor in his voice. The gin seemed to be cheering him up.

"We're both writers ourselves," Chris answered. "We came here so we could meet you. Share some of our experiences. Talk about writing."

"Oh Christ," my father said. "Give me a fucking break." He shook his head.

"I just wanted to meet you... and find out if you really were my father," I said. "I thought maybe I could get to know you, but I guess that depends."

"Depends on what?"

"On whether you'll let me."

He stared at me, as if I had said something profound. He looked as if he were deciding what to say next, then he shook his head, as if dismissing whatever comment he'd been about to make. "Why aren't you in school?" he asked.

"I'm in grad school—at Stanford," Chris answered.

"I don't care a rat's ass about you," my father said, looking at Chris dismissively. He turned to me, waiting for my answer.

"I was in school at Oregon. I finished my freshman year."

"So you went to college—even after your mom died?"

I nodded.

He looked as though he was impressed. "You must be pretty smart. No one else has been able to find me. Sylvia Prentiss was just an accident."

"Chris helped me." I was feeling sorry for Chris. So far every attempt he'd made to ingratiate himself with my father had been rebuffed.

"Which of you knew the Mafia guy—the Chinese—Lee what's his name?"

I looked over at Chris. You explain the kind of people you associate with, I thought.

"He's an old friend. I used to live over here," Chris said. He looked embarrassed.

"He's an odd person to have as friend," my father said. "He's a criminal. He does some pretty nasty things."

"He's not a close friend," Chris said. "But he knows a lot of people, and we thought he could help find you."

"So are you two a couple?" He looked at both Chris and me.

"Sort of," Chris answered.

"Not really," I said. "So why don't you want anyone to find you?" I asked.

He sipped on his coffee. "I don't like people, and my publisher is trying to get some money from me. Besides, Saigon is a good place to write." He frowned across the table at the two of us. "Except when I get interruptions."

"Last night you were drunk and this morning you were sleeping off a hangover," I said. "Tell me again what we were interrupting?"

He stared at me for a moment, and then laughed. "I wonder if you get that tongue from your mother or from me?"

"Mom didn't say mean things," I said.

He continued to stare at me, as if he was thinking. "No she didn't. You're right."

"Your daughter's a writer, too. She got that from you," Chris said. "Both of us are."

My father's expression became serious. "So you've said—a couple of times." He turned toward me. "Is that true? Are you a writer?"

I felt self-conscious. "I like to write and I like words, but I haven't tried to write anything but term papers for school."

His face showed more interest than I had anticipated. "Term papers about what?"

"Kingsley Amis, James Joyce, Thomas Hardy, Kazuo Ishiguro."

He nodded approvingly. "Not a bad selection. How did you pick those writers?"

"They were some of my favorites, and they were on the list of those we could read."

"How'd the papers come out?"

"I got A's."

He nodded again, as though he was impressed. It felt eerie, as if I was discussing my school grades with my father. In fact, I was, and that really felt weird.

"Are those some of your favorite writers?" Chris asked him. The poor guy was still trying to become part of the conversation.

"I'm my own favorite writer," my father answered. "But Joyce and Hardy are favorites of mine. Ishiguro is OK. Kingsley Amis is a toot... in more ways than one, and he and I have a lot in common, lifestyle wise."

"His son is a writer," Chris said.

181

"A good one," my father said. He looked over at me. "There's something in the genetic argument."

I looked at him. Even though he was saying what I wanted to hear, I was getting the feeling that I was being seduced, and I felt a stab of anxiety, which I interpreted as a ghostly nudge from my mother warning me to be careful. "That's why I don't drink," I said.

"Ouch," he said, then lifted his second gin sunrise and toasted me. "That's a good choice."

I couldn't tell if he meant it or was being sarcastic. I was having a hard time accepting anything resembling parental concern from this man who'd ignored me all of his life.

Our food had arrived, and we all took a few minutes' respite from our strained conversation to distract ourselves with eating. My father ordered a third gin sunrise. I had heard of heavy drinkers before, but I'd never seen anyone drink this way so early in the day. He'd already had almost half a bottle of gin in his room that morning.

"Everyone says that you're a recluse," I said... "it even says so on Wikipedia." *And that's something the two of us have in common*, I thought to myself.

"Really?" he seemed amused by my comment. "I've never thought of myself as a recluse. If people weren't trying to get so many things out of me—money, my next novel—I'd be perfectly happy to be around them. But most people bore me. I don't want to spend my time talking to the average Joe who worries about his bills, is busy saving money to send his kids to college, and who spends his free time watching football on TV. I can use him as a stereotype for one of my stories, but there's not anything interesting going on in his head. Not interesting to me, anyway. But I've met lots of people I do find interesting. The thing is, though, you never get it right when you actually interact with them—or at least I don't. That's why I prefer interacting through my novels. I can make sure that I say everything just the way I want to."

"And the average Joe isn't going to read your books, anyway," Chris added.

"Probably not. I think I write for people like myself. I think most writers do."

"That's what I've always said," Chris said, triumphantly. "A writer has to write for himself... not for others."

My father heaved another long sigh, but again he seemed to will his irritation to leave. "No. I write for people *like* myself. Not for myself. But as I said, maybe that's just me."

I think I understood what my father was saying. At least it fit with the feeling I'd had when I'd read my favorite writers—that they were actually communicating with me. I even felt as if he was right about wanting to communicate with people like myself—assuming there were such people—but from the safety of the printed page, rather than in person.

"So how did you get your first book published?" Chris continued, doggedly.

My father looked as if he was becoming irritated, but he nodded and continued talking. "First of all, it wasn't my first book, it was my eighth. The first seven never saw the light of day."

"You mean they were just ideas in your head?" Chris asked. I knew why he asked it, because that's what his own writing was at this point.

"An idea in your head is an idea, it's not a book. I finished seven novels, which I sent to every agent and publisher I could think of, and they were all turned down. The eighth one was the charm. I'm not sure it was any better than the first seven—maybe it was, since I never tried to publish any of the earlier ones after I became known—but I sent it to an agent who had just moved back to his home town after being gone for thirty years. Since that was the plot of my novel, the story hit him right where he was living at the time... literally. It was blind luck. He read the synopsis, became intrigued, then read the book, then sent it to his uncle, who was a publisher, and bingo, I was in print."

"*A Memorial to Time*," I said.

"That was the one."

We'd all finished eating, and my father suggested that we leave the café and walk to what he called a "real bar," down the street. He said he always went there after breakfast. I couldn't imagine that he was going to drink more, but it sounded as if that was his intention. Since I wasn't here to alter my father's habits, no matter how destructive they were, I agreed and so did Chris.

When we got to the bar, which was inside, off the street, Chris ordered a beer and my father continued with his gin, this time without the orange juice and grenadine. He looked a little drunk, but I wasn't really sure he'd ever sobered up from the night before. Maybe he just stayed drunk all the time.

"What are you writing now?" Chris asked. "Or are you like me and you don't like to talk about it until you're sure you've got it right?"

"Oh hell, I can talk about it," my father said, his voice a little slurred and his gestures more expansive than they had been earlier. "That's about all I can do these days is talk about it."

"What do you mean?" I asked. I thought I'd detected a note of despair in his voice.

"I've lost my touch," he said. He had almost sobbed the words. Either he was really drunk or we'd brought up a very sensitive topic for him.

"Like a writer's block?" Chris asked.

"Like a damn writer's brick wall." He picked up his drink and downed it in a gulp. "Thank God for this or I might get worried."

I just stared at him. After coming all this way to find out if Martin Bloom was my father and, if so, what we had in common, thinking that it might help me find myself, I was beginning to feel sorry for the poor man. He was pathetic. He was a pathetic drunk who was blabbering about his misfortune to a daughter he'd abandoned and hadn't even cared about. Now he was acting as if I was supposed to care about him. I felt my stomach beginning to churn again. I hadn't expected it, but I was feeling angry with him.

"You've become a hopeless drunk," I said. "You're not even a writer anymore."

He directed an angry gaze at me, and then grabbed the new drink the waiter had brought and downed it. His anger dissipated. His face sagged, and he looked as if he was about to cry. "I always hoped that someday my daughter would come to see me and she'd be proud of me. I didn't think you'd despise me." He hung his head and looked up at me from under his eyebrows, his darkly circled eyes clouding with tears.

I felt a moment of pity, but then I caught myself. "You always hoped you'd never see your daughter again. Don't make up a past that never existed. I'm real, not a character in one of your novels." This was my father and he was a slobbering alcoholic who just wanted sympathy. He had nothing to give back to me. Suddenly I was too angry to remain in his presence. "Let's get out of here," I said to Chris.

"We don't have to leave," Chris answered. I could hear the disappointment in his voice.

"I do. You can come if you want," I said.

"You're just like your mother," My father said, his voice bitter. "So high and mighty and judgmental." He had already ordered another gin. I was surprised that they continued to serve him.

"Absolutely," I said, getting up from the table. "I'm exactly like my mother, except I'm leaving you this time, not vice versa." I turned and walked out. Chris waited a few seconds—to see if I was coming back, I guess—then followed me out the door.

Chapter 32

"Your father was just drunk," Chris said, a note of pleading in his voice. "You knew he drank before you even met him. It's no reason to pack up and leave. He could still help us."

Chris had no idea of the depth of my disillusionment. In a matter of weeks I had gone from believing my father was dead, to building up the hope that he was alive and someone with whom I could finally share myself, to finding that he was indeed alive, but that he was a selfish, hopeless drunk. I'd been happier when I'd believed that he was dead. I was truly alone in the world. The only one I had ever been close to was my mother, and it had turned out that, in sparing me from the knowledge that my father was alive, she had understood me better than I'd understood myself. My father offered me nothing except the false hope that there was someone else like me in the world.

"What do you mean, 'help us?' " I asked Chris.

"He knows a lot of people. He might be able to introduce us to someone or at least give us some names of agents or publishers. Remember, he said it's blind luck and so every little edge helps."

"I didn't come here to use my father," I said. "I wanted to learn something about him. But in the condition he's in, there's nothing to learn, except that I don't want to end up like him."

"I think he sold out anyway," Chris said, "...trying to write so that he pleases everyone. He's lost himself in the process. That's probably why he drinks."

Chris had missed the whole point of my father's explanation about writing, but I was almost as fed up with Chris as I was with my father, so I didn't feel like getting into it with him. I got my suitcase back out and started taking my clothes out of the drawers.

"We don't have to go today," Chris said, still pleading. "Besides, if you leave, I may stay here for awhile."

As soon as he said it my legs became weak, as if their muscles had just turned to liquid. I couldn't believe it. I felt something close to loathing for Chris, and yet, when he said he would stay behind after I

186

left, I had begun to panic. What was wrong with me? Had I become a helpless bimbo? I wished my mother were here to take my hand and lead me away.

"What are you going to do here?" I asked, trying to keep my voice as casual as I could, but aware that I was feeling terrified. "I thought you came here to meet Martin Bloom. We've done that."

"I haven't given up on him like you have. I was thinking that maybe I would put some of my ideas down on paper and ask him what he thinks."

All of a sudden I felt sorry for Chris. Martin Bloom was still his hero, even though Chris was mostly interested in using him as a steppingstone to promote his own writing career. But he also desperately wanted to have my father praise his writing ability. I knew that he was doomed to failure on that account. My father was too selfish to praise anyone but himself.

Just as suddenly, I knew I was ready to go back to Eugene and resume my education. Hoping to find a kindred spirit in a ghostly father who had suddenly emerged from the dead had been a bad idea. The only good thing about it was that I'd gotten it accomplished, and hopefully, out of my system in a fairly short period of time. I could find out if I was a writer by trying to write something. If anything had changed in me as a result of this odyssey, it was that I now felt a little sorry for my father. He was degenerating about as fast as anyone I'd ever seen. He was drunk all day and he was no longer able to write. I remembered Professor Truong's message about repaying my father for giving me life, but I wasn't going to give in to that message. I'd never been my father's responsibility, and he wasn't going to become mine.

"How about one more night—just to give yourself enough distance to gain some perspective?" Chris interrupted my thoughts. "If you still want to leave tomorrow, I won't stand in your way. And tonight, just to take your mind off of today, I'll take you out to dinner."

One more day in Vietnam wasn't going to make a difference. I couldn't start school back in Oregon until the next term anyway, and it would take some time to arrange my return flight. Besides, Chris owed me a dinner.

We left the backpacker district and went to a fancy-schmancy restaurant with white table cloths and a maître d' to lead us to our table. It was called the *Vietnam House* on Dong Khoi street in the heart of the business and hotel district. Because it was Saigon, the prices were still well below anything that could be found in the U.S., and Chris insisted on steak and lobster for both of us. He even ordered a bottle of wine, although he was going to have to drink it all himself, because if I'd learned one thing about my newly discovered father, it was that he was carrying a full load of alcoholic genes, and I had a good chance of having inherited them.

"Are you sure you can afford this?" I asked, when he started picking out a fancy dessert that took so long to prepare that it had to be ordered in advance of the meal.

He was already tipsy from the wine and he pulled out a wad of bills from his pocket and fanned them with his thumb. "I've got tons of money," he said with a smug grin.

Suddenly I had a flashback to the picture of him at the café at the end of the alley exchanging something for money with all of those so-called artist friends of his. "How did you get so much money?"

"I told you some people owed me money from when I was here before and they paid me."

"What did they owe you money for?"

"Just loans. I was pretty rich back then with my Alaska money, compared to them, anyway."

To quote my dead mother, did he think I'd just fallen off the turnip truck? I didn't buy his story, but there was no way I was going to get him to admit to something else and, anyway, I was leaving the next day, so what did I care where his money came from? I just looked at him without saying anything.

I could see the waiter behind Chris, bringing our food, but Chris' face suddenly went white. He was looking past me. I turned around and saw Lee Cheung walking toward our table, his eyes fastened on Chris. He wasn't wearing his cargo shorts but instead was dressed in a crisp, grey suit and his mouth was set in a grim line. He looked like a character from a Saigon version of *Goodfellas*.

"Hey, Dillon," Lee said, managing a quick smile. "Did you and your father finally hook up? I hope he was more sober than he was last night." He was talking to me but he was still eyeing Chris, who looked as if he was about to lose his steak and lobster before he'd even had a chance to eat them.

"We met him. It was OK." I wasn't going to share anything personal with Lee. Even my lowlife father had warned me about him.

The waiter served our meals. Lee made a big deal about looking impressed. "Wow, treating yourselves to the very best tonight, I see. And such a fancy restaurant. Whose treat is this?" He looked from Chris, who was staring at his plate, back to me.

"Chris is taking me out," I said.

"Really?" Lee said, putting a hand on Chris' shoulder. "Feeling flush, are you, Chris?"

Chris looked up at him. Despite the air conditioning, his forehead was shiny with sweat and I could see the fear in his eyes. "It's her last night here. She's going back to the States tomorrow. I wanted to treat her."

Lee looked at me, his face showing concern. "You're going back, after finding your father?"

"We had our meeting. I don't need to see him anymore."

He shrugged. "Well, I'm glad I was able to help." He turned back to Chris, who was fiddling with his fork and the rice on his plate. "You weren't thinking of going back with her, were you, Chris?"

Chris shook his head. "I told her I was staying." He looked at me with a pleading expression on his face. "That's right, isn't it, Dillon? I said I was staying here, didn't I?"

I nodded. "Yes, you said you were staying." Something weird was going on between Lee and Chris, and Chris was scared out of his wits.

"OK," Lee said. He looked back at me. "Have a good trip back, Dillon. It's been a pleasure meeting you, and I'm glad I could help." He walked off and, so far as I could tell, out of the restaurant.

"What was that about?" I asked Chris.

189

Chris shrugged. "I borrowed a little money from him, and he knows that I got paid back by my friends, so he's afraid I'm gonna leave without paying him."

"Why did you borrow money from him? I have money, you know that."

"I didn't want to bother you again after borrowing the $200 already."

"The $200 was for Lee to find my father. It wasn't a loan to you."

He shrugged again, as if none of it mattered. "I'll deal with Lee tomorrow. Let's enjoy our last meal together."

I took him at his word and we ate, although since both my father and Lee were sensitive topics that we both had decided to avoid, there wasn't much to talk about. After we ate, we took a taxi back to the motel.

"When are you going back to Stanford—or are you?" I asked as we entered our hotel.

"They're on a quarter system, so I have until February to sign up for spring classes," he answered. "I'm sure I'll be back by then. Are you really going back to Eugene?"

"I might as well finish school. I did pretty well my first year, and I took an extra course over the summer term, so I'm not really behind, even after missing a quarter."

"I'm gonna keep trying to make a connection with your father," he said, as he unlocked his door.

"Good luck," I said, turning to go into my own room.

I entered the room and, turning on the light, was immediately confronted by three armed men. They'd been waiting in the dark.

I felt as if I were in the middle of an Asian action movie. The men were shouting things in Vietnamese. They had their guns drawn. They were also pointing at the bed. I looked down and lying on the bed was a plastic bag containing what I recognized was at least a half a pound of marijuana. I was stunned.

"It's not mine," I shouted, although I doubted any of the men understood me.

One of the men stepped forward, and I recognized him as Detective Nguyen. "I'm disappointed in you, Miss Bloom. Always seeming so innocent, and yet, look what we've found in your room." His tone was sarcastic, but he wasn't smiling.

"You know it's not mine." Even though I was trembling with fear, I was becoming angry, realizing that I had been set up.

"Perhaps it is your friend's," Detective Nguyen suggested. At that moment the door opened and two more men shoved Chris into the room.

"Is this junk yours?" I screamed at him, my anger turning into full-blown rage.

Chris was white as a sheet. He had a guilty expression on his face, but then his face became serious. "This is your room, Dillon. That must be your stuff."

What an asshole! I could tell it was his pot and he'd probably put it in my room just in case something like this happened.

"We know that you've been selling this," Detective Nguyen said to Chris. He turned to the two men who'd brought Chris into the room. "Did you find anything in his room?" They seemed to understand his English because they both shook their heads.

"We're going to take both of you in," the detective said, looking first at me, then at Chris.

"I didn't have any drugs," Chris said, his voice becoming whiny. "They're hers."

"Bullshit!" I yelled at Chris. I faced the detective, my hands on my hips. "This is crap! I'm not going anywhere with you. Those drugs are that bastard's, not mine." I was hoping that my defiance concealed my terror.

Detective Nguyen said something in Vietnamese and two of the other policemen stepped forward; one of them held out a pair of handcuffs. Another policeman reached over and snapped a cuff on Chris's wrist. I hid my hands behind my back.

"Do what they ask," Chris hissed at me, "...or they'll start hitting you. I'll call Lee and get this fixed."

I held out my hands. I didn't want them to hit me or pull their guns again. I was mad as hell at Chris. "Lee?" I shouted. "This is why you owed him money, you freaking scumbag! He gave you these drugs to sell. That was what you were doing in that cafe and that's why you had money for dinner." I turned back to Detective Nguyen. "He's the drug-dealing asshole, not me!"

"Shut up!" Chris yelled. "Don't say anything. They'll use it against us."

I hated him. What a fool I had been to ever team up with someone like him. I hated my father for being a drunk, and here I was being arrested because the man I was with was a drug dealer ... and no doubt a user, too. I bit my lower lip so I wouldn't cry. I was going to get through this somehow, and not by relying upon Lee and Chris and for sure not my father. I thought about my mother. She wouldn't have hesitated to tell me that I had been a fool.

Chapter 33

The pounding on his door was deafening to Martin's hangover-sensitive brain. *Don't tell me it's my daughter again*, he thought. He had only a foggy recollection of their previous day together, but he knew that it hadn't ended well. He had gotten sloppily drunk, and she had walked out. What was puzzling was that it was his attempt to be conciliatory that had driven her away. Had he actually said he had hoped that she'd be proud of him? What a bunch of hogwash, he thought. When he was drunk, he had a tendency to become maudlin, and invariably it got him into trouble. He never knew if he sometimes meant the things he said when he was drunk or if it was always the booze talking.

The hammering on the door was louder, and he struggled out of bed and lurched to the door. When he opened it, Lee Cheung was standing there, his fist raised, ready to pound the door one more time.

"What the hell?" Martin said.

"Still drunk?" Lee asked. He pushed past Martin and entered the tiny hotel room. He was dressed in a pair of cream-colored linen pants and a flowered silk shirt, open at the collar. Once inside the room, he removed his dark glasses.

"What the hell do you want here?" Martin asked, trying to resurrect some semblance of dignity, although he was dressed only in his underwear and, in fact, his head hurt so much that he didn't really care about anything but making the pain go away.

"Your daughter's in jail, and I've been asked to act as intermediary to arrange for you to pay to get her out."

"What are you talking about? In jail for what?"

"Drug possession."

Martin sat down heavily on the edge of his bed. "My daughter? She doesn't even drink. You're the fucking drug dealer— you and probably that idiot boy she's with. What do you mean you're the intermediary?"

"You pay me, and I can get her out of jail."

He looked wildly around for his bottle of gin. The only one he saw, sitting on the top of his dresser, was empty. Had he really finished all the gin last night? "I don't have any fucking money," he said. "If I did, would I be living in this flea-bitten motel?"

Lee was still standing in the middle of the room. He looked around. "You've got a point, Martin—I hope it's all right to call you Martin. But you own a boat, am I not correct?"

"It's getting fixed."

"I'm aware of your mishap. The dockmaster says the boat is worth at least $60,000."

"It's worth more than that, but that boat is my home. I'm not giving up my boat."

"Then access your accounts in the U.S. You're a famous writer. You must have considerable money. The price for your daughter is $100,000."

The figure was so far beyond his means that there was no way Martin could even think about paying it. In a way he felt relieved. It made the decision not to help his daughter easier. "I haven't got that kind of money."

Lee's cordial smile faded. "She is your daughter, Martin. She will remain in jail for years, maybe for the rest of her life, if you don't do something to help her. What kind of father are you?" He leaned down, his face right next to Martin's and looked him in the eyes. His breath had a peppermint smell, like fresh toothpaste.

Martin's shoulders drooped. "I'd do something if I could, but I can't help her. She shouldn't have been involved with drugs."

Lee shook his head. "You are shameful, Martin. You daughter is innocent, and you know it. She was arrested because of the young man she was with, who, I am sad to say, was not only selling drugs but also failing to pay his supplier. But he has rich parents and he had no drugs on him when he was arrested, so he will go home to the U.S. while your daughter remains here, in jail."

Martin sat on the bed and covered his face with his hands. "I can't do anything. Now get out of my room."

"Ah, Martin," Lee said, making a clucking sound. "If you change your mind, you can reach me at the Mekong Bar in Cho Lon. I am sure you remember the restaurant."

Martin continued to sit, holding his head in his hands. He heard the door close as his visitor left.

What was he going to do? The only thing he owned in the world was his boat, damaged as it was. But it was still his, and with his boat, he could travel anywhere, get away from anything. If his boat was repaired right now he'd be out in the middle of the South China Sea headed somewhere like Malaysia, somewhere where no one would find him. How could he give up his boat?

But what about his daughter? A week ago that would have been an absurd question. But now she had intruded into his life. Why? Because she'd wanted to know her father. Fucking shit, he thought. Why couldn't Regina have remarried? Why didn't Dillon have a caring stepfather to relate to? All she had was him and a no-account drug-dealing boyfriend who'd gotten her arrested.

He glanced over at the empty bottle of gin on the dresser and thought that it was time to go to the bar. Then he hesitated. He had to come up with a solution. That was *his* daughter languishing in jail. Was he really going to drink his way through her conviction for a crime she hadn't committed? The drug laws in Vietnam were severe, even though it was unusual for Americans to be charged with anything so minor as marijuana possession. But this wasn't about a crime so much as it was extortion. That was why Lee Cheung was involved. Dillon's case was never intended to come to trial. Both the Mafia and the police assumed that Martin would pay before things went that far. But he didn't have the money ... unless he sold his boat. He looked longingly at the gin bottle. Why did life come down to this kind of choice? He got up and walked over to the dresser and picked up the gin bottle and threw it in the wastebasket. Then he went in the bathroom and turned on the shower.

Without his usual complement of gin sunrises to accompany his breakfast, the sight of the mushroom omelet on his plate was nauseating. He wolfed down the coffee, but even that made his stomach churn and his hand was shaking so much that the coffee splashed across his food and left dark puddles on the top of the table. He had intended to go straight to the marina after breakfast and talk to the dockmaster about selling his boat, but he felt too sick to do anything but walk back to his hotel and crawl into bed. He knew he ought to visit his daughter in jail, but such a trip and the confrontation with both the authorities and his daughter, was too much for him to consider at the moment.

His bed wasn't as comforting as he'd hoped it would be, but at least it kept him warm. Despite the heat outside and the lack of air conditioning in his room, he was chilled to the bone. None of what he was feeling was new to him. He knew it was alcohol withdrawal. He'd always stopped the symptoms with several quick drinks. That was still an option.

One side of him was fighting with the other. Every time he told himself that he would be able to help his daughter even more if he wasn't going through withdrawal, he reminded himself that it was exactly those kinds of rationalizations that had derailed every other attempt he'd made to stop drinking. If he picked up a bottle now, he would go from feeling sick, to feeling better, then feeling normal, then feeling drunk and finally to being unable to do anything but crawl back into his bed, exactly where he was right now.

He pulled the covers over him and shook with cold. If he'd had any more to eat he would be throwing up. He knew he had to get out of bed and talk to the dockmaster, but he also just wanted to sleep. At least if he was asleep he wouldn't be cold and he wouldn't feel nauseous. Finally his hopes were answered, and he drifted into a fitful sleep.

When he awoke, it was three in the afternoon. He felt marginally better and he dragged himself from the bed and took a shower under steaming hot water—the one luxury the hotel seemed able to offer. He felt as though he was thinking straighter and he was still resolved not to take a drink. He got dressed and headed for the river.

He'd paid a bargain price of $110,000 in Manila for his boat two years ago and, except for the damage from running into the dock, it was still in pretty good shape, even though it was twenty years old. He knew that in the States he could probably get $150,000 for it, but he needed the money now and he wasn't in the States. The dockmaster was essentially the only game in town.

"You'd better sell me your boat today, Ong Martin," the dockmaster said. "That Chinese is not someone you want to mess around with. If you need to give him money, then give it to him."

Martin figured that the dockmaster was remembering the Australian couple whose bodies had been found floating in the river. Martin didn't have to worry about that, at least he didn't think he did. He didn't owe Lee any money; he was just going to pay him to pay off the police to drop the charges against his daughter. If he couldn't come up with the money, nothing would happen except his daughter would remain in jail. "How can I pay him if you won't pay me what my boat is worth?" he asked.

"This is Saigon, Ong Martin. I run a nice marina, but we don't get many customers wanting to buy boats. I am offering you as much as I can."

He managed to finagle another $5,000 out of the dockmaster, bringing the amount he would receive for his boat to a total of $65,000. It was still less than half of what he could have gotten in the states, and at least $40,000 less than he would get in Manila, or maybe even in Vietnam if he'd been able to wait for it to be repaired and taken it to a resort area, such as Nha Trang. But he couldn't wait. And he was still $35,000 short of what Lee was demanding. He had another $5,000 in the bank, but that still left him $30,000 shy of the $100,000 he needed to come up with.

He called Sidney Duckworth.

"I can't get you another cent," the agent said. "That damn Marilyn Reams wants the $150,000 back that they already gave you. She doesn't think you're ever going to write anything for them."

"How about another publisher? We could promise them a different book. I only need $30,000."

"Your name is mud in the publishing industry. Reams has been spreading the word that you welshed on your last book deal with her and have spent all of the money and disappeared. Nobody else is gonna touch you."

"How about you, Sidney? You've got that kind of money. You know I'm good for it. When I finish the book I'm working on, it will bring in a lot more than the $150,000 they gave me. I'll even sign a new contract giving you 20% of the royalties."

"Twenty percent of nothing is nothing," Duckworth answered. "You've made me too many promises in the past ,and you've never kept any of them. I'm not risking my own money on you."

"It's not for me, Sidney, it's for my daughter. She's in trouble."

"Your daughter? You mean that kid who called me on the phone?"

"Her name's Dillon. I was married to her mother years ago, and her mother died last year. My daughter tracked me down, but now she's in trouble with the police over here, and I've got to help her."

"Are you sure she's your daughter, Martin? She could be anybody, just trying to get your money."

"She's my daughter. All you'd have to do is look at her and you'd see it. Besides, I remember her and her mother. I was married for two years ,and I was there when she was born."

"Jesus Christ, what a fuckup," the agent said. "OK, Martin. Against my better judgment I can loan you $10,000. And I will rewrite our contract at 20% because I know you can't pay me back except through royalties and that's if —and in my mind it's a big if —you actually write something."

"You're a prince, Sidney, a real prince. But that still leaves me $20,000 short. You couldn't find another $20,000 where the first $10,000 came from could you?"

"No deal. I'm willing to risk $10,000 because this is the most human thing I've ever heard of you doing, but that's my limit." He was silent for a moment. "I'll tell you what I will do, though. If you can send me something—the first third of the next book, or a rough draft of the damn thing, not the fucking synopsis, I've already got that—if you can send me something, I'll go over Reams' head and talk to Gerald Litton, the Editor and Chief and ask for another $20,000 so you can finish the book. I can't guarantee that he'll give it to me, but I'll ask. I think if they have something concrete in hand, especially if it's good, they might free up a little more cash."

Martin felt his anxiety mounting. How could he send anything to his publisher? He hadn't written more than a few pages on the book and those were crap. He would never be able to write without drinking and if he started drinking again, things would spin out of control so quickly that who knows what would happen? "I'll do it, Sidney," he said on impulse. What the hell, he didn't have any choice. "Give me a couple of weeks and you'll have something. Start setting up your negotiation with the editor right now."

"I'd prefer to wait until you send me something. I don't want to end up with egg all over my face."

"Trust me, I'll send you something." Even as he said it, he wondered if it was true.

"OK," the agent said. "But don't screw this up, Martin. It's my reputation you're playing with now... and my $10,000. I'll deposit the money in your account tomorrow."

"I love you, Sidney," he said, kissing the receiver loudly.

"Save it for you daughter, and, Martin... good luck."

Chapter 34

They drove us to Cho Lon. The District Five police station must have been the most rundown building in the city, and this was a city full of rundown buildings. It looked as if it had been built sometime during the century before the last one, and the walls on the outside hadn't been cleaned since that time. They were covered with mold; large scabs of paint were falling off onto the sidewalk. The whole building looked as if it were suffering from leprosy. Detective Nguyen told me that the cells to which we were headed were in the basement of the building. I couldn't imagine what they were like. Public bathrooms in Saigon looked as if they should be condemned, so a jail cell and its facilities would probably resemble something out of Devil's Island. The detective joked that Chris and I were being taken to the "Saigon Hilton," an obvious reference to the prison in Hanoi where U.S. flyers, such as John McCain, had been held during the Vietnam War. I didn't feel like laughing. I would have called him an asshole, but I figured that would have gotten me a pistol whipping. I wasn't absolutely sure what a pistol whipping was, but the name was pretty graphic, and my imagination filled in the gaps.

Speaking of assholes, I hadn't seen Chris since we'd been arrested and driven to the police station, both of us sitting handcuffed in the back seat of the same police van. I was too angry with Chris to say anything, and, anyway, he kept giving me looks that told me I should keep my mouth shut around the police. When we arrived at the station, we were both fingerprinted and photographed and then separated. I didn't know where they took Chris, but I was uncuffed and marched downstairs to a cell—surprisingly clean, given the condition of the rest of the building—where three other women, one of them a young Australian and the other two a couple of very old Vietnamese women, both of whom had bruises and torn clothing as if they had been in a fight and who looked as if they were sleeping off a drunk, were already incarcerated. There was a vague smell of vomit and pee in the air and I looked around but the floor of the cell had been hosed down recently so I didn't know where the smell was coming from. I finally decided it must be coming from the old women themselves. From all of the TV shows I'd watched, I'd expected to find a cell full of hardened prostitutes, but then I realized that over here, they probably didn't arrest the prostitutes. Their pimps, like Lee, probably paid the police to leave them alone.

I asked the Australian girl, whose name was Ashley Donner, what she was in for. She was a couple of years older than I was, sort of heavy-set and dressed in a pair of shorts and a tank top that showed off her muscular arms and her tan. I guessed she was one of the backpackers that I had seen in the area near my hotel. She looked scared out of her mind. Her face had shown her relief when they'd brought me into the cell. I'd thought she was going to run up and hug me.

"They caught me with pot," she said. "I thought no one ever got arrested for that shit over here."

And I thought that I was naïve. "Did you buy it here?"

"A friend gave it to me. Everyone I was with was carrying it. They bought it here."

Great, her friends were probably Chris' customers. "Are you alone?"

"I was with friends, but they split when the cops came up to us and they just left me standing there. Nobody's been to see me since I got arrested. I guess they're too scared to come here."

"How long have you been here?" I asked.

"Two days. They're contacting my parents in Brisbane. They said if my parents can pay the fine, then I can get out."

Super. So that was the scheme. Who would they contact in my case? My dead mother? My no-account drunk of a father? "How much is the fine?"

"$20,000."

"For pot?"

"That's what I said. But they told me that I could get life in prison, or even the death penalty if the judge was a strict one. They told me about some other people from my country who got hanged in Singapore for carrying heroin. They showed me a newspaper article about it. I think they base the fine on what they figure the parents can

201

pay. They asked me all this stuff about my father's income. I took a guess, since I'd never paid much attention to that, but he's got a steady job managing a grocery store and I know my parents have some savings." She looked panicked. "They're gonna kill me when I get home."

I had almost $35,000 in my bank account and I could access it here in Saigon. If $20,000 was the going rate for possession of pot, I'd be OK. "So who talked to you?" I asked.

"A detective. I think his name was Nguyen or something, but all their names sound alike to me and every other person over here is named Nguyen."

I knew Detective Nguyen quite well by now. "I'm gonna talk to him myself."

"Just tell the guard. He'll get him for you."

I banged on the cell bars and yelled for the guard. When he arrived—a fat, sloppy young man about my age, his shirttail hanging out, looking angry at having to make the walk back to the cell—I asked for Detective Nguyen.

In a few moments, Detective Nguyen, dressed as usual in his neat gray suit, a white shirt and tie, ambled back to the cell. "So you want to talk to me, Miss Bloom," he said. "Are you ready to confess?"

"I'm not confessing anything, you asshole."

His face broke into a grin. "I'm glad to see that jail hasn't dampened your spirit. But you are in a lot more trouble than Miss Donner over there. You and your boyfriend were dealing."

Super. I'd already been judged guilty. "No, I wasn't," I said. "I didn't even know there were drugs in my hotel room. My friend— and trust me, he's not my boyfriend—was the one doing the dealing, if anybody was." I knew that there was supposed to be an unwritten rule among young people not to rat on each other about drugs or stuff like that, but Chris had already tried to claim the drugs were *mine* and, at this point, I was so pissed off that I felt as if Chris deserved whatever he got.

"That's what your boyfriend says. He says the drugs were yours." He shrugged his shoulders. "That's how it always is with you drug dealers, you always blame each other."

I couldn't believe that Chris was still telling them the drugs were mine. He was a bigger bastard than I'd thought he was. "I told you, he's not my boyfriend. He's just a friend... or at least I thought he was. And he got the drugs from this Chinese friend of his–I'm sure you know who–and was selling them downtown. You probably even watched him doing it, since you were hanging around us most of the time."

The detective pretended to yawn. "You are right, I was an eyewitness to your boyfriend selling drugs. But you and he must have been partners, since you're obviously close to each other. And it won't do you any good to try to accuse anyone else, such as the Chinese person you mentioned. You and your boyfriend are both guilty as far as I'm concerned."

"I want to see a lawyer."

"Really?" he asked, looking amused. "If you see a lawyer we will have to charge you in front of a judge. The evidence against you and your friend is overwhelming. I'm afraid I will be unable to keep the judge from convicting you. The penalties over here are very severe, Miss Bloom. You don't want that to happen I assure you." His amused expression was gone.

His words frightened me. He knew that Chris was selling drugs, perhaps even had witnesses or pictures. I'd seen Chris doing it myself, but I'd been too stupid to believe my own eyes instead of Chris' stories. I was sure that a judge would convict us both. "So can I just pay a fine, like she's doing?" I looked over at Ashley.

His smile broadened. "Of course. If you pay a fine we do not have to go to see the judge. That is easier for everyone. The crime will never appear on your record."

That sounded good to me, but he hadn't named a figure. "How much?"

"For possession of marijuana with intention to sell, the fine is $100,000."

I heard Ashley gasp.

"I haven't got that much money!" I said, trying not to shriek.

"I guess you will have to contact your parents."

"I don't have parents!" I shrieked.

He didn't look perturbed by my outburst ... or my information. "That's not what I hear. Your father is a famous writer. And he lives right here in Saigon."

I wondered how they knew that, and then I realized that Chris, with his big mouth, must have told them. "My father is a drunk, and he's broke."

He shrugged his shoulders. "Lee Cheung, perhaps you know him—you did mention a Chinese gentleman earlier—has volunteered to represent our department with your father. He will ask him for the money."

That scumbag Lee again! This whole thing was a scam between Lee and this weasly little detective. Chris may have been selling drugs, but Lee must have set him up to be arrested. Lee knew that I was leaving Saigon, and maybe he thought Chris would go with me. This was his way of getting as much money out of us as he could before we were out of his reach. I wondered if Chris had told him about my HSBC bank account. In fact, I began to wonder if Chris hadn't set this all up with Lee in order to get to my money. But then Chris knew that my father was broke so he wouldn't have told Lee to ask for $100,000.

"Lee's the asshole who gave Chris the drugs that you found!" I yelled at him. "He's guiltier than either one of us."

He frowned and shook his head. "I wouldn't say things like that if I were you. Lee Cheung is acting as your friend by contacting your father. He is not a man you would want as an enemy." His eyes became hard pinpoints as he said these last words. I knew that I was being threatened. "Besides, your friend has already contacted his parents, and they are wiring his fine to us. He will be out of jail within a day or so. I'm sure your father will be just as cooperative."

The news about Chris just made me hate him even more. He'd go free and I'd rot here in this Vietnamese jail. "My father doesn't have the money, I told you. I have some money of my own. Not that much, but I can pay a smaller fine. Trust me, that's all you're gonna get from anyone. My father doesn't care and can't pay anyway. You're better off getting something instead of nothing, and my father isn't going to give you or that Chinese shitball anything"

He looked offended by my outburst. "You slander both Mr. Cheung and your own father. You are a mean bitch, Miss Bloom. I hope your father doesn't think about what a bitch you are when Lee Cheung asks him to pay your fine." His eyes were laughing this time. He was getting off on calling me a bitch.

"And you're an asshole," I said. I quickly looked at his face to see if I'd gone too far. I hadn't thought before I'd called him an asshole. It was just a reflex.

To my relief, he laughed at me. "Such a bitch," he laughed. "Maybe your father won't pay. If that's the case, I guess we will get to know you pretty well, miss bitch. Life can be boring here at the police station and we usually just get these old crows in here," he glanced over at the two sleeping old women. "We will have some fun with you, I think."

Oh, shit. My worst fears were going to come true. I was going to become a sexual plaything for a bunch of horny policemen. I turned away to hide the fact that I was about to cry, and I heard the detective walk away.

Ashley came over and put her arms around me. "Your father will help you. He has to."

I burst into tears. "He's never been my father."

## Chapter 35

Martin debated whether or not to go to the jail in Cho Lon and visit Dillon. He didn't have the $100,000 yet, and he didn't want to give her any false hopes until he was sure he had the whole amount. On top of that, she'd probably berate him or refuse to see him. He didn't want to risk his shaky, one-day sobriety by having a stressful meeting with his daughter.

Whether he would drink or not was still touch and go. He couldn't go ten minutes without edging dangerously close to heading for the nearest bar. But then the urge to drink would subside just enough for him to come to his senses before he walked out the door. How the hell was he going to write when he felt like this, he asked himself.

The story was outlined in a fair amount of detail in his mind. And he had a written synopsis on his computer... the synopsis he'd turned in to his publisher in order to get his advance. But the plot wasn't the problem. It was the words and images—the actual sentences, which he felt required inspiration in order to construct. In the past, his inspiration had come from a bottle. But then the bottle had begun to kill the words. The more he'd drunk, the slower the flow of sentences until finally the stream of words had turned to nothing but empty, parched dust, a barren desert instead of the torrent of words he was used to when he was writing.

He tried to remember if he'd ever been completely sober when he'd written. Of course he had been. He'd written *A Memorial to Time* and the seven unpublished books that had preceded it without ever taking a drink until he'd finished each day's writing. It was only the fear that he'd never be able to write another book to equal *A Memorial to Time* that had started him trying to generate an extra "oomph" of inspiration by consuming alcohol while he wrote. At first it had worked. Despite the fact that *A Memorial to Time* had been nominated for a Pulitzer Prize, his next books were all better than his first—both in his opinion and in the critics'.

But the drinking had gotten out of hand. When he'd started drinking during the day, even if he had a class to teach, he'd recognized that he was losing control. But he hadn't really liked to teach anyway, and when he was sober he'd felt intimidated by the students and inferior to the other faculty, who'd seemed to know what they were doing. Then he'd come to Saigon and begun drinking from the moment he woke up in the morning and his writing had stopped completely.

It was just a matter of doing it, he told himself. You put the computer in front of you and you began typing. No matter what kind of garbage you produced, you just kept typing. Everything could be changed later if it needed to be. But there was a deep chasm between booting up the computer and putting words in sentences. How could he compose a story if he had nothing but glasses of gin parading through his imagination?

Think of a picture, he told himself. Think of a picture and then describe what you see, what you smell and feel. Are there background sounds? What are they? How can they be described? And is it outside? If so, is the wind blowing? What does the sky look like? Is it near enough to the ocean to smell the salt from the sea? Or is it in the city, where the smells from the ethnic restaurants drift onto the sidewalk to snare the potential customers strolling by? He thought of a scene and began to write.

He wrote steadily for an hour. Then he stopped and re-read what he'd written. It wasn't bad. He'd written better, but he'd also written worse. He felt like celebrating. Would it hurt to have a drink now, now that he'd conquered his demon and begun to write again? He left the computer running so that he could resume his writing when he returned. Then he went into the bathroom, splashed some water on his face and left the hotel room. He got halfway to the bar when he felt that old feeling, the anticipation of the first drink, taking hold of him. He checked his wallet to be sure he had enough money to last the whole evening—maybe even find a woman. Then he stopped. What was he doing? He'd written five, at best mediocre, pages. He had to complete at least a third of a novel, a really good novel—a hundred pages or more of the "dazzling prose and bejeweled sentences" his publisher and critics expected—before he could give it to Sidney Duckworth to use as a bargaining chip for negotiating enough money to pay his daughter's fine.

He turned around and trudged back to his hotel.

## Chapter 36

Ashley was going home. I'd also heard that Chris had gotten out and would be going back to California with his parents. The two old drunks had gone the evening I'd arrived and the cell smelled better. Whenever new prisoners showed up, they put them in another cell. I wasn't sure why. Maybe they were trying to isolate me. Anyway, it looked as if it was just going to be me sitting here by myself. Me and all of those oversexed cops who came into the station. Periodically, Detective Nguyen stuck his head in and said something like, "how's it going, miss bitch?" What a joker.

Ashley's parents had flown to Singapore and then to Saigon and were waiting outside the jail when she was released. She was almost as afraid of seeing them as she had been of being locked up for life, but it sounded to me as if they cared for her very much. She'd turned out to be so sweet and naïve that I couldn't even be jealous that she had a family who loved her and I didn't.

We kissed and hugged, and she asked me if there was anyone I wanted her to contact once she was reunited with a computer and a cell phone, since her laptop and phone had both been confiscated by the police, along with the marijuana, and they claimed to have no clue where either of them had gone. I debated about letting Candy and Betsy know what had happened, but then I decided that they would only worry. They didn't have enough money to be able to help and if they'd had, I wouldn't have asked them anyway. Besides, I was embarrassed to have them find out what a fool I'd been.

"To quote Paris Hilton, nobody turns up his nose at money," I told Ashley. "These guys will take my offer eventually." I was acting more confident than I actually felt. "They think my father will do something, but when it's clear that he won't, I'm sure they'll prefer getting my $35,000 to getting nothing. I mean, how are they gonna explain to a judge that they arrested two of us but they let Chris go? They're not gonna let me appear in court."

Ashley seemed convinced by what I'd said, even if I knew it was just bravado on my part. Detective Nguyen had made it pretty clear that he could keep me in jail indefinitely without a court appearance. He acted as if he were looking forward to it.

I had the cell all to myself, but I didn't feel very privileged, even if it was as large as my hotel room had been. I still had my clothes, which they had given back to me to wear and had even laundered for me. Two tiny women, who spoke no English but looked concerned about me and smiled and nodded in a friendly way, came in each morning and cleaned the toilet, the floors, and took away my dirty clothes and, on my third day, changed the sheets on the cot. Maybe this really was the Saigon Hilton.

The afternoon of the third day, the guard announced that I had a visitor. I wondered if Chris had come to say goodbye before he left for Palo Alto. I was ready to tell him what a shithead fucking assholecreep he was for getting me into this mess. Only it wasn't Chris. It was Lee.

"Ah, my poor little Dillon," Lee said, smiling behind his dark glasses. "First your father turns out to be a loser, and then your boyfriend turns out to be a loser, too."

He was lucky that there were bars between us. If there was ever a time that I wanted to kick a man in the balls, this was it. "What do you want?" I asked. I remembered that Detective Nguyen had said that Lee was approaching my father to try to get the money to pay my fine. I couldn't imagine that he had any news except bad news in that regard.

"Your father may not be the loser you thought he was," Lee said. "I think I succeeded in pricking his conscience. You know how I value loyalty, and family loyalty is the most important kind of all."

"What are you, some kind of dope-peddling philosopher? To quote the Dalai Lama, why don't you find some lonely mountaintop and go there and fuck yourself?"

I thought I might have made him angry enough to hit me, but instead he broke into laughter. "Detective Nguyen was right. You can be a bitch. But I am being serious. Your father is trying to raise the money to get you out of here."

*And swines are great aviators.* "He hasn't got that kind of money. They want $100,000."

"He says he can get it. He's already sold his boat."

I was dumbfounded. My father had sold his boat just to get me out of jail? That didn't make any sense. "Why would he do that?"

"Like I said, I convinced him that he needed to be a good father. You see, I have your best interest in mind, Dillon."

Despite not being able to see his eyes behind his glasses, I had the feeling that he was leering at me. "You're a fucking asshole," I said.

He gave me a cruel smile. "Your bitchiness can become tiresome. I'd be more careful what you say to me if I were you. I can have them raise the fine even more if I decide it's needed in order to teach you a lesson. Or better yet, I can have them release you into my custody. Perhaps you would like a job at the *Mekong Bar* entertaining the customers? Young American women are a prize commodity."

He wasn't kidding. I could tell by the look on his face. I resisted calling him any more names, but that didn't mean I didn't think them in my head. "Why hasn't my father come to see me?" I asked.

"Who knows? Perhaps he's embarrassed. He's a drunk and now he has a daughter who is a druggie. It's unseemly for a famous writer to be in such a situation."

"I'm no druggie, you shit-for-brains, and you know it." I wondered if my father thought I was guilty of the drug charges. He wouldn't have any reason to think otherwise. He didn't know me at all.

"Such a nasty mouth," Lee said, shaking his head. "Let's hope your father can raise the rest of the money. Meanwhile, Detective Nguyen will take care of all of your needs, as I'm sure he has so far. I won't see you again unless your father fails in finding the money. Then I'll see you at work." He laughed and turned and walked away.

I hated men. I hated Lee and I hated Detective Nguyen and I hated Chris. But I hadn't started hating my father until I'd met him and found out that he was a self-centered alcoholic who only wanted my sympathy. Did I still hate him? I was mixed up. I had learned nothing

211

about him that would have suggested that he would lift a finger to help me. He hadn't even come by to see how I was doing. Maybe he really was embarrassed, like Lee had said. I was embarrassed. Not because of the drugs. I hadn't had anything to do with them. I was embarrassed because Chris had taken me in, and I'd thought that I was too smart for that. I'd also been embarrassed by my father when he was drunk in front of me. Now, I felt guilty. I had come all the way to Vietnam to get to know my father, and I didn't know him at all.

Chapter 37

Martin hadn't felt this good since he didn't know when. He clicked away on his computer and realized that he had just reached 100 pages and it was less than two weeks since he'd resumed writing. He wanted to finish this chapter, then he would send the manuscript by email to Sidney Duckworth and see if Sidney could get his advance increased by another $20,000 over what he'd been given two years ago so he'd have the money to get Dillon out of jail.

He hadn't seen Dillon yet, but he knew that she was OK. Duc had an aunt who cleaned the cells at the jail, and she had reported that Dillon was healthy and unharmed. She still hadn't officially been charged with anything, which meant that the police were holding off appearing before a judge until they determined if he could come up with the "fine," which was really a bribe, to get them to drop the case. Duc's aunt had also said that his daughter's friend, Chris, had been released. That meant that Chris' parents had come through with the cash to get him out.

Lee had been by several times inquiring as to whether he had the money yet. The Chinese's manner was becoming increasingly less friendly. On the last visit, he had hinted that, if Martin couldn't come up with the payment soon, he might find his daughter turning tricks at the *Mekong Bar* in the future. Martin had been so incensed that he'd threatened to kill him if such a thing happened, but the Asian drug dealer had only laughed at him. "You'd better remember who you're talking to," he'd told Martin.

He finished his typing and then attached the manuscript to an email and sent it off to Sidney Duckworth. Sidney had not had good things to report so far with regard to his talks with Marilyn Reams' boss, but Martin hoped that the quality of the manuscript, which he felt was the best work he had produced so far, would change the Editor-in-Chief's mind. Only the exercise of more will power than he had ever thought he possessed kept him from taking a drink while he waited for Sidney's reaction.

The morning after he sent the manuscript to his agent, Martin got a telephone call from the United States. Sidney was ecstatic. "This is fantastic. How do you do it? You haven't written like this in years."

"Never mind your reaction," Martin said. "Will it get more advance out of Gerald Litton?"

"If these pages don't do it, nothing will," Duckworth answered. "This one might actually get you a Pulitzer. Can you keep it up for the rest of the book?"

Martin felt the same way his agent did about the work. "I can keep it up. I can't stop myself from writing it anymore. It just flows out of me. I feel like the old Martin Bloom rejuvenated."

"You've got your daughter to thank for that, then," the agent said. "Is she still in jail?"

"Of course she is. That's why I need the extra $20,000. They won't take any less."

"I'm hand delivering the manuscript today. Straight to Gerald. I should have news by this time tomorrow," Duckworth said. "Wish me luck."

"You damn well better have luck," Martin said. He didn't even want to think what would happen if the publisher refused to advance him any more money.

He felt an urge to buy a bottle of gin and celebrate that he'd finished the first third of his novel, but he knew that it was his addiction to alcohol causing him to use any excuse to resume drinking. He told himself no and went to a restaurant, had a big bowl of noodles, and then went back to his hotel room and wrote six more hours, then went to dinner and came back, typed another three hours and went to bed. Tomorrow was the day he'd find out whether or not he could get his daughter out of jail.

The telephone woke him up. Martin knew that New York was twelve hours behind Saigon in terms of time, and Sidney had given Gerald Litton the manuscript first thing in the morning, which would have been last night. Litton must have already read it and this had to be Sidney calling with the news.

"He loves the manuscript but he won't budge on the advance," the agent said, by way of greeting. "Marilyn got to him, I think. He gave me a bunch of excuses about your drinking history, your disappearances, and the whole scenario that Marilyn likes to throw in my face every time I talk to her."

Martin felt himself panicking. "But I need the money, Sidney."

"Hey, I'm on your side with this. I've got ten thousand of my own money invested in getting your daughter out of jail."

"They're threatening to turn her over to a local pimp and turn her into a prostitute," Martin said. He could hear the panic in his own voice.

"What the hell kind of police force have they got over there? Can't you go to the U.S. Embassy?"

"She's accused of selling drugs, Sidney. And this is a Communist country. The embassy can't do anything."

"I don't know what to tell you, Martin. I really don't."

He thanked Sidney and hung up. What was he going to do now? He'd felt good about his writing. Hell, he'd felt great. But for the first time in his life, his writing hadn't been an end in itself; it had been done to earn him some money. And that was exactly what it hadn't accomplished.

His thoughts were interrupted by a knock on his door. It was more like a pounding and he recognized the signature announcement of Lee Cheung, come, no doubt, to check on his progress on raising the last $20,000 dollars.

"What do you want?" he asked trying to keep the Chinese man outside.

The taller Lee just pushed him out of the way and walked into the room. "Got the money yet, Martin?"

"I'm having a little trouble with the last $20,000," Martin said. The question and answer had become a routine between the two of them.

Lee's expression became stern. "This can't go on forever, Martin. Do you have any chance of raising the last $20,000?"

Martin sat down on the edge of his bed and hung his head. "Eventually. I'm a third of the way through my next book and it'll probably earn millions. I just can't raise any more money right now."

Lee sat down beside him and draped one arm around Martin's sagging shoulders. "I understand. You are a famous writer. You are in between books right now, but the next one will be a best-seller, eh?"

"No question about it," Martin said. He didn't know what Lee was up to, but Martin felt relief that he wasn't threatening either him or his daughter at the moment.

"Then maybe I will loan you the money. What do you think? I give you $20,000 now so you can pay your daughter's fine and you give me $30,000 back... unless it takes you 6 months to achieve that best seller. Then you give me $40,000." He tightened his grip on Martin's shoulders. "And if it takes you a year, you owe me $50,000 and so on. That's how my loans work."

"That's not even legal," Martin said, standing up, just so he could get Lee's arm from off his shoulders.

"The police won't complain," Lee said, smiling. "How about it? Do you want to borrow the money, or should I make your daughter earn it at the *Mekong Bar?*'

Martin felt as if he had no choice. At least he could get his daughter out of jail and then out of Vietnam. He'd deal with the consequences later. "OK," he said. "I'll take your money. Just tell the police to release my daughter."

Lee stood up himself. He put his arm around Martin's shoulder again. "You are a fine father, Martin. You can be proud of yourself for doing the right thing."

## Chapter 38

Martin was standing outside the run-down police station when Dillon emerged. She was carrying a suitcase and she looked healthy, but lost. With her skinny frame and funny-looking hair she looked like a 13 or 14 year old. He approached her hesitantly.

"Father?" Dillon said. She put down her suitcase. "They said you'd paid my fine."

He shrugged. "You're my daughter."

His statement was absurd, given their history. Dillon began to laugh. So did he.

"Do you need a place to stay?" he asked, knowing that she did. Her boyfriend had already flown back to the U.S.

"I have money. I can get a room."

"Suit yourself. There's a vacant room in my hotel if you want to stay there."

She nodded.

"Are you hungry?"

She shrugged. "Sure."

He picked up her suitcase and led her over to Duc's waiting taxi, which had brought him to Cho Lon from his hotel in the backpacker district.

"We can go to District One," he said. "I know a great Italian restaurant there. You must be tired of Vietnamese food by now."

"The food at the jail wasn't half bad," she said. "In fact, it wasn't that bad as an accommodation. I've been in worse motels."

"But you could always leave them," he answered.

She laughed. "Right."

On the way to District One, Martin took her hand. "By the way, I think you should leave tomorrow. Don't give the authorities another chance at you."

Dillon hesitated. "I came here to get to know you."

"What's to know? The first priority is your safety."

He'd said it so forcefully that she just hung her head and meekly agreed with him.

They arrived at the restaurant and each ordered. He had Steak Milanese and she had spaghetti. "You're not drinking," she said.

"I'm writing instead," he answered, a note of pride in his voice.

"I heard you sold your boat."

"Easy come, easy go. I never really did anything on it except use it as an apartment. I can do that a lot more cheaply on land."

"Thank you," she said. "Why did you do it?"

He didn't know how to answer. He'd tried to come up with a reason... partly because he'd known that she would ask him for one. What could he say? Was it guilt? Was it a chance to make up for what he'd failed to do for eighteen years? "Did you ever read *A Dead Man's Tale?*" he asked her.

She nodded. "It was assigned for my sophomore English lit class."

"Remember the character's attempt to pay everyone back whom he owed for all of the years in which he'd only thought about himself?"

She nodded.

"Well, remember that nobody needed anything from him. There was no way he could expiate the debt that he owed. Well, this was my chance with you." He held up one hand. "Before you tell me that it wasn't enough to make up for eighteen years of neglect, let me agree with you. But it was a chance to do *something.*"

"It was a big gift," she said." Who's to say what's enough?"

He reached over and patted the back of her hand. "Thank you."

"I'd like an explanation, though," she said, staring him in the eyes, then dropping her gaze, as if she were embarrassed.

"An explanation?" He felt a sense of dread. Automatically he looked around the room for the waiter. He had an overwhelming urge to order a drink.

"Why did you leave us?"

He sat silently, his eyes lowered.

"Mom said some friend of yours died. You left while she was at his funeral."

His stomach felt queasy. He looked around wildly, searching for the waiter.

"You don't have to talk about it," Dillon said. Her face showed her concern. "I guess it bothers you."

He took a deep breath, then looked her in the eyes. "I've never told anyone. Not even your mother."

She waited, afraid to say anything.

He looked away, wondering if he could go on. Suddenly his anxiety seemed to disappear. He felt he could trust his daughter, although he wasn't sure why. "I killed my best friend," he said.

She stared at him in disbelief.

"Not directly. He committed suicide. But it was my fault." He lowered his head. "I've never talked about this."

"You don't have to if you don't want to."

He looked up. "I want to. I need to share it with someone. The burden has become too great."

She waited in silence.

"His name was Jeremy Slater. He and I had been friends since high school. We had bummed around together after high school, traveling, seeing what life was about. We were both writers. He was a better writer than I was, more serious about his craft. I still had romantic notions about what it meant to be a writer, what it would feel like to achieve fame ..." he looked up and, for the first time in several minutes, smiled, "how I could use my writing to find dates. That's how I met your mom, by the way. She came to listen to me read poetry."

"I didn't know you wrote poetry."

"It wasn't good. Even I knew that. Jeremy was the real poet."

"So what happened?"

"After a few years of the two of us just fooling around—we told ourselves we were collecting stories—I enrolled in college. Jeremy kept writing, supporting himself with whatever jobs he could get that gave him time to write. He continued sending stuff to agents and publishers and literary magazines—both his poetry and a novel he'd written. Nobody was interested. Meanwhile, I was achieving minor fame within the university community for my writing. I got a scholarship that paid a few of my expenses, published a couple of short stories in the school literary magazine, read my poems at coffee houses at night. Jeremy was getting more and more discouraged. I told him to enroll in school, but he didn't want to. He was busy on his magnum opus—a novel he was convinced would make his career."

"Was it any good?"

"Better than anything I've ever written." He looked at the floor. "I was jealous," he muttered.

"Because he was a better writer than you ... in your opinion?"

"That and he had a crush on Regina, your mother. We competed for her. I won, even though I'm sure he loved her more than I did. He was too introverted to really compete. Besides, he had kind of a hero-worship thing going with me." He stopped talking and swallowed hard. He wished he had a gin and tonic in his hand, but he knew that if he took a drink, he'd never finish his story. He'd never finished it before, even to himself.

"Regina and I got married. He was a good sport about it. Stood up at our wedding. Was excited when you were born." He paused again. Should he tell her everything? Hiding from the truth was too difficult. This was the time. "I reacted poorly when you were born. I panicked, felt as if I was losing my freedom, like the world was closing in on me and I'd never be my own person again. I don't know why I felt that way. I guess that at my core, I'm a selfish person. Anyway, I withdrew from Regina, didn't relate to you at all. Jeremy stepped into the chasm and gave Regina the support she needed. I could feel her slipping away from me, and even though I was the one who was pushing us apart, I was jealous of Jeremy. Knowing that he was the better writer added to my jealousy."

The food had come. Both dove into their meals, a respite from the intensity of his confession. After a few bites of his steak, Martin put his fork down and resumed his story. "Jeremy wanted me to critique his new novel before he submitted it anywhere. It was his best work, and he knew it. His whole identity as a writer was riding on acceptance of that novel. I read it. I was flabbergasted. I'd never read anything so good. He'd done things with words and character that I had never come close to doing ... still haven't. I hated him for it. Here he was, stepping in to take my place with my family, and now he was going to become a success as a writer. I told him the novel was terrible, immature, self-indulgent, no one would ever publish it or if they did, it would become a joke within the literary community. If this was the best he could do, then he should give up writing. He believed me. I was still his mentor as far as he was concerned, and my words carried the weight of a divine judgment. He withdrew. He didn't show up for a few days, and Regina asked me to check on him. I found him in his apartment; he'd cut his wrists, torn his novel into shreds and strewn it about the apartment. He left no note, but it was clear to me why he'd killed himself."

Dillon had stopped eating. She looked stunned. She stared across the table at her father, as if she were seeing him for the first time.

Martin looked across the table at her. "What I did was unforgiveable."

"That's why you didn't jump all over Chris when he was spouting all of that nonsense about writing for himself and composing books in his head. I could tell you thought it was bullshit."

"I'm not going to make the same mistake with another young writer."

"Elizabeth said that you were unable to criticize any of your students' writing. She said it was your one fault as a teacher."

He shrugged. "I couldn't risk doing what I did to Jeremy. There was no way for me to forget what I did."

She looked back at him. "And you haven't ever forgiven yourself for it. I can't believe you've lived with that all these years."

"I've been running away from it. I ran away during Jeremy's funeral, left you and your mother, vowed to save myself at any cost, but it hasn't worked. The guilt never left. I only kept it in check with booze."

"But you wrote, you became a great writer. You sold your boat to get me out of jail, and now you've stopped drinking."

"For now," he said, avoiding her eyes. "Nothing guaranteed."

"And now you've admitted what you've held inside for all these years."

He looked at her. "I don't know why. It seemed safe to tell you. But admitting it doesn't take away the guilt."

"So what? Do you know how guilty I feel about the way I treated Mom? She gave up everything for me, and I treated her like shit most of the time. Now she's dead, and I can't do anything to make it up."

"You're a kid. Kids always treat their parents like shit."

"And you were jealous, you said you were panicked about having a kid. I didn't make Mom die, and no one commits suicide just because someone criticizes his novel. Pardon me for saying it, but your friend must have been pretty mixed up already. If his novel had gotten rejected when he submitted it, he probably would have killed himself, even if you'd told him it was great."

He shrugged. Maybe she was right. The truth wasn't something written in plain sight. Jeremy had been on the brink of suicide before, when his earlier novel had been rejected. For some reason, the truth didn't seem to matter as much anymore. His fear of the truth had dissipated. He still felt guilty, but he wasn't afraid of the feeling anymore. It was just something he had to live with; he didn't need to let it dominate his life.

"I want to write," she said abruptly. "I want you to know that. One of my reasons for wanting to find you was to see if I was like you, had I inherited any of your gifts?"

He felt embarrassed. He still felt guilty just by being around her, and now he'd even told her his darkest secret, but here she was, talking about inheriting his gifts. "You'll have to find out for yourself."

"I know that. But two weeks ago I was determined not to be a writer because I didn't want to be like you. That's changed. I'm going to go back to Eugene and keep going to school."

She actually admired him; he almost couldn't speak. "That's a good idea," he finally managed to say, avoiding commenting on her change of mind about him. "The more educated you are, the better writer you can become."

"Maybe someday I'll even be able to sprinkle my books with *fustian*," she grinned as she said it, even though she wasn't sure that he'd get her joke.

"A great word, don't you think," he said, grinning back. "It can be a noun or an adjective. In fact as a noun, it's more descriptive than most adjectives."

She laughed. "My friend Betsy and I said almost the same thing... not quite so cleverly."

Their food came and they ate in silence, both of them feeling a sense of relief that the forbidden had emerged into the open. Finally Dillon spoke. "You could come back to Eugene with me. I mean, you're broke and you don't have a boat to live on anymore and I've got mom's condo and her insurance money..."

He shook his head. "I'm honored that you'd ask, but I have a few loose ends to tie up down here." He was thinking of the money he owed Lee. He'd never be able to make it to the airport alive if Lee thought he was skipping out on his debt.

She shrugged. "Just thought I'd ask. Are you gonna finish your book here in Saigon?"

He nodded. "I'm on a roll. All I have to do is keep writing." *And stay sober*, he thought to himself. "But you ought to leave as quickly as you can. I don't trust the police down here—or that Chinese guy, Lee."

"He set Chris and me up, you know. Chris was selling drugs, but they were Lee's drugs. I didn't know anything about it. Do you believe me?"

He nodded. "Of course I do. Believe it or not, it was Lee who told me that you were innocent."

"Really?" she looked surprised.

"He was trying to convince me to pay him to get you out of jail. It worked, although I would have done it anyway."

She looked at him, her expression softer than he had ever seen it. "Thank you, again."

They walked together back to the backpacker district, which was only about a half mile, and then to his hotel where she checked in, but took a different room. They said goodnight and, awkwardly, gave each other a hug.

Chapter 39

When I had read *Jude the Obscure*, I'd had a glimpse of some of the yearnings that may have provoked my father to leave my mother and me in order to pursue his dream of being a writer. Even while reading *A Portrait of the Artist as a Young Man*, I'd gotten a feeling for the sense of isolation that could cause a true artist to separate himself from family and friends in order to pursue his art. But the father whom I'd grown up thinking was dead had turned out not only to be alive, but even more complex than the characters in those novels. He was selfish enough to have left my mother and me to follow his own path, but he was also troubled and plagued by guilt. Yet he had saved me, whom he hardly knew at all.

So who was this man who'd given up everything he owned to rescue his daughter from jail? I had no idea. His story about his friend's suicide completely threw me off. It had never occurred to me that my father's absence, much less his alcoholic lifestyle, might be related to a concrete event over which he had spent a lifetime wrestling with his conscience. I had only thought about his irresponsibility toward me and my mother and had attributed it entirely to his selfishness. I felt like the character I was reading about in *A Memorial to Time*, the man who'd returned to his hometown determined to wreak revenge on the people he'd hated all of his life and then discovered that he hadn't really known them at all.

And what about my reason for being here? I'd tracked Martin Bloom to Vietnam so that I could find out if he was my father and if I shared any of the traits that had made him a writer. He'd told me I would have to find out for myself. The only way to find out if I was a writer was to write. I thought about Chris and his story being constructed in his head. My father had told him that that was an idea, not a novel. Chris had been full of bullshit. I didn't know if he'd believed any of the crap he had said about knowing that he was a writer, about living for his art and all the other blah, blah, blah that had spewed from his mouth during the few weeks I had known him. He was a bastard; I knew that for sure.

I'd gained a thread of faith in my father and a lot more distrust of men in general. When I returned to the hotel after having dinner with my father, I fell asleep with the echo of my mother's voice saying, "I told you so," in my head.

The next morning my father and I had breakfast together. Neither of us was completely comfortable. We were two antisocial people trying to establish a relationship. Social skills weren't our strong points. "Still no alcohol?" I asked, when my father turned down the gin sunrise the waitress had automatically brought him.

He held up two crossed fingers. "So far so good. No promises, though. It's still nip and tuck as far as I can tell."

"But you're writing," I said, reminding him of the bonus he'd gotten from avoiding alcohol. I felt motherly and became embarrassed. "Sorry for meddling," I said.

"Writing isn't life," he said, looking at me so closely that it felt as though he were trying to memorize every feature on my face. "That was my friend Jeremy's mistake to think that it was. It's what I do to earn a living. It's the only skill I've got, actually." He raised his eyes to look directly in my eyes. "But you finding me here in Vietnam has reminded me that there are things in life more important than writing."

"You missed knowing Mom," I said, surprising myself at my own words. I guess his honesty had lowered my defenses.

He wagged his head as if to indicate that he wasn't sure that had been such a loss. "I knew your mother. She was a great person— very down to earth and practical. We were a poor fit." Then he looked me in the eyes again. "But what I really missed was getting to know you."

"I'm still alive," I said. "So are you. We can still do that. Are you sure you don't want to come back with me?"

He frowned. "I've got some business to finish over here. Not just the novel, although that's part of it. But I'll come and visit as soon as I've tied up all the loose ends."

"You could teach at Oregon."

He wagged his head again to signal his dubiousness at my suggestion. "I'm not a great teacher. Too much discipline required."

At least he had some self-insight. He had echoed Professor Chappell's assessment of him.

"Maybe your book will be a best seller."

He smiled. "It actually might be." He looked down at his plate. He'd already finished everything on it. "I owe you for giving me back my ability to write. If I hadn't needed to raise some money, I'd never have stopped drinking and started writing again."

That was the first I'd heard that he'd used money from his new book to pay the police. "You mean you got an advance for this book from your publisher?" I remembered the woman I'd talked to at his publisher's firm and she hadn't sounded as if she were ready to give my father any more money.

"My agent and I worked a deal. They gave me enough to make up for what I didn't have after selling my boat."

Maybe I really had given my father something, although I was probably just kidding myself. He'd had to give up $100,000 on my account. That was hardly a gift.

"Duc will take you to the airport. Have you got money for the plane?"

"I've got plenty," I said, realizing that he was saying goodbye.

We went back to the hotel and I got my suitcase. Duc was there with his cab. I guess my father had called him. Neither of us knew what to say, so we just hugged.

"I love you, Dillon," he said. "Too little, I know, but I hope it's not too late."

"I love you too, Dad," I said, feeling as strange hearing those words come from my mouth as I had ever felt in my life.

I wasn't very talkative on the drive to the airport. We had driven for about fifteen minutes through the usual circus of Saigon traffic when I finally asked Duc if he thought my father was going to be OK.

"He is better since you came, miss," Duc answered. "I am just worried that he owes money to the Chinese."

"What do you mean?"

"He borrowed some of the money to get you out of jail. The Chinese does not forgive those who do not pay him back."

I had thought that my father had raised all of the money himself. He had never said that he'd had to borrow some of it.

"Do you know how much he borrowed?"

'It's not my business, but I think it was about $20,000."

"How long does he have to pay it back?'

"Till his book is published. But the amount goes up every few months. That's how the Chinese does business. And if your father doesn't pay...."

"What? What happens if he doesn't pay?"

"The Chinese is not a nice person."

What had my father done? I couldn't believe he'd put himself at risk to get me out of jail. Why hadn't he told me? I guess he felt he was being a good father by keeping the burden all on his own shoulders. "Turn around, Duc, we're going back."

"Back where, miss?"

"To the *Mekong Bar*. I need to talk to Lee Cheung."

He kept driving. "That's not a good idea, miss. You don't want to talk to him."

"Oh, yes, I do," I said. "Stop the car and turn around or I'll jump out right here, and walk back."

He made a U-turn. In Saigon, such a change of course in the middle of the road attracted no attention at all. Traffic just swirled around the taxi as if a U-turn in the middle of the street were perfectly normal. "Ong Martin is going to be very upset," he said, shaking his head, but now heading back the way we'd come.

"Ong Martin doesn't need to know. I'm going to talk to Lee—the Chinese as you call him—and then we can drive to the airport, just like my father wanted us to do."

He continued shaking his head but he didn't say anything. We continued driving to Cho Lon.

The *Mekong Bar* had a sizeable lunch crowd. I had no idea if Lee would be inside, but I figured that, even if he wasn't, I could leave word that I wanted to see him. As luck would have it, he was eating in the restaurant and he was alone.

"Congratulations, you are free," Lee said, when I sat down across from him. "Martin is a responsible father after all." He smiled, but it wasn't his usual broad, disingenuous smile. It was more like a quick, almost painful grin. "What can I do for you, now that you have disturbed my lunch?"

I told him that I wanted to pay him what my father owed him.

"He owes me a great deal of money. I am content to wait until he finishes his book and can pay me."

"Doesn't the amount go up the longer he doesn't pay?"

"Of course. That is the way with interest."

"And what if he can't pay?"

He shrugged his shoulders. "Everyone pays me... one way or the other." He wasn't smiling at all anymore.

"How much does he owe you?"

"$30,000."

"I thought he borrowed $20,000."

"He did, but interest accumulates rapidly." He looked around the restaurant and then, somewhat longingly, at his food. "I think you had better leave this up to your father. You should go home to the United States."

"I have $30,000."

His eyes widened in surprise. "You have that much money?"

"I inherited it from my mother. It's in a savings account. My bank has a branch here in Saigon and I have enough ID to withdraw the money. I want to give it to you. I want my father free and clear of any debts to you."

He looked at me, as if he was deciding if I was telling him the truth or not. "Does your father know you're here?" he asked.

I shook my head. "He doesn't even know that I know he borrowed the money from you."

"Why are you doing this? You only met your father a little over a week ago."

"I owe him something."

"Because he paid your fine? That was his duty. He is your father." He had a very serious look on his face.

"I owe him something because he gave me life."

He seemed to think this over. "In my culture we have a similar philosophy." He looked down at his plate. "I have had enough to eat. We can go to your bank."

The HSBC bank was only a few blocks away and I had all of my ID in my purse in preparation for the plane flight to the U.S. We entered the bank together.

"I know the manager," Lee said. We walked to the back of the bank lobby and a uniformed guard let us through a small gate. The manager, a short, fat, middle-aged man with glasses, wearing a black suit, was sitting behind a desk that had a view of the entire lobby. Lee greeted him. The man looked frightened. He removed his glasses and looked at me with suspicion.

"I have a savings account in this bank," I said. "I set it up before I left the United States to come here. I want to take out almost all of the money and transfer it to Mr. Cheung's account."

The manager still looked as though he was suspicious, but he looked at Lee, who nodded his head, and then the manager took out some forms. He asked for my savings account information and my passport and driver's license as well as my bank debit card.

"I can transfer the money to your checking account and you can write a bank check for any portion of it that you wish," the man said. He didn't look me in the face.

"Go ahead. I will write a check for $30,000. I am repaying a debt."

He nodded as though he understood, although I could see that he just wanted to get the transaction over with as quickly as possible.

We completed the transfer, and I wrote the check to cash and Lee deposited it in his account.

"Please let my father know that he no longer owes you any money," I said. I started to walk away. I knew that Duc was still back at

*Mekong Bar* waiting for me and I preferred returning to the restaurant and Duc's cab, alone.

"Wait a minute," Lee said, grabbing my hand.

I pulled my hand away from his. What now? Was there still another condition I needed to fulfill before my father was off the hook?

"I just wanted to tell you that I admire what you have done," he said. He didn't appear to be joking. "You and your father have each put the other one first. I have rarely seen that."

"I don't need your admiration," I said. I still regarded him as the scum of the earth.

"Of course you don't. But I am going to tell your father why he no longer owes me money."

"I'd rather you didn't."

"You don't want him to know how much you care for him?"

"I don't want him to think he has to pay me back. He and I are even now."

"You have given him the gift of money. Now give him the gift of knowing that you love him enough to want to help him."

"You're an asshole, you know that, Lee. I don't know how you can talk about love and caring, when you sell drugs, you cheat, you steal, you run whores, for all I know you kill people."

He shrugged. "I am a businessman. That doesn't mean I can't recognize good people when I see them. I'm not like you, but I'm glad there are people like you in the world."

I just shook my head. I was finding out that I didn't really know anyone. "Do whatever you want to do," I said as I turned and headed back to Duc's cab.

Chapter 40


I was back in Eugene, I had a condo and a car, and I still had my bicycle and a little less than $5,000 left in my bank account. I'd enrolled in classes for winter term at the U of O, and now I was looking for a part-time job so I could pay my utility bills, my grocery bills and my tuition. When I'd registered for classes, I'd changed my major from *Undeclared* to *English*. The only regret I had about having missed a quarter of school was that none of my father's books was on the reading list for any of my classes this term.

Mrs. Fuller asked me how my aging relatives were getting along, and I'd said that they were doing better than I had expected. Randolph Fuller reminded me that I wouldn't be able to graduate on time unless I took extra classes to make up for the quarter I'd missed. I thanked him for his concern and told him to go back to his room and finish memorizing the rest of the college rules.

After I got home, I wrote down everything that I could remember about my search for my father and especially my trip to Vietnam. If I was going to write a story, I might as well use my experiences as the basis for it. I couldn't help wondering how my father was doing. He called me a week after I had gotten back.

"Lee Cheung told me what you did," he said right after he asked me how I was doing. "I didn't want you to do that. I bawled Duc out for telling you about Lee's loan to me. I'll pay you back when my book gets published."

"How is the book going?" I asked. I didn't want to dwell on who owed what to whom.

"I'm more than half way through with it. I'm finishing five to ten pages a day."

"You must not be drinking."

There was a pause on the other end of the line. "Well, actually, I am. But not so much as before. I write every day first and start drinking afterward. It seems to be working."

I could feel my stomach churning. I had serious doubts about whether my father could control his drinking. But at least he was still writing, so maybe, for a while anyway, he hadn't descended back into the alcoholic nightmare in which he'd been living when I'd arrived in Saigon. It wasn't something I had any control over. It was all up to him.

"When do you expect to be finished?" I asked.

"I told Sidney Duckworth I would deliver the manuscript to him and the publisher at the end of next month. I think I can make that deadline...or at least close to it."

"Once you've finished the book there's nothing keeping you there. You could come visit me. You'll probably have to come to the States to do a book tour anyway, won't you?"

"Yes, unless I can get out of it. But I'd enjoy visiting you. No promises just yet, but, when you see the book being advertised, remind me that I'm invited to come."

I was disappointed and I wondered what fears of attachment were still ruling my father's life. "What's the book called?"

"*Life Choices.*"

We were both still making them. "I'll keep my eyes open for it. Then, if you're not here, you'll get a call from me."

"I'm looking forward to it."

That was my last conversation with my father. *Life Choices* was published in the spring, posthumously. It garnered a Pulitzer Prize. Sidney Duckworth had called just before the book came out to tell me that my father had died of liver cancer. He had left all of his royalties to me, but there would be some time for probate to determine his tax obligations. Sidney said that at least half of what he would get from his new book was owed the federal government for back taxes.

I asked Sidney about the funeral arrangements in Saigon, and he said that they'd been taken care of by a man named Lee Cheung. Go figure.

I'd never counted on receiving any money from my father, but I'd assumed that I'd see him again. I really was the orphan that I'd thought I was before. But now it hurt a lot more than it had when I'd never known my father.

For my spring quarter composition class, I chose to write my term paper on *Life Choices*, even though it was too new to be on the reading list for the class. The professor never made the connection between my last name and the author's. My grade on the paper wasn't very good because I couldn't help but use the composition as an excuse to launch into an attack on academic conformity and its incompatibility with literary creativity. That was the theme of my father's book, but I got carried away, remembering the attitude the department chairs at Harvard and Stanford had had toward my father. I couldn't help but think that if they had been more tolerant, my father might have stayed at one of their schools and maybe he'd still be alive. But probably not. The life choices he had made had been his own.

I was working my way through my own book about my search for my father and my trip to Vietnam. I was disappointed in my writing. I knew what I wanted it to sound like, but it never quite came out that way. I remembered my father's experience of having completed seven books before he finally got the eighth one published, and I eventually just wrote this first effort of mine off as manuscript number one. If I was going to follow in my father's footsteps, I still had seven more to go before I'd get anything published.

Professor Hendrickson continued to be interested in me as a student and, once again, I had turned out to have been a poor judge of people. He didn't show any interest in getting me into bed. In fact he had a wife and kids, and he and his wife sort of adopted me. He seemed to really believe in my talent as a writer and continued to push me to write. He told me I had it in my genes. At first I was skeptical about my talent, but I could tell that I was getting better and better. Maybe it was in my genes. My father and I had an awful lot in common.

A few days after I'd gotten back to Eugene I called Candy and Betsy in Yuma. They both wanted to know if Martin Bloom had turned out to be my father, and if I was still with Chris, whom I'd written to them about.

"Martin Bloom was my father," I told them. "But nothing else was what I expected. Chris turned out to be a real bastard. My father might have been one at one time in his life, but he's not anymore." I told them about my father freeing me from jail after Chris had gotten me thrown into it. The whole story left them amazed.

"Are you going to see your father again?" Candy asked.

I told them that I hoped so, and at that time, I had thought that I would. "But even if I don't, I've finally gotten what I needed from him."

"He saved your life," Betsy said, a note of awe in her voice.

"And he gave me inspiration to pursue the real gift he might have given me," I said. "The gift of writing. Now I have to find out if I have that gift myself."